I0662824

He was tired of the ridiculous traditions and restriction imposed by ignorant priests...

Suddenly, the family priest returned and joined the crowd. He shouted loudly, "Sisters and brothers, Saina's marriage is not valid. She is still married to her previous husband. Did you hear me?"

Harshpat heard him and dragged him out. He said to the priest, "Pandit ji, don't shout and please listen! My father already went before the court with Saina and got her previous marriage annulled. So what's your complaint?"

"That priest didn't say the mantras of *kanya dan*. So both marriages are not legal," complained the sulking priest. "What a joke! She didn't even wear a veil to cover her face."

"Pandit ji, *kanya dan* means a gift of the girl. A girl is not a cow to be given as a gift in a *go dan* ceremony during the wedding. Tell me. Is there any *purush dan* in your ceremony where the groom is offered as a donation to the bride? Pandit ji, India will not be truly liberated until we treat men and women as equal partners. Women are going to behold a new dawn without any veil."

"Your dawn will be clouded. You will be a *vajrapat*, not a Harshpat!" Pandit ji had declared him a thunderstrike and not a joy-strike, the latter being the meaning of Harshpat's name.

"Pandit ji, priests are deadly social pests. Science education will sooner or later develop a pesticide to kill their reproduction of sickening rituals." Dr. Harshpat then left the priest standing there alone and joined the wedding party to mingle and enjoy the sweets of the wedding celebration.

Mutilating Women is the story of an honor crime. It follows members of the Kotwal Clan during the chaotic months before and after Indian independence in 1947, a time of upheaval and of hope. The members of this Himalayan clan would be termed liberal/progressive in their stance toward the many issues they faced: from questions of equality for women and untouchables, to the role of religion in thwarting both and changing marriage practices to what modernization might look like for India. However, this book, based on the fictional interviews with the offspring of some of the "characters," is an accurate portrayal of the many obstacles the people of India faced during this time—the cultural and psychological barriers that confronted them at every turn.

KUDOS for *Mutilating Women*

In *Mutilating Women* by Anoop Chandola, we follow members of the Kotwal Clan of India during the difficult times around the fight for Indian independents. The clan faces many issues, not the least of which is women's rights not to be beaten, sold, and treated as chattel, as well as their right to remarry after a divorce. The traditional and repressive practices of the Indian establishment are brought to light, along with the more enlightened citizens' fight for equality and justice. Giving us both a glimpse of life in India in the forties, as well as an educational look at their fight for equality for women, this is a great read. ~ *Taylor Jones, The Review Team of Taylor Jones & Regan Murphy*

Mutilating Women by Anoop Chandola is the story of the struggle for women's rights in India. The story follows the members of the Kotwal Clan in the chaotic times in 1947 while India was fighting for its independence. As the story opens, a new member of the clan describes how she took revenge on her abusive husband and fled. Now in hiding, she wants to remarry, but it is forbidden and the clerics will not preform the wedding. As the story progresses, we see the traditions that allow arranged marriages in which the women have no say, and other inequities heaped upon them and the enlightened men who fight for their rights. *Mutilating Women* is both entertaining and educational, a realistic look at life in India in 1947 when women were denied even the basic rights that most of us take for granted. It's a book that everyone should read. ~ *Regan Murphy, The Review Team of Taylor Jones & Regan Murphy*

ACKNOWLEDGMENTS

Many thanks to Black Opal Books and its team of Faith, Lauri, LP, and Jack.

My wife Sudha and son Varn deserve my sincere thanks for their invaluable help.

Mutilating Women

ANOOP CHANDOLA

A Black Opal Books Publication

GENRE: HISTORICAL FICTION/FAMILY LIFE/MULTI-CULTURAL

This is a work of fiction. Names, places, characters and incidents are either the product of the author's imagination or are used fictitiously, and any resemblance to any actual persons, living or dead, businesses, organizations, events or locales is entirely coincidental. All trademarks, service marks, registered trademarks, and registered service marks are the property of their respective owners and are used herein for identification purposes only. The publisher does not have any control over or assume any responsibility for author or third-party websites or their contents.

MUTILATING WOMEN
Copyright © 2019 by Anoop Chandola
Cover Design by Jackson Cover Deisgns/Anoop Chandola
All cover art copyright © 2019
All Rights Reserved
Print ISBN: 9781644370698
Library of Congress Number: 2018967052

First Publication: JANUARY 2019

Printed and published in the United States of America

All rights reserved under the International and Pan-American Copyright Conventions. No part of this book may be reproduced or transmitted in any form or by any means, electronic or mechanical, including photocopying, recording, or by any information storage and retrieval system, without permission in writing from the publisher.

WARNING: The unauthorized reproduction or distribution of this copyrighted work is illegal. Criminal copyright infringement, including infringement without monetary gain, is investigated by the FBI and is punishable by up to 5 years in federal prison and a fine of $250,000. Anyone pirating our ebooks will be prosecuted to the fullest extent of the law and may be liable for each individual download resulting therefrom.

ABOUT THE PRINT VERSION: If you purchased a print version of this book without a cover, you should be aware that the book is stolen property. It was reported as "unsold and destroyed" to the publisher, and neither the author nor the publisher has received any payment for this "stripped book."

IF YOU FIND AN EBOOK OR PRINT VERSION OF THIS BOOK BEING SOLD OR SHARED ILLEGALLY, PLEASE REPORT IT TO: lpn@blackopalbooks.com

Published by Black Opal Books **http://www.blackopalbooks.com**

DEDICATION

For my granddaughter Prasha "the Great Expectation"

Chapter 1

Nanda and Murti looked about, to make sure there were no men nearby, then lifted their saris to their knees and climbed the oak tree without knowing that a tiger was hiding below. For them, summer was the best time to climb up an oak tree because, come winter, this Himalayan forest would be white with snowfall and very cold. They positioned themselves halfway up the tree.

Nanda was riveted, amazed by the distant views. Toward the north, the sun's rays had made the snow-clad towering tops of the Chaukhamba Himalayan range so shiny. And toward the east, stood Mt Rama Rana. The Chandrabhaga rivulet looked like a trickling stream as if reluctantly released down that lazy mountain, between the Kotwal and the Gadoli forests. Come heavy rains and it became a raging river for the next twenty miles before merging with the overflowing Ganges. The soil of the mountain was studded with *burans* rhododendron. Murti hummed in Garhwali, the local Himalayan language, "*burans phulyo rato rato*...(the rhododendron flowered red and red...).

Nanda didn't appear to react to Murti's singing. Murti grabbed one twig of oak, with which she touched Nanda's face. Nanda shook her head with a smile. She came out of her ecstasy. "I was smelling the pollen of the *ku-lain* trees," she said in Garhwali. The swirls of the *kulain* pines on top of Mt Rama Rana were blowing the yellow pollen.

"Did you see a pair of *karain* birds gliding down with their extra-long tails? The female ahead and the male behind her?" Murti asked with a smile.

Nanda reciprocated a smile, as her gold nose ring, the sign of a married woman, shined brightly.

They started cutting a long oak branch, taking turns with their large well-sharpened axes. The long oak branches were used to create a trellis to give support to sun-loving hyacinth vines.

In this central Himalayan region hyacinth was known as *chhimi*, which was called *sem* in Hindi and spelled *seim* in English. The supporting branch was inserted in a one-foot hole next to the little vine which then climbed to the top of the supporting branch, covering its sub-branches along the way. The whole dry oak branch experienced a sort of metamorphosis. It didn't look like a part of an oak tree when it was fully covered by the green leaves, purple flowers, and pods of hyacinth. One vine could grow to more than six meters if the supporting branch was that tall. One single vine could yield a huge number of bean pods, roughly sixty to one hundred pounds, depending on the size of the branch and the number of its sub-branches. The more sub-branches, the greater the yield. The fresh pods were eaten as a vegetable and the beans were also dried. When the vine itself dried up, it was converted into mulch, which was used to make the garden soil more fertile.

These women didn't need such information on *chhimi*, for this knowledge was in their blood. They severed the oak branch from the helpless host tree. Its breaking noise was so sharp, as if the oak tree was screaming. The noise scared the *baters* (quails) below as they fluttered away for shelter.

"Ah, those *baters*!" Murti shouted. "You made me addicted to their soup."

"Me too. My husband would have shot them if he was here, and you would have enjoyed more *bater* soup."

"He would have shot the *malyo* pigeons. See their flock flying up."

"Yes, their spicy and soupy meat." Nanda sucked her saliva.

She paused momentarily then resumed talking with eyes glancing toward the east. "I can see Pauri from here."

The town of Pauri spread all over on the lap of Kandoliya Mountain, offering the best view of the Chaukhamba Himalayas, which looked even taller when viewed from the mountain top.

"Can you see the Messmore High School's big building?" Murti said, pointing with her index finger to the east.

"Yes, big for our husbands. They studied there. We didn't."

"If we were sent there, then we wouldn't be here cutting oaks," Murti said with a sigh.

That Christian School was nestled in an oak forest, separating Pauri from Gadoli. Today was not Sunday. Otherwise, they would have heard the big gong of the bright white church, perched like a dove on a little hilly hump below the school.

Instead they heard the drums *dhol* and *damau*. "I think they are going to sacrifice a ram to please the goddess." Murti was looking at the Devi temple, situated on a saddle half a mile below the church.

"I know, you like the roasted legs of goats. So chewy!"

Murti ground her teeth.

Suddenly, the women smelled, *baghyan*, the Garhwali word for the tiger odor. Murti shouted "*Hwa, hwa,*" several times to scare the tiger.

Nanda didn't shout. "Murti, the *hwa, hwa* words work better with hands up. Our hands are tied here. Let us ignore the *baghyan*, so long we don't see any tiger."

Then they dragged the two branches to a slope especially prepared to slide the cut trees down. Once the branches hung over the slope, the tree branch was given a push and slid down the hill, aided by gravity, until it reached the banks of the Chandrabhaga.

Murti took a deep breath of relief and moved a few yards away, slipping under a bush to pee. A tiger appeared as if out of nowhere and grabbed her from behind. As the male tiger dragged her toward the slope, Nanda came from behind, quick as lightning, to scare the tiger. "*Wha! Wha!*" she yelled.

But the tiger continued to drag Murti down the slope. Then Nanda stepped up to the tiger with her axe and chopped his tail. That didn't scare the tiger either, and so she hit his testicles, which were situated near the bottom of the tail, with her large axe. The tiger ran away, his tail bleeding and his testicles ruptured.

"You saved my life, didi." Murti wanted to hug Nanda to show her gratitude, but her neck was bleeding.

Murti, being the younger sister-in-law, had to address Nanda as didi, never as Nanda. Nanda could address Murti by her name or affectionately call her bhuli, junior sister, for sisters-in-law were considered sisters. Murti's husband, Balram, was Nanda's husband's junior cousin. Pawan would address Balram affectionately as bhula, little brother, and Balram would address Pawan very respectfully as bhai ji, big brother.

Nanda put her hand on Murti's shoulder. "You are my bhuli. I was only doing my duty." To lighten Murti's unbearable trauma, she added, "He will never be able to fuck any tigress. I have made his balls—" She made a fist of her left hand, which she then hit with the fist of her right hand in downward motion to mimic her chop with her axe.

Murti's bleeding would not stop. Nanda quickly tore a piece of her sari's corner with her teeth and then made a bandage. She bandaged Murti's bleeding neck, which had no deep wounds, just a few scratches. *The tiger must have been too old to do her much damage*, Nanda thought.

"You are so tall, didi. If I were not tiny, the tiger wouldn't have attacked me."

"That's not true. If they can kill buffalo, they can kill me as well."

Murti pressed her upper lip over her lower lip as if trying to suppress her laugh.

Old tigers were known to become man-eaters because they could no longer take bigger or faster animals such as wild deer, hogs, monkeys, langurs, jackals, and buffalo. Calves, children, and women were easier targets.

Though her name meant "statue," like any Himalayan woman, Murti could run like a mountain goat. She was barely five feet tall, of average height for a Himalayan woman, but Nanda was very unusual for a Pahari woman, in that she was four inches over five feet.

Murti had no children, thus making her free to leave home and go out with Nanda to enjoy their gossiping. Hence, they were given euphemistic names: Nanda was called Naranga and Murti was Saranga. In the Garhwali society, Naranga was associated with Narada, an ancient sage known for gossiping and roaming. Saranga was associated with Sharada, the goddess of speech who goes to any home where she was worshipped as the goddess Sarasvati. This goddess gave false hope of giving knowledge and therefore most people who worshipped her remained illiterate. These mythical names from folk custom were very popular in local Garhwali culture. Naranga was also the color orange and had passed as such into other languages (the Spanish word *naranja*, for example). Saranga was also a species of deer and a species of bird, known for running and flying fast, respectively.

Murti was still shaking. Nanda gently put her arm around Murti's shoulder and led her down to the creek, the Chandrabhaga. Both drank a lot of water and felt better, but as they walked up the bank, Murti looked around because she was apprehensive of another tiger attack. Nanda kept her engaged by talking about family matters.

Then they reached the place where their felled oak branches had stopped sliding at the foot of the embankment. They began to drag them toward the creek. Near the creek was a huge *dalchini,* a cinnamon tree. They cut smaller branches to use the leaves for the beds of livestock. The Paharis did not know that cinnamon trees produce an internationally coveted spice but only used it as fodder and as the bedding for cows.

Then they kept calling, rather yelling, "Mussi! Hey, Mussi!"

Disappointed they did not hear a response, Nanda said, "Let's go home, Murti! That man must have heard our call. Maybe, he is still sleeping with that woman."

Murti understood who she meant by "that woman." She always believed that Mussi was a decent man. He was not remorseful for keeping "that woman" as his mistress. He did not believe in using women for carnal pleasure, nor was he a religious man or a sadhu. Then why should he be remorseful for keeping a mistress? Was

Lord Krishna, who had eight wives, ever remorseful? And who knew about his other girlfriends. Lord Krishna's flute had a purpose—to lure the gullible *gopi* girls. Mussi was not guilty of such lecherous behavior as that.

Mussi was a Rajput, not a Brahmin. His full name was Musa Singh, but many local Rajputs considered him very low in their caste hierarchy. His name was fun for kids. How could he be a female mouse, musi or mussi, and a lion, Singh, at the same time!

Nanda and Murti knew that Mussi was a man with authority, even though he was just a *chaukidar* (guard). His job was to keep an eye on the neighboring village women who would steal trees and fodder from the Kotwal forest. He was tough with those women. The owners of the forest didn't pay him anything for his services.

However, the Kotwals didn't call Mussi a *chaukidar*. They considered him as their forest's *patraul*, which in English was "patrol." It was a term used for the government forest overseer, and hence a very prestigious position, unlike *chaukidar,* a watchman. However, the local Pahari people were not aware of the word's prestigious derivation.

Mussi was a farmer, too. He grew lots of fruits and vegetables: beans, big Himalayan cucumbers, pumpkins, mangoes, oranges, peaches, apricots, apples, lychees, peppers, tomatoes, lemons, limes, onions, garlic, turmeric, ginger root, corriander, peas, and much else. He knew the folks of the neighboring Pauri town were desperate to get this kind of produce. As long as he continued patrolling the forest, the owners allowed him to use four acres of land near the bank of the Chandrabhaga. That chunk of land was his remuneration for his services, and Mussi was completely attached to it, using it for commercial gardening.

And for additional cash, he sold sickles. One of his duties as guard included stopping illegal woodcutting. If he found any outside woman cutting little trees with their sickles and axes, he would snatch those tools along with the cut trees or plants. Before selling the snatched tools, he would show them to the owners as proof of his honesty, proof he was carrying out his task patrolling the forest.

He could have made more cash, however. Some women did not want to go through this humiliation, and they offered him cash, and even their bodies, which he declined.

He was given the task of dragging those heavy oak branches up to these women's home, about half a mile, across the creek. Mussi knew that Murti's husband Balram was an accountant and Nanda's husband Pawan was a lawyer and judge, and these men would not do this kind of menial job, but their wives would do whatever was needed to live with their "classy" husbands under the same roof.

The Kotwal clan had no village, just five family ranchettes and three cowsheds with large barns. Each ranchette was a sort of joint residence of several brothers and cousins and their families. For drinking water, the ranchette area had two springs, one on each side. For washing clothes, the Kotwals used the Chandrabhaga creek.

The Chandrabhaga was not a glacial creek. Its source was ground water from the Rama Rana mountain. Its water was drinkable except during the rainy months when it became a raging muddy torrent. Many villages and hamlets thrived near its banks. Also, like the Kotwals, there were many other ranchette owners with their own forests and fields scattered along the entire length of this waterway.

The Kotwal forest had a couple of other creeks that were tributaries of the Chandrabhaga. The Kotwals owned several terraced fields and the orchards surrounding the ranchettes. The Chandrabhaga also made it possible to grow basmati in the wet fields on its right bank. The terraced fields were used to grow rice, wheat, and beans as staple crops. Additionally, they grew vegetables and fruits in their orchards. They never sold any produce of these orchards or fields. Although all farming was done with the help of hired labor, gardening was a hobby, not a menial chore, for all the Kotwal men and women.

Mussi could pick any produce of the Kotwal gardens for free. It was up to him how he wanted to use that produce. The bhang plants grew wild here and there. No Kotwal was interested in using the cannabis, but they used to see some hired workers picking the bhang during two sacred festivals: *Shiva Ratri* and *Holi*. During sacred occasions, all hired workers were free to pick the produce from the orchards, including bhang. The *pakoras* of fresh bhang leaves would get them high, but Mussi was not one of those workers interested in bhang.

In the evening, Murti told Balram what happened to her. He almost fainted. Murti calmed him down.

Chapter 2

The next morning, Mussi, accompanied by his mistress Saina, knocked at the door of Nanda's house. Nanda came out and was shocked to see Mussi had a black eye. "What happened, Mussi?" she cried.

Mussi said, "First, I apologize for not responding your call, which Saina heard. Why were you calling me, by the way?"

"To bring some oak branches up here for us."

Mussi had done this task several times. He knew the place where he would retrieve such branches, and he began to walk in that direction. "Hey, Mussi. Don't go away. Tell me what happened? Come on over and have some snacks."

He responded, "Saina will tell you what happened. I will come back for snacks later."

Saina was understood to be Mussi's woman but not really Mussi's wife. Everyone seemed to accept them as an unmarried couple. Some remembered he had considered marrying another woman, his older brother's widow, before Saina came into his life. That woman declined his request, and he didn't attempt to marry again. He was well aware of what happened to Sakar's Brahmin parents.

Saina liked Nanda and Murti very much. When she came to live with Mussi very recently, these two women welcomed her.

"So tell me why Mussi got that black eye," Nanda reminded Saina.

"Mussi was out overseeing your forest," Saina replied. "There he found a woman cutting small plants. He grabbed her sickle and confiscated the plants she had cut. She begged him to return her sickle. He refused. Then she raised her sari up, offering him sex, and Mussi noticed blood spots. Obviously she was in her menstrual cycle. Instead of accepting her offer, Mussi began to drag the two loads down the mountainside. The woman fled crying. Mussi ignored her crying. The whore was crying because she was not fucked!" Saina couldn't stop laughing for several moments. When she regained her composure, she said, "In a few minutes, a man came from behind him and slapped Mussi several times. That's when Mussi received that black eye. Mussi realized quickly that the man must be her husband. That man had an axe in his hand. 'What can you do about the wild cherry tree that I have cut over there with this axe? Going to drag it down?' he challenged as he raised his axe. Mussi quickly grabbed the axe as soon as the man lowered his hand. 'I am going to chop your head,' Mussi said loudly. The man ran away quickly." Then Saina showed her the sickle and the axe that Mussi had confiscated.

"Keep them safe to prove Mussi's courage," Nanda said. "Let me take you to Murti's house. She would love to hear this story."

When they met Murti, she was flabbergasted to hear Mussi's courageous story. Then she said, "Would you like to hear Nanda didi's courageous story?"

"Sure! I am eager to hear," Saina replied.

When Saina heard her story of the tiger attack, she remarked, "Mussi's fight with that man is not as courageous as your fight with that tiger!"

Nanda smiled. She asked Saina to have lunch with
them.

"I would love to eat with you, but Mussi wanted me to
cook a special lunch for him today," Saina said, politely
declining the invitation.

"How about some snacks?" Murti asked.

"Sure," Saina replied.

Over the snacks Saina saw an opportunity to unburden
herself by telling them her story. "You two are my *didis*."

"Yes, we are your elder sisters," Murti assured her,
and Nanda nodded her agreement.

"Would you like to know who I was before Mussi
came into my life?"

Both women looked curious and nodded their heads.

"My name actually is not Saina," she revealed. "Mussi
changed my name from Bidya to Saina. He believed me
when I told him that my husband might come after me. I
told him that I can fight him again if he shows up, and so
he need not change my name, but he named me Saina,
which means army, because of my claim that I would
fight him. Mussi and I tried to get a pandit to marry us
properly. There are only three pandits in this area, and we
tried all three. They refused. Not only did they refuse but
they would not even share cooked food with me anymore."

"But why?" Nanda asked.

"They found out that my name Bidya is my Brahmin
name—"

"How did they find out?" Nanda interrupted.

"Mussi told them. So no pandit would perform our intercaste marriage. No woman can remarry, every pandit
told us, but I am now an untouchable for these pandits.

As you know, untouchables are not allowed to go through the standard Hindu rites. One pandit asked me why I left my Brahmin husband. He had no right to ask me about my married life. I kept my secret to myself. But I had to open up to Mussi. Can I share my secret with you?"

Nanda and Murti looked at each other and nodded their assent.

"Sure, you can if you feel comfortable."

"I do, but this story must remain with you only. One late night, my husband came home drunk and began to beat me. Then he forced me on the bed. I considered it rape, but nobody would take the charge seriously because, for him, I was not just any woman. I was his wife, his possession. But I refused to be treated thus, as a slave, and I found a solution, revenge."

Both women became very curious.

"I let him sleep. He was completely out of his senses. I cut his *kujaga*."

"What?" Murti was shaken.

She was already shaken by the tiger attack and didn't need any more shocks the next morning. Her wide-open eyes indicated her shock.

But Nanda laughed and laughed. "Shabash! You taught him a good lesson. You handled that dangling pen very well." She gently slapped her back in praise and continued to laugh. Finally, she closed her mouth with her fingers.

"I ran away that night," Saina continued. "He knew I had left him forever. I stayed with my cousin, a widow, in her village of Malli. She had no problem with my decision. Fortunately, my ex-husband never looked for me. He better not, for he knows that I will expose his mutilation."

"It is good to hear your courageous story, Saina!" Nanda sighed. "How sad it is that there is no concept of divorce in our hills!"

Murti remained quiet. She looked shocked, in disbelief.

Nanda complimented her more. "Saina, your story is far more important than you think. You know my brother-in-law Sakar. He believes that in every family's history you will find cases of men abusing women. Women feel helpless. He thinks that there is an *upaya*. My husband uses the legal word for it: remedy. He explained to me what Sakar meant. The *upaya,* he suggests, is *Stri-Sangha-Shakti*, women organizing to utilize their collective power. Women have to stand together to change our stupid society. Sakar strongly believes that in a free India it will happen. Your story is a sign of that. You didn't try to defend your husband's violence. I am glad that you don't cover your face. Men have forced women to cover their faces. How can a woman with a cover raise her voice openly? If my husband knew of your case, he would have found the right place for your husband: a jail. My story is pale compared to yours."

Murti agreed. "Your move with Mussi is also a bold step. How did you meet Mussi?"

"That's another secret. Can we meet some other time? I better hurry up. Mussi will come home right after he delivers those oak branches. He expects that special lunch to be ready."

"That sounds good. Right, Murti?" Nanda turned her face toward Murti.

Murti nodded her head.

"On the day we meet again, I will have that special lunch for you, too," Saina said.

"How about tomorrow at the spot from where you heard our call for Mussi?" Murti proposed.

"Good. I will be there," Saina replied.

Chapter 3

The following day, Nanda and Murti arrived at the designated spot. Saina was not there. So they shouted, "Saina! Hey, Saina!"

Saina responded by shouting, "Ho, ho, ho!" Then they saw her walking toward them very slowly with a big basket on her head.

Finally, she arrived at the spot and met Nanda and Murti who smiled to greet her. Saina also reciprocated with a faint smile while holding the big basket with her trembling hands. Nanda helped her unload the basket from her head.

"Why did you cook so much food, Saina? Murti has brought enough *biranji*."

Soon they started eating, enjoying all of the food and praising each other's cooking as delicious. As soon as lunch was over, Saina said, "Now I am ready to tell you the second half of my secret story."

"Yes, how did you meet Mussi?" Nanda asked her.

"It all started in your forest and at the Chandrabhaga!" Saina responded as she stared at Trishool, a very high peak not far from the four majestic Chaukhamba peaks. She appeared as if in ecstasy.

"What are you thinking?" Nanda attempted to remind her of her present company and bring her out of her reverie. "How are our forest and the river related to your meeting with Mussi?"

"That is what I was dreaming," Saina replied. "My cousin sent me out to collect fuel wood from your forest. I had cut a few branches of an *amla* tree when I heard a man's distant voice warning me. The voice belonged to your *chaukidar*, Mussi—"

"Our *patraul*, not *chaukidar*," Murti corrected Saina.

"Your *patraul* but my *chaukidar*," Saina smiled, a smirk on her face. "I ran toward the Chandrabhaga and tried to cross it. I had no idea that this big creek could become a raging river during rainy season. I was swept away by its currents and hit some rocks. I lost consciousness but somehow kept my head above the gushing water. When I woke up, I was resting on Mussi's shoulders. He took me all the way to his house. I don't know how he was able to carry me that far."

"Of course, you are lighter than those oak branches he carried!" Nanda commented.

They all laughed.

"Then what happened?" Murti looked very inquisitive.

"He wanted to take me to the Pauri hospital, but I begged him not to admit me there. Everybody would know that I was stealing from your forest. When I said this, he felt guilty for he thought it was his shout of warning that made me try to cross the river."

Saina blushed and remained quiet momentarily, but then she composed herself. "The first thing he did was help me change my clothes for I was not able to use my hands. Those river rocks to which I tried to cling hurt my hands."

"And then he nursed you while you were recuperating in his house! Right?"

"Right. I was in a lot of pain. We entertained each other with stories. One of the stories I told he found very moving."

"Can you tell us that moving story?" Murti requested her.

"I told him how King Dushyanta and Shakuntala met in Garhwal."

"Where in Garhwal?" Nanda pretended she didn't know.

"At an ashram of Kotdwar. For deer hunting!" Saina responded as if they didn't know their meeting place. The moment he saw Shakuntala in Kanva Rishi's hermitage, the king forgot about deer hunting. He was eager to sleep with her but didn't want to violate caste rules for he thought she was sage Kanva's daughter. The sage was a Brahmin. And so he was delighted when he found out she was a love child of sage Vishvamitra. Dushyanta knew that this sage was a Kshatriya like him.

"And thus Shakuntala became pregnant in Kotdwar with Dushyanta's son Bharata. Eventually India would be called Bharat, after Bharata. Isn't that amazing, honoring the son of parents who were not married properly? Mussi interrupted me at this point in the story, saying, 'You mean they were not married and had a son?' I told him they were married in a way. 'In what way?' he inquired. I told him by *Gandharva Vivaha*. The king said, 'I love you!' And he asked her if she, too, loved him. She instantly repeated, 'I love you. I love you, my lord!' Mussi looked puzzled. Then I mustered my courage and asked him, 'Mussi can we get married that way?' He looked upset as he said, 'Look, I brought you into my house to save you, not to marry you.' He went in his sleeping room and left me sobbing in my sleeping room.

"The following morning, he came into my room with two parathas along with chutney and a tea cup. He saw me crying. 'Don't cry. People will not accept us as a married couple simply because we said to each other: I love you. I love you.' His concern made me laugh. He also laughed. But he believed my story. We did exactly what Dushyanta and Shakuntala did. I was in shock. What did he see in me that changed his decision overnight? I have no sure answer."

"I'll tell you why," Nanda said. "He must have been in shock because of your beauty when he started nursing you!" Nanda pressed her lips into a smile.

Saina blushed. "Not because of my beauty perhaps, but because of my helplessness!" She paused for a few moments as if she was in reverie. Then she began to talk again. "After we took the love vows, we began to behave like a married couple. The next morning Mussi took me to the hospital on a bus that was traveling from Srinagar to Pauri."

"You mean he stopped a bus that passes through our forest?"

"Yes, and he told me why and how Wakil Sahab got that bus road." Then Saina added a sort of request. "Mussi still wants our marriage to be legal. I know your husband can help us. He is a judge."

"Does anybody else know that you are secretly married to Mussi?" Nanda asked.

"My cousin. She found me and wanted me to come back to stay with her. I had to convince her, and convinced she was! 'I know the Shakuntala story,' she told me by way of her answer."

Nanda shook her head. She was not sure if her husband could fulfill Saina's request, even though it was clear to her that Saina was not a *rakhail* (mistress) of Mussi. Saina was a married woman, not merely a woman living with Mussi for fun only. Nevertheless, Saina's 'love marriage' would be considered a farce by society, which was a double standard because they did not think that way about the marriage of Shakuntala, the marriage out of which Bharata was born.

Pawan, too, might not take this request seriously. However, Nanda had a glimmer of hope as she knew Pawan's philosophy. His mantra: practicing law is like hunting—change strategies as necessary to hit the opponent. Animals hunt without double standards because they don't have the advantage of language. Our human ancestors began to have double standards when they became able to speak.

So, she reasoned, he might argue in favor of Saina, but Nanda's optimism in this regard was no more than lukewarm.

Pawan Kotwal only acted as a judge infrequently, on a part-time basis. He was a wakil, a lawyer, and he was addressed as such: Wakil Sahab. Every case he adjudicated earned him a court-fixed rate, but as a lawyer, he had reasonably moderate income.

Pawan was also an outstanding hunter and licensed to have a gun. He would put on an English type hunting hat and shoot wild animals, mostly for food rather than for fun. His forest was being considered to become public land, but he fought for the Kotwal clan to retain ownership of the forest. All other Kotwal families, nine in all, give him credit for having saved their forest.

Another of his achievements was arranging convenient travel for the Kotwals. When the first bus road to connect the entire district from one end to another, including the Tibetan border, was planned by the government, it did not go through the Kotwal forest. Pawan pressured the planners to change the route and the road now passed through this forest, which made for easier access to the bus for the Kotwals. It was hardly a half-mile walk to access the road, and all they had to do was raise their hands

and the bus would stop to give them ride to Pauri or Srinagar, the closest towns. They didn't complain that
Pawan took the major portion of the bus road compensation paid by the government or that the forest had lost a
lot of land when a bus route was carved through it. They
liked the convenience he had negotiated for them.

Thus Pawan became a representative of the literal
meaning of his name, pious, for the Kotwals. All adult
Kotwals believed his advice: We live in the world of
changing relationships, so observe and absorb then decide.

Nanda was not still sure that Pawan would follow his
own advice in Saina's case, however. For her, Saina's
story was a case of pliable relationships, and she thought
Saina was coping courageously. And Mussi, too.

"I like Mussi. He is courageous," Saina said

"Indeed. Rajputs are known for their bravery. He can
'fix' your ex-husband if needed. My sister and I recognize your marriage to Mussi. We are Brahmins."

"But you cannot perform our marriage. Women cannot
act as priests."

"We are Bharadwaj Brahmins, but we don't write
Bharadwaj. *Desi* Brahmins write their *gotra* name. We
don't. We use Kotwal, after our ancestral village Kot,
which means fortress, as our family name. Kotwals don't
do priestly tasks, but my brother does. My father was a
Maithani priest, although he didn't make it his profession.
He didn't teach me his profession, but someday women,
besides being wood-cutters, will be priests."

"I like your huge forest," Saina said, changing the subject. She recognized not only *amla* but oak, *toon*, deodar,
cypress, *hard*, *kaphal*, figs, wild pears, *tungu*, *ghingaru*,
timru, *bhinlu*, *khair*, *kharik*, *haira*, *baira*, *almora*,
lemongrass, *kulain*, bushes of black and golden raspberries, *kingor*, and *kukurdara*. She named them aloud.

Nanda laughed. "Your list is not complete without *dalchini*, which is so important for fuel wood."

"And the incredible view of the Chaukhamba peaks where nothing grows. They say that you can see this range from Tibet. So many rivers flow down from those glaciers. Without them northern India would be like Tibet, hardly any forests, hardly any of the plants you just named."

"I know. We are so lucky! But the Chandrabhaga's origin is not any glacier."

"That's true. The source is underground water. Mussi enjoys bathing in it, and fishing, too. We love trout curry. I am happy that you have appointed him as the *chaukidar* of your beautiful jungle."

"You mean our forest *patraul*!" Murti corrected her again.

Saina added, "My ex-husband's village, Amkoti, doesn't have such views as you have here. But it, too, uses the Chandrabhaga's water."

The Chandrabhaga passed through Amkoti, ultimately draining into the Alaknanda, which joined the Ganga at nearby Dev Prayag.

"Yes, Chandrabhaga begins to look like a small river by the time it reaches your village. It is joined by many smaller creeks along the way. Amkoti is named after its many *am* trees. Great Amkoti mangoes! Any passerby is free to pick them. Very generous men and women, the people of Amkoti. We don't have such a variety." Nanda said.

"But you have six trees of Bombay mangoes. Nobody around here knows that Bombay *am* is the king of mangoes," Saina complimented in return.

"You are free to pick up our mangos, Saina." Nanda got up. "But be careful, for there may be a bear or two enjoying mangos up on the treetop!"

"I keep my sickle tucked below my navel!"

They all laughed and then departed.

"Tucked below her navel! Nearer the *kujaga*, the right place to hide the secret sickle," Murti exclaimed. "She managed to cut the *kujaga* of her former husband. I can't believe it!"

They laughed.

In Garhwali, women used the word *kujaga*, a euphemism, for male or female genitals. It meant "bad place." But men used other words, all obscene. If a woman was found using those obscene words, people lost respect for her. Nobody seemed to be bothered by men's use of these terms. Men used the word *kujaga* when talking to women without being considered uncivil. Other organs had no taboos. The only word for male genitals was *ling*, from *linga*, and *yoni* for female genitals. But these Sanskrit words were rarely used here.

"Can you imagine doing such a horrible mutilation, didi?" Murti asked.

"Bhuli," her senior sister-in-law said with a laugh, "I don't have to imagine. I would not hesitate to do it if I were in her situation. You too would do it, my little bhuli. Otherwise, men will continue to use women as sex slaves."

"I would never, didi. You are very brave. You saved me by mutilating the tiger's tail and much else. I will never be able to return this life-saving favor."

The tall Nanda just smiled and put her hand on Murti's shoulder to show her affection for her.

Chapter 4

The next Sunday, the judge got up early. After breakfast, he dressed up like a hunter, grabbed his hat, rifle, and a lunch pack, which contained seven big stuffed *parathas* and chunky chutney, all prepared by Nanda. Last night, he told Nanda of his plan to avenge Murti by killing her attacker—the tiger.

In late afternoon, he returned with a fowl but no tiger. Nanda understood. "Well, a fowl is a better revenge. I will send some of its *shorwa* to Murti. Balram loves spicy chunks in saucy soup."

"I will try again next week. I have an idea. Are you planning to go to the forest this week?"

"Yes. Murti is not scared anymore. But why do you ask?"

"She can ask Mussi to bring me a goat. Big or small, male or female, it doesn't matter. Any tiger can be lured if a goat or sheep bleats occasionally. Even if it doesn't bleat, its smell is enough for the tiger."

Three days later, Mussi brought a good-size sheep.

"Good. This big ram will be better bait," Pawan said appreciatively.

"My cattleman friend, Mattu, didn't take any money."

"But why?" Pawan asked.

"I tried to convince him that Wakil Sahab wants it as a loan for a day or two. He won't take any money from you. It's a gift, he insisted. He has a big flock and so no shortage of sheep."

"I heard bad news about a month ago. A tiger killed some stray goats in Batha village. Could they be his goats?"

"Maybe. The villagers often complain about Mattu's cattle trespassing into their fields."

Pawan smiled as he understood the *quid pro quo* in play. "Do you want to come with me to hunt?"

"That's a good idea."

"Then we can carry the tiger, and you can take its skin and sell it." Pawan was aware of people's desire for tiger skins, which they thought good to display in their sitting rooms.

Mussi knew that the judge had several skins in his house, but these were proof of his bravery and not just for decoration or for sitting. Beside the skins, he had no interest in other organs. What he wished for was a bear, from which he would carefully remove a special part such as the spleen, the source of a powerful aphrodisiac for men. The judge was a typical Indian male in that he appreciated aphrodisiacs from any source, including the organs of a bear. In India, aphrodisiacs were more in demand than copies of the *Kamasutra*.

Except for the skin, the other organs of the tiger were not used, the body left out in the open at a reasonable distance to avoid the rotten smell. Other wild animals finished all the flesh. Vultures were usually the first to notice the dead animal with their kaleidoscopic aerial survey capability. The other leading omnivorous scavengers were very keen observers as well—the jackals. They had terrific olfactory receptors and easily locate the dead animal and clean up every bit of the carcass.

❧❧❧

The next day Mussi led the ram from his home. He had a bundle of green grass and offered it a little portion intermittently while holding the rope tied to the ram's neck. Mussi had his axe tied to his belt, and Pawan was behind the ram with his gun.

When they reached the spot where the tiger attacked Murti, Mussi tied the ram to an oak tree, and he and Pawan made a small *machan*, a sitting place like a miniature tree house made with ropes and branches of the oak tree, for hunting purposes. No grass or water for an hour for the poor ram. From a distance, Mussi showed the ram a bundle of green grass and a bowl of water. The ram bleated. They left him alone and hid themselves up on the *machan*.

In a few minutes, two jackals showed up ready to grab the ram. The ram's bleats exploded, and with frantic semi-circular movements, it tried to free itself from the tree.

Mussi heard the panicked calls of the ram and shouted as he ran toward it. The jackals speedily disappeared. As he returned to the tree's *machan*, the ram continued bleating.

In a couple of hours, a tiger showed up. It looked around. Then, without growling, it stood still. The hunters also kept quiet and waited for about two minutes. But the black-striped beast still appeared silent, still looking around. No movement, no growls.

More than four minutes passed. Mussi began to show impatience. "Wakil Sahab," he whispered, "Shoot now!"

"Not yet," Pawan whispered, "The tiger has some meaning in its silence."

"What meaning?" Mussi whispered.

"Its own meaning of the situations, its own interpretations."

"Interpretations?" Mussi looked at Pawan with blank eyes. Pawan knew his blank eyes were expecting more—anticipatory meaning or action, beyond the intended meaning and action of the speaker. This is what Sakar had told him about *anticipatory meaning* and *anticipatory action*.

But Mussi thought that Pawan intended to wait more and watch a little longer.

After waiting for about four minutes, Mussi's anticipated meaning became *presupposed* meaning. Pawan wanted to tell Mussi that meaning was never static. Just like us and all animals, the tiger *thought* when awake. That was, it constantly formed mental images of one situation after another, a sort of silent syntax.

However, Pawan didn't say that. He doubted if Mussi would understand. Instead, he gave a simple answer, "Thinking means interpreting. Right now, it is interpreting—attack or not to attack. I have to understand the meaning behind its waiting before I shoot."

Pawan was also thinking of the Buddhist *apoha*, a theory of *opposed* meaning, as explained to Sakar by his lama guru. A word or sentence is understood not only by what it means but also by what it does not mean. As a hunter and lawyer, Pawan loved to use *apoha* in court and hunting. In court, he would try to understand his adversary's words, include their *main* meaning and exclude their *associated* opposed meaning and then attack the argument of his adversary. Sakar liked his brother's use of *apoha* in court, but not in hunting. Pawan remembered how one day Sakar acted radically when he took Pawan's gun in his hand and said in a respectful, but angry tone, "Bhai ji, the sole purpose of guns is to shoot or kill. I am going to deposit your gun with Pauri's jailor. Those who hunt have not yet gone beyond the hunting-gathering stage. My lama guru would be stunned by your cruel use of *apoha.* True religion for a Buddhist is non-killing, kindness." A month later when Sakar left home, Pawan retrieved his gun from the jailor.

Pawan kissed his gun. Mussi nodded his head with a funny smile. Suddenly, the tiger moved a little farther toward the ram. Mussi looked into the eyes of Pawan and then blinked.

Pawan understood what Mussi wanted him to do. He too blinked back. He wished to tell Mussi that like us, the tiger knew what its closer movement meant and what it didn't. Its knowing meant it formed in its mind some images that made its interpretations or situations. Then it converted one situation into actual action—the movement.

Instead, he whispered, "Mussi, the tiger is thinking, meaning some action. Its movement is the symbol of its readiness to attack. But we wait until it actually attacks." Then he added, "Note Sakar's advice: Never attack any animal unless it attacks."

Mussi nodded his head, apparently out of respect, but he knew the lawyer would have shot the animal without any delay if it were a deer. He was aware of Pawan's taste for venison. He was looking at Pawan with excitement, not because of his nonsense philosophical applications, but because of the tiger's intent gaze at its prey.

Suddenly, the tiger adopted its typical attack pose, the sign of its next move. Pawan understood the meaning of that sign—to jump or not to jump over its prey. That meaning prompted Pawan to place his hand on the trigger of his gun. Mussi didn't need to query again as he too remembered Sakar's advice or rather his guru's advice: *No need to discuss what is obvious.*

All of a sudden, the tiger took the ram to the ground,

choking it in its fierce jaws. A gunshot rang out as the tiger tried to drag the ram away. The tiger was wounded very badly and left the ram. Another gunshot hit the tiger in the head when it inadvertently moved in the direction of the two hunters. The tiger died instantly.

They felt sorry to see the bruised ram. Mussi and Pawan made a stretcher out of two oak branches and carried the ram on it all the way to Pawan's home.

Just before evening, Mussi and his neighbor brought the dead tiger on a stretcher made with oak branches.

"Nanda, I have killed that tigress. Bring Murti along. She will see the dead tigress before we skin it. We have avenged her," said the elated judge.

"Did you say a tigress?" Nanda inquired.

"Yes, a real tiger."

"I asked, was it a tiger or tigress?"

"No, no. I killed a tigress."

"Then it is not Murti's attacker."

"Are you sure it was a tiger?"

"Yes, an old male. Didn't I mutilate his tail and what is directly under his tail?"

The judge didn't say a word further. With Mussi's help, he quickly skinned the dead beast and threw away the rest of the body.

ᘒᘓᘒᘓ

The next day, Pawan noticed the ram was in excruciating pain. He shot it in the head and the misery of the poor ram was over.

In the evening, Nanda prepared a mutton *biranji* (biryani). She sent a *digchi* filled with about two pounds of biryani to Murti, whose husband Balram devoured the chunky mutton pieces, emptying the whole pot.

A month later, Pawan went to the forest again to kill the tiger. This time, thinking that the tiger could attempt again to attack them, he went with Nanda and Murti.

Murti was not scared because she had full confidence in the hunting skills of her brother-in-law. She even kept herself a few yards away from Nanda and Pawan to lure the tiger.

In less than an hour she heard one shot. Then another shot. Then another shot. She ran scared toward Nanda, who told her she didn't know if it was the tiger Pawan was shooting. Then the two women saw Pawan slowly dragging an animal in their direction.

"Nanda, could you go down the mountainside and call to Mussi! I need his help."

"What is it? I have to tell him why you need him."

"Come see this big wild hog. This bastard was hard to kill. Very thick skin."

In the evening, all of the Kotwals gathered to barbecue the big hog. Nanda gave two legs and the head of the hog to Mussi to take home and share with Saina. They all loved the fresh pork.

The judge finally lost interest in locating the tiger that had attacked Murti. He believed that the tiger didn't taste human blood and so there was very little chance he would become a man-eater. Pawan was more interested in hunting animals they could eat.

ርዓርዓ

One evening Pawan brought a deer, an immature adult, almost a fawn. Nanda hesitated to cook it for dinner. She told Pawan to give it to Murti. He was surprised for venison was prized meat for Paharis. But her parents, the Maithanis, never allowed any meat to enter their home and Nanda had a very difficult time adjusting to her husband's meat-eating Brahmin family.

"Oh, come on! You know the Sanskrit word *mrigaya*, meaning deer hunting. King Dushyanta came to Garhwal to hunt the Pahari spotted deer, not to meet that Pahari girl Shakuntala.

"Let me caution you. Never tell *desi* Brahmins that Sita loved venison."

"Look! We are genuine Vedic Brahmins. We follow what our oldest scriptures say." It was clear that he was referring to the Vedas, which tell how Aryans enjoyed all sorts of meat, the flesh of many kinds of animals. "I read a D.Lit. thesis by a Banaras Hindu University Brahmin, a vegetarian *desi* Brahmin. Being a scholar he had to tell the facts and leave the myths out," Pawan said, stretching his hands.

"What sort of facts are you trying to tell me?"

"Just one fact. Our early Vedic ancestors enjoyed not only venison but steak as well. Beef steak was their favorite. Therefore, this vegetarian Brahmin scholar says the *godan* ceremony was very common. During marriage, a cow gift to the groom by the bride's father was a requirement, primarily for steak. Much later for milk. Like many *desi* Brahmins, your father would like to kill this fact."

Doubt showed in her eyes. "Whatever you say, but my father didn't even touch garlic, let alone any meat."

"Yes, if he had eaten garlic then he would have more children. We eat garlic regularly, however, and we have just three children. Why does garlic affect only Indians this way and not the other people of the world? Stupid discrimination by garlic!"

"Not so. I heard most Indians eat garlic. Garlic chutney is the best. A swami ji told us how garlic is useful to treat many health problems. And vegetarians should not have any objection."

Pawan seemed to be happy to hear that from her. "I agree with the swami ji. I am sure all Paharis would agree with him. They cannot imagine a meat dish could be zesty without garlic."

Nanda used garlic and onions in every vegetable dish and *dal*, not to mention meat dishes.

"But some say that they don't like garlic because of its awful smell," she said while looking into Pawan's eyes.

"That's a lame excuse. Roasted garlic or raw garlic with *tarka* loses its smell. Indians have no taboo against black salt in snacks to make them taste better. If they can use *kala namak* why can't they use roasted garlic! This black salt is farty, cooked or uncooked. That's why we Paharis call it *padya lon,* farty salt."

Nanda laughed hard at Pawan's facial expression of disgust!

Chapter 5

"You look happy, very happy," Nanda said to Pawan, who had just returned from his Pauri office. "What makes you so joyous, happy, as if you were high?"

"It's not *bhang*. You know I don't smoke. What I had today to get high is far more potent than *bhang*."

"Can I share it with you?"

"In fact, I wanted to celebrate the occasion with venison, but I can't hunt deer anymore."

"Just tell me clearly."

"We have to celebrate without any meat dish."

"Again, the same *nautanki* drama! If you keep doing this, I will leave to cook."

"I have a letter in my pocket." He handed the letter over to her. "Read it. It's in Hindi."

As Nanda read it, she burst into tears.

"Isn't that proposal for Prachi fantastic, my dear?"

Nanda composed herself. "The boy is twenty-four years old and a graduate of Roorkee."

"Yes, the best engineering college in India. But did you understand why I said I can't hunt anymore?"

"I wish you could have stopped when my father objected to your meat-eating. Are you saying that now you understand why the girl's parents must yield to the requirements of the boy's parents?"

"I know. You yielded to our requirements, and now you have to yield to these forthcoming Arya Samaj in-laws."

"That's the destiny of a Hindu girl."

"Now we have to tell our girl. Where is Prachi?"

"Murti is teaching her how to make a special dish."

"What dish?"

"Balram has brought some goat liver from Hussain's Pauri butcher shop."

"Maybe this will be the last meat dish for Prachi."

"I know. I read in the proposal: 'We are Arya Samaj Brahmins. Pahari Brahmins may not follow our Vedic traditions. So, your daughter must accept or reject this proposal based in part upon whether she follows those traditions.'"

"Very funny! Right?"

"What's so funny?" Nanda wanted to know.

"They consider themselves Vedic Brahmins because they are vegetarians. We Pahari Brahmins consider ourselves Vedic Brahmins because, like our Vedic Brahmin ancestors, we eat meat!"

"Anyway, let's wait for Prachi."

When Prachi returned around eight p.m., they showed her the proposal. She understood the demand to accept or reject the proposal regarding following Vedic practices. Her knowledge about Arya Samaj was almost zero. She had studied in Pauri's Christian Messmore High School and finished two years ago. Now she was eighteen years old. After high school, there was no college in Pauri and her parents didn't want to send her outside the region. Achieving a high school education was very rare for girls in these hills, which made Prachi and her older married sister Uttara unusual.

Her brother Harshpat's medical education in Lucknow's King George Medical College was hurting her father's pocketbook more and more. So Prachi also understood that now was the best time for her to become engaged. Would she give her consent? Would it matter? Only Arya Samaj Hindus believed in the equal rights of men and women, gender equality unheard of among these Himalayan people who seldom cared about a girl's choice in such matters.

A little blush was visible all over Prachi's face as she began to read the proposal. She seemed surprised and she placed her palm over her lips. Her parents reacted quickly.

"Are you looking at the line where they mention getting your approval?" Pawan asked Prachi. "I admire them. As a lawyer, I would like to represent them. I believe they will treat you as good as their son."

Prachi blushed again. "But I don't know what Arya Samaj principles are. I need to know them in detail before I say anything about their proposal. Can you both tell me tomorrow?"

"Yes, tomorrow, but in the evening after I return from my office," Pawan responded.

"That's a perfect time for me," Prachi responded instantly.

ෆ๑๛

The following evening Pawan and Prachi were on the sofa in the sitting room after dinner, which had been all vegetarian. Prachi was surprised to observe a change so soon. Last evening, her parents didn't even touch the liver dish that Murti had sent for them.

"I already told your mother about some views of the Arya Samaj earlier," her father said. "At that time, I hadn't expected you would receive a proposal from someone who follows those views. You can get at least some idea of those views from your mother."

"But give me some general idea of their Vedic principles."

"Number one: They don't believe in idolatry. The Vedic religion is without idols, without temples. Their mantras are recited in the early Vedic language, not in later Sanskrit. Number two: They believe in one Supreme Self called *Parmatma*, just one god. Indra, Yama, Varuna, Pusha, Agni, and several others are aspects of, manifestations of, that one *parmatma*. Got it?" Pawan asked Prachi, his disbelief in such ways of thinking obvious because of the smirk on his face.

Prachi agreed with Pawan. "Baba, nobody in our hills believes that Ganesh and Hanuman are one and the same Supreme God. Do you think my grandparents would have believed Hanuman and Ganapati as aspects of one god?"

"These two gods are not Vedic," Pawan said. "There is a Vedic hymn in which Indra and Varuna boast about their superiority. Shouldn't these two gods have realized that they are one and the same god?"

"And how about goddesses? Are they too aspects of the one god?

"You have seen in our *pujas* that Lakshmi and Sarasvati sit with Ganesh and Hanuman. We worship each of them as if they are different from each other. Ganesh has an elephant head and Hanuman has a long tail. And these vegetarian deities don't mind sitting with flesh-eating deities. Due to our animal sacrifices, *desi* folks consider us Paharis big dunces."

"No wonder so many men from here are employed in the military and police, Baba!"

"Clerks, too. But these are low-paying government jobs...By the way, did you ever imagine a Pahari from here could be the first premier of the largest province of India? The population of UP must be more than that of England. I hope that, in free India, the head of this Himalayan chief minister does not evolve like the head of that Himalayan god, the first god of *puja*, Lord Ganesh who was born human and then evolved as a big hard-headed animal!"

They both laughed.

Pawan resumed speaking. "I will not go hunting anymore. No meat will be brought into this house, at least until you are married! The only time I maintained this principle faithfully was when I was at your mother's parents'. That was our wedding day!"

"But nobody here can afford meat even once a month. Most are lucky to taste a small portion of the free meat, the *prasad,* from a *bali*. Even we eat meat not more than twice a month, and then only because you are a hunter. The other days we are vegetarian."

"But your mother's priest considered me a regular non-vegetarian. He performed a purification ceremony on me before our wedding."

"What purification ceremony?"

"You know the *panchagavya* ceremony in which I had to drink cow urine. Why didn't that adamant Brahmin priest allow me to add sugar to the cow urine? Mixing a spoonful of sugar would have made that stale cow urine more drinkable!"

They laughed and laughed.

"Baba! Seriously speaking, I am not interested in meat-eating anymore. And you know I left believing those idols after our history teacher told us what happened to the god Somnath's statue at the hands of Mahmud Ghaznavi," Prachi said to her lawyer *baba* (daddy). "Temples will not save us but King George Medical College will. I heard that a religious businessman from the plains plans to build a huge temple some-where between Rishikesh and Hardwar. Harshpat bhaiya told me that he has seen people defecating all along the railway lines from Dehradun to Lucknow, and so he sug-gests rich religious business leaders use some common sense and spend that money on toilets, not temples."

"I agree," Pawan said then changed the conversation to the proposal. Now, regarding our business. Can we tell your brother that you can live with these basic principles of an Arya Samaj family?"

"Yes, you can write to Harshpat that I have become a vegetarian. I appreciate his King George Medical College doctors, not our temple priests. These Pahari priests don't have the common sense to persuade their rich visitors to donate for building toilets around the temples. Anyway, as time goes by we will add more Arya Samaj principles to your appreciation list. This list you just gave me is good enough for me right now." Prachi sounded very firm in her convictions.

"Then let's tell your ma in the kitchen."

Nanda hugged Prachi with tears in their eyes. "Victory to gender equality!" the judge shouted with tears in his eyes.

They all enjoyed their vegetarian dinner.

ഇൗഇൗ

In about two weeks the future groom's parents' letter arrived, a thank you for accepting their proposal. They wanted to discuss the wedding plans at the convenience of the Kotwals.

Pawan showed the letter to Nanda when Prachi was not present.

"Nanda, I am hoping for a happy relationship with these Arya Samajis. Sometimes I am worried that, as they say, history will repeat itself. I never told you why we have very little contact with Bhagbati Prasad and Uttara. It's not our daughter who is the cause; it's our son-in-law. Bhagbati Prasad's father is a scholar of Sanskrit, but very fanatical. Bhagbati thinks his father is right, and why not? After all, Sundar Mani Pokhriyal is his father. Pokhriyal ji is a member of Hindu Mahasabha and so Bhagbati Prasad supports his father's Mahasabha views. I had arguments with Bhagbati Prasad but never with his father."

"What arguments?" Nanda was curious to know.

"Look, I am a lawyer, and Bhagbati and his father think lawyers are quarrelsome. Bhagbati told me that not only are Gandhi and Nehru lawyers and so quarrelsome, they are womanizers too. He said his father told him so. I asked Bhagbati how his father found out. 'Oh, my father has his sources,' he replied. Gandhi and Nehru are known for their open lives, like open books, I told Bhagbati. But Uttara agreed with Bhagbati. I revealed a secret to Uttara when she was alone. She asked me how I found out. I said I have my own sources. Then I told her what the sources told me. Since then Uttara and Bhagbati Prasad are sulking and keeping their distance from us."

"What secret did you reveal?"

"Bhagbati Prasad's nana, Badri ji, was a womanizer. His first wife died and his nana had to raise his daughter and son. After his children were married, Badri ji felt free to roam around. He brought a woman into his home and lived with her for one year—unmarried. Then he left her for another woman. He lived with her for only a couple of months. She left him. He used to beat her. Then he became interested in a beautiful Pauri Christian lady. He asked a friend who knew her personally to propose to her on his behalf. The friend was a relative and a lawyer—and my source. He tried to convince Badri ji that his thinking about himself was flawed. He said, 'Why would that Christian girl marry a Hindu who was much older and with married children?' The friend was very clever. He came back and told him that she said 'no.' But Badri ji advised his friend to try again: 'When a woman is in love and says no she really means yes.' The friend didn't buy Badri ji's behavioral analysis. Moreover, Badri ji was a high school dropout and the lawyer who was his friend was a college graduate.

"So you told Uttara this whole story?" Nanda asked Pawan.

"Not only this, but I argued against raising Sanskrit up to be the national language. Uttara's father-in-law wants Sanskrit to be the official language of an independent India."

"What? Did you ask him if his grandma and ma can speak correct Hindi?" Nanda asked in disbelief.

"She is lucky to speak correct Garhwali. Forget Hindi! Forget Sanskrit!" The two smiled while they nodded their heads.

"Worse, he wants the *Bhagavad Gita* to be the national book."

"But why does he want a dialogue between two polygamists honored? Doesn't he know that Krishna and Arjuna of the *Bhagavad Gita* had several wives? Does he want women to be objects of men's desire? We need women's rights in a free India, not any outdated religious stuff propagated by polygamists."

"I didn't ask him that. It is true there is much exploitation of women by religions. I should have brought that up. But I did ask him why not the Bible or Quran? He told me those books were not of Indian origin. I was dismayed that he didn't mention our own books, like the holy scriptures of Jainism and Buddhism. And their founders were not wife-collectors! I was a little tough on him when I told him how people around the world admired

Gandhi and Nehru. He tried to cut me out, saying, 'But they don't know their secret lives.' I retaliated by saying, 'And how many people heard your grandfather's name in your small town of Rishikesh?' I think that hit a nerve."

"Obviously, good enough to make him sulk," Nanda said.

"But let us leave this obscene topic and be ready to discuss our plans for the wedding."

"Yes, we don't know how much cash they demand in dowry and *tilak*. Dowry on the plains is much higher than in our hills. I will be ready even if I must take out a loan...But right now, we better enjoy the great news."

They looked out the window together at the clear sky with a nearly the full moon. They could see the shiny snow over the tops of the Chaukhamba Mountains.

Chapter 6

After the proposal was accepted, the next phase of preparation for the wedding was the most important. The following month Pawan went to Jaipur to discuss the plan with the Bharadvaj family. They were not exactly living like the Maharaja of Jaipur, he noted, but their house was above average for some of the middle class. Pawan was very happy to know that his daughter could live here far more comfortably than in her Himalayan home. He was highly impressed by the future son-in-law Shashi and his mother Chandrika. Shashi offered to take him around Jaipur city after lunch.

The discussion started before lunch. They talked in Hindi. The first thing Chandrika assured Pawan of was they had no gift demands. No jewelry, no dowry, no *tilak* money, no suits for the groom, no honoring of the guests with cash. That relaxed Pawan. The other thing that concerned him was the family name: Bharadvaj. The groom's father, Dhirendra Bharadvaj, was not interested in the family name of the Kotwals. But Pawan knew that his own family *gotra* was also Bharadvaj. He asked Dhirendra if he had any objection to a matrimonial relation with a Bharadvaj. Unlike the Paharis, many *desi* Brahmins would not marry within the same *gotra*.

"Nice to know that we share the same *gotra*. You have been living in those remote green and cool mountains and we in this hot and dry desert city for centuries. We don't think we are close relatives. We have no problem with intercaste marriage."

They all laughed. They all knew theirs was not an intercaste marriage, but Dhirendra's words made Pawan very comfortable to go further. Nevertheless, he wanted to make one thing clear: jewelry. "Excuse me for bringing up one more matter about material gifts. You said 'no' to jewelry," he reminded them.

"Yes, and we mean it," Chandrika responded. "We have enough jewelry for Prachi."

"But in our Hindu tradition the mother passes her jewelry to the daughter. Will you have any objection to that?" Pawan looked at Chandrika, probing her eyes for an answer.

"Such inheritance is a private matter between mother and daughter." Chandrika's answer made Pawan very happy.

They continued their discussion while having lunch at the dining table. The main topic of the discussion was dietary restrictions and appropriate food items. They seemed easy for Pawan. In fact, the Bharadvaj folks showed their curiosity to know the Pahari customs of cooking party food and their serving style.

"Let us know them. If we see any conflict, we will let you know."

"Our marriage lunch follows very different rules from the rules of breakfast and dinner. Anyone can prepare breakfast and dinner, so long as the cooks are not untouchable—"

"We don't care if you have untouchable cooks," Chandrika interjected.

Pawan was surprised, but he was not uncomfortable.

"I don't believe in untouchability. I agree with the news that Gandhi ji would prefer Dr. Bhimrao Ambedkar to be the future framer of the new constitution of independent India. We have to wipe out untouchability."

"Swami Dayanand had started his Arya Samaj effort to remove untouchability much earlier than Gandhi ji," Shashi commented.

"Yes, and both came from the same region of Gujarat. I wish Swami ji had the legal expertise of Dr. Ambedkar. Ambedkar ji is the only untouchable educated at the top universities in England and the USA. It's a shame how he was mistreated by the upper castes despite his excellence. Thanks to Gandhi ji for thinking of Dr. Ambedkar."

"Be sure that you eat enough." Chandrika smiled. "So, what are the Pahari customs of cooking and serving food for weddings? Give us some idea."

"Oh, it's a mess. Rules and more rules. We have the most idiotic dietary model in the world," Pawan responded, "but I will give you a short summary." Pawan started to explain, "The most important man is a Sarola Brahmin who is in charge of cooking, but only for lunch."

The Bharadvaj couple thought that it was a sort of *Kacchi-pakki rasoi* cooking convention among the *desi* Brahmins.

"Who are Sarola Brahmins?" Chandrika asked.

Pawan gave a brief historical background of the "raw and cooked" meal-convention.

"Many Pahari Brahmins are actually *desi* Brahmins. Their ancestors came to our hills from different parts of India. Two of them are noteworthy: *Sarola* and *Gangapari* Brahmins. One clan lived across the river Sarayu and the other across the Ganga, thus *Sarayupari* and *Gangapari* divisions of the U.P. Brahmins. These clans feuded to establish superiority in the plains, and when they came up to the hills they, continued their quarrels.

The *Sarolas*, meaning the *Saryupari* Brahmins, consider themselves the supreme Brahmins of all India. The Kotwals are *Gangari*, meaning *Gangapari*. They are happy that they are not chefs. So, these two clans cannot intermarry."

"Imagine, Pawan ji," Dhirendra joked, "Dr. Chandrashekhar as a Sarola chef instead of an astronomy professor. The astronomer would have wasted his time cooking dishes over hot coals instead of looking for white dwarf stars!"

They all laughed.

They knew that the famous astronomer belonged to a south Indian Brahmin community, even though he was born far in the north, in Punjab.

"Yes, the astronomer could qualify for a Sarola chef if he was born in our hills. We have always accepted a south Indian Brahmin, and only a south Indian Brahmin, to be the Badrinath temple's head priest and share all foods with him." Pawan added this information to the joke.

"Now let's be serious," Dhirendra said. "We are compatible, Pawan ji, for we are neither Saryupari nor Gangari." Dhirendra didn't look serious.

Pawan responded with a good laugh then replied, "Actually we Kotwals have become *Anari*. We live near a huge forest."

"Ah, the word *Anari* is from the Sanskrit word *Anarya*," Dhirendra joked again, "but now it means uncivilized."

"True, we are non-Aryan, a mixed people, part Indian and part Tibetan. Look at my face," Kotwal joked.

"In Arya Samaj anybody is Arya: brown, black, white, yellow. That includes those who are part Indian and part Tibetan. Color variations by Mother Nature have nothing to do with *Aryan*. For Arya Samaj an *Aryan* means any civilized person. Do you see Chandrika's complexion?"

Pawan looked at Chandrika with a smile. She returned his smile. Chandrika's complexion looked black to Pawan, though her name meant "Moonshine."

"The Arya Samaj believes in the equality of men and women," Dhirendra continued. If a widower can remarry then a widow can remarry too. A woman can also leave her incompatible husband and remarry, just like men, but there is no tolerance for polygamy in Arya Samaj. The founder of Arya Samaj was not a womanizer, but a monk, a swami. Yet he fought for equal education for boys and girls. As you know, Chandrika and I are college educated. Pawan ji! Have you ever seen a woman officiating as a priest at a Hindu wedding?"

"Never. Only male Brahmin priests every time," replied Pawan, his eyebrows raised.

"The Arya Samaj has changed that Hindu custom. I am not proselytizing for your daughter's conversion to Arya Samaj. Prachi is free to be or not be an Arya Samaji. She can pursue higher education here."

"As a lawyer and judge I believe in the basic rights you just mentioned." Pawan nodded his head. "The new constitution must guarantee them."

After lunch Pawan and Shashi went out to see the city. They had a good time.

The most fascinating site was the Maharaja's Hawa Mahal (Palace of Wind/Breeze), though Pawan hoped to get rid of all the maharajas and nawabs in an independent India for they plundered India's wealth more than any foreign invader.

౦౨౦౩

The next day Pawan left very happy. The Bharadvajs'

full approval of his plan for the wedding day was totally unexpected.

Upon his return home, the first thing Nanda asked him was, "How did it go?"

"No need for a loan," said the elated lawyer. "Oh Nanda, you won't believe how friendly they are. They relaxed me with so many jokes and discussion of all sorts of topics. In short, everything went smoothly."

Nanda was delighted by the approval of the Bharadvaj family.

"Let's keep this confidential, but Harshpat, Mussi, and Saina must be included for the wedding to be successful. Let's give them the news and instruct them to wait for the detailed work plan."

"And what about Uttara and her husband?"

"We don't have to worry about them. We must inform them, but they may not even attend the ceremony. Anyway, their cooperation is not so vital. Saina alone can manage the evening feast. At the most we can expect Murti's assistance. The Bharadvaj party will consist of fewer than twenty-five guests, and none of their guests will want to eat the soupy intestines of a goat like we do. Mussi will be surprised to learn that no ram sacrifice will take place!"

They laughed.

"We will be the first Kotwals not to do the Nagraja Puja before the wedding, offering no goat to the lord of snakes. Everything vegetarian!"

Chapter 7

Murti informed Mussi and Saina of the wedding, and he only gave them that part of the news. They were very excited and wanted to surprise Nanda and Pawan as soon as possible. The following day Mussi visited Mattu's cattle ranch. He could hear the cattleman yelling down near the creek. He was trying to lure some cows that were trying to go beyond the creek, the divider between Mattu's terraced fields and Batha village.

Mussi helped Mattu herd all seven cows into the barn. "You need a farmhand to take care of your animals, Mattu."

"I can't afford one."

Mussi gently tapped Mattu's back as he recommended, "Then get married. Your wife will look after your animals."

Mattu smiled. "Only if she is as tall as I am!" He looked to be five feet, nine inches tall and was very muscular.

Slowly they walked up to Mattu's house. Mussi lay on the long wood bench in the verandah while Mattu went inside. In a few minutes, he came out and brought his portable hookah with a tobacco pot on top of it.

The two friends began to smoke. "So what brings you here this morning?" the cattleman asked.

"I need a ram," Mussi responded after a puff and exhalation of smoky air.

"The tiger problem again?"

"No tiger this time. I will explain later."

"Then let's visit the goats in the barn. There you can select a ram, but first let me take one more puff."

Mussi passed the hookah to him.

When Mussi entered the barn, he found over two dozen goats and kids. He selected the biggest ram.

"That's the costliest ram. Why don't you select a good but less costly one?" the cattleman advised Mussi.

"How much is the ram I want?"

"It's much more than you think."

"How do you know what I am thinking?"

"Last time you got a free ram."

"Not this time. I will pay your price."

"Hussain has offered me thirty rupees, but my asking price is forty. He will buy this giant ram at my asking price eventually and sell its meat at his butcher shop for a good profit."

"You are joking, Mattu! You know I am not buying it for profit. I just want to celebrate the news of Prachi's wedding. Your price is too high for me."

Mattu scratched his head. "Oh, for Prachi's wedding? Then why don't you select some lambs over there. I guess everybody will enjoy lamb curry."

"No, no. No lambs. Just a fat ram."

"I have a deal for you," Mattu said. "The less costly ram can be free if you tell Wakil Sahab to take care of my recent legal problem."

"What's the legal problem?"

"Some of my goats crossed over that creek and grazed in the paddy fields of Batha village. Just to teach me a lesson, those sister fuckers slaughtered all of my goats. I want to teach them a lesson."

"That's awful, Mattu Singh. Why didn't you tell Wakil Sahab?"

"I hesitated."

Mussi paused while massaging his head. Then he looked into the eyes of Mattu. "Listen! I mean seriously. Here is a deal for you. I will get you invited to the wedding of his daughter."

"I accept and you can have the ram I am offering. And I will be happy to slaughter it for you."

Mussi was now staring at the ram. Then he said, "Thanks. I will take it. Its meat will be enough for nine Kotwal families."

"I think so. I will get fresh *malu* leaves to make packets. I will wrap each share in them. How do you want me to mix the meat?"

"I will save the *lwekhuru* for myself. You can have the head."

"That's a very nice thought. I love to eat the baked brain."

Mussi laughed. "Wakil Sahab deserves it, too. He is a Brahmin. You are a Rajput."

"Wakil Sahab does not need it. He is a judge and so knows what's right and what's wrong."

"I know. You definitely need to improve your brain. Otherwise, you would have been married long ago."

Both men laughed.

Mattu Singh was only twenty-two when he joined the Indian British Army as a *hawaldar* during World War II. He dreamed of capturing Hitler and leaving him near Garhwal's Rupkund, a lake surrounded by snow-covered mountains where an entire platoon died long ago due to landslides and avalanches. Being a petty sergeant, Mattu was released from his military service at the end of 1945. He joined his father's cattle raising business.

Now he was facing his enemies from Batha village, but he had no gun and didn't need one. After all they just killed his goats because they trespassed on their territory. If Hitler had killed Poland's "trespassing" goats only, then nobody would have considered him the enemy of all humanity—and Mattu knew very well what butchery Hitler had committed in Poland.

The next Sunday morning, as planned, Mattu slaughtered the ram. Mussi lifted the dead ram upside down and drained the blood into a large pot. He immediately placed the pot on the oven beside the pit, which was for roasting. The coagulated blood was heated slowly until it dried and thickened. Coagulated blood, or *lwekhuru,* is a favorite meat dish in these hills. Then Mattu roasted the head and the torso over the pit. Mattu kept the roasted head (*siri*) aside for himself. Then both began to cut the torso into chunks.

Out of eleven packets of meat, two were specially prepared for the judge: one contained intestines and the other the thigh meat, which is the best cut for Pahari-style steak.

The two friends tasted a few squares of the *lwekhuru.* Mussi took the rest. "Saina, too, loves *lwekhuru,*" he said as he spread his tongue out and then closed it with a sipping noise.

Then Mussi bundled up all the packets into a bag and quickly moved to the Kotwal residence. He distributed the nine packets among the nine Kotwal families. Then he came to see Nanda and Pawan. He handed the two special packets over to Nanda. She was totally surprised just like the other Kotwal families. Pawan was working in the garden. She called to him.

Pawan came up and hugged Mussi. "I am glad to see

you. We wanted to discuss the wedding plan with you."

"I just brought two special packets to celebrate the great news."

"What packets?"

"Your favorites: the intestines and the steak to celebrate the news!" Mussi looked at Pawan's face, anticipating signs of surprise and joy. Instead he saw a slight sadness.

"Mussi, we have reluctantly become vegetarians. Let's go inside and I'll give you all the details."

When they went inside, Nanda went in the kitchen to prepare tea for the two men in the sitting room.

When Mussi came out of the Kotwal house after an hour's meeting he burst into tears. He had the two special packets in his hand. He ran back to his home and showed them to Saina.

He discussed the wedding plan with Saina. She, too, burst into tears. They collected all the meat and proceeded toward the Chandrabhaga, where they saw a herd of *Kakhar* deer drinking water from the creek. If he had seen them one day ago he wouldn't have cared for Mattu's ram. The Kotwals would have preferred venison. He ignored the herd, but Saina threw all the meat toward them. They ran away faster than tigers.

Then Saina and Mussi took a bath. After bathing, both bowed down with folded hands and took three sips of the Chandrabhaga water. They muttered words of prayer, joined hands, and vowed to be vegetarians.

"Now I must meet Mattu tomorrow," Mussi said to Saina.

"Why? You are not negotiating for another ram, are you?"

"I am, in a way. Wakil Sahab has given me thirty rupees to pay him for the last one."

"Thirty rupees? That's not right."

"Wakil Sahab trusts Hussain more than Mattu. Hussain wouldn't have given him more than twenty-five rupees. That ram was smaller than the ram I had selected. Wakil Sahab didn't even touch its meat. He wants me to tell Mattu that he was invited to Prachi's wedding. He also wants Mattu to arrange for two pairs of drummers and bagpipers."

"That's so good. The invitation should make Mattu very happy."

"But not the news that we are now vegetarian. He would have been happier if Wakil Sahab had given him his gun instead of thirty rupees. He would have killed a couple of Batha village men. He had no problem slaughtering the ram and boasted of fatally shooting many enemy soldiers."

Saina laughed, but then she became serious. "He fought in Europe, and now he faces a fight in his backyard. Wars out there in the world and wars here at home, they never end."

"I agree," Mussi said as he briskly mocked a fist attack on Saina.

The couple laughed.

Chapter 8

The wedding festivities started on a Saturday evening. The month of June was not hot here for the Jaipur's little Arya Samaj *barat*, the bridegroom's party. That the groom's party consisted of fewer than twenty-five people surprised the local hosts and their guests, who numbered over one hundred friends and relatives from adjacent villages and Pauri. More shocking to the locals than the low number of guests in the *barat* were the six women included in that number. The local people were accustomed to all-male bridegroom's parties. All the Arya Samaj men wore English-style outfits, mostly shirts and pants, but the women wore blouses and saris.

The Arya Samaj people didn't care about the astrological time or *muhurt* either. Their convenience, congenial weather in the Garhwal hills, was more important matter. For the local people, the weather was hot, but for the Jaipur folks it was so cool! And the following Sunday was also very convenient for everybody, courtesy of the British Raj, which introduced Sunday as a regular holiday in India.

On Saturday evening, the *barat* was welcomed in the front yard of the Kotwal residence. The local musicians headed the host party, which included the Kotwals and their relatives and friends. The *barat* was headed by its own musicians, just one *shahnai* player and a *nagara* drummer, one word from Persian and the other Arabic. The local musicians consisted of the drummers of *dhol* and *damau* and a bagpiper. The bagpipe, which was called *mashak baja* (*mashak* a Persian word, *baja* a Hindi word), was the Scottish bagpipe! Everyone applauded without knowing that the auspicious musical fusion had nothing to do with the Vedic tradition!

The real shock came to Murti and Balram, who were very active, that the only persons more active than they were Uttara and her husband Bhagavati Prasad (locally pronounced as Uttra and Bhagbati). Indeed, Nanda and Pawan had low expectations of their older daughter and son-in-law.

Murti said to Nanda, "You were not sure if Uttra and Bhagbati would even attend this marriage. And here they are the most active family members. What happened?"

"Ha, ha! It's a long story. But let me tell you quickly. Bhagbati Prasad likes to be addressed as just Prasad because it is a boy's name, unlike Bhagvati the 'goddess.' However, people here prefer to use the first name and so everyone is calling him Bhagbati instead of Prasad. And he has another reason for wanting to be addressed as Prasad. Bhagbati left the Hindu Mahasabha and joined the Congress Party, and to make fun of him, some friends began to call him *Bhagabhagi Prasad*, a runaway pleasure, in reference to moving from one party to another."

"That makes sense, but why didn't his father pick a boy's name? What's his father's name anyway?"

"Sundar Mani Pokhriyal, a Sanskrit-knowing pandit who became a member of Hindu Mahasabha early on. One reason he hates the Congress Party is because it has an English name! He wants no English influence on India after independence," Nanda responded. "However, he accepted the fact that Bhagbati was a teacher in the Dharma Samaj School of Dehradun, which included English in all classes. Uttara also was employed in the same School."

Murti said to Nanda, who had already started to move away, "Wait, one more question: Why are Mussi and Saina nowhere to be found?"

Nanda laughed. "They are busy solving their marital problem, but they have sent Mattu as their representative to help us."

"Mattu has been very helpful. He has just placed all the heavy items that I need for the evening. Quite a *pahalwan*!"

Mattu was not a *pahalwan* (wrestler) but did look like one because of his muscular build.

"I've got to go. Thanks to you and Balram for all your hard work." Nanda then all but sprinted away.

The evening dinner feast, all vegetarian dishes, was prepared by Murti, Balram, Bhagbati, and Uttara. The guests seemed to like the local cuisine, which was very different from the Jaipur's.

The next morning around ten, the marriage ceremony started with all the musicians playing their instruments by rotation. Shortly, the bride was escorted by her brother to the altar, the *Vedika*. She looked beautiful in her *ghagri* skirt with her *dupatta* scarf and *sehra* crown set on her head. She wore no veil. She welcomed her groom with folded hands as she saw him stepping up toward the altar with his parents.

Suddenly, everybody saw Mussi coming out with seven or eight guests. The only surprise guest was Pawan's brother Sakar, now Swami Nirakaranand. Mussi had his own bagpiper and dhol-damau drummers, who headed this small party marching toward the altar. Many had confused looks to see Mussi dressed up as a typical

Garhwali bridegroom in a *kurta* shirt, tight white pajamas, and Jodhpuri sandals. He also wore a turban from which hung the *sehra* crown, its colorful strings covering his face.

To many, Mussi looked like a rival bridegroom as he was dressed up like Shashi. But soon his role became clear when Saina was escorted to the altar by Uttara and Bhagbati. She was dressed up just like Prachi in a colorful sari and blouse with *dupatta* scarf and a *sehra* crown. She too wore no veil. Now everyone understood she was Mussi's bride when she welcomed Mussi with her folded palms and stood beside Prachi.

There were audible whispers from the crowd. The whispers made it clear that those in attendance were in disbelief.

Pawan Kotwal, the judge, offered the hand of his daughter to her groom. It was the *pani-grahana* or handshake ritual for Prachi and Shashi. There were some faint whispers and pleasant looks around.

But soon the soft whispers began to evolve into soft noise when the judge acted as the father of Saina and offered her hand to Mussi after the hand-shake of Shahsi and Prachi.

The priest, Maitri, seemed to be an expert at crowd management. She said loudly, "Please talk outside, not in here. We are performing the most solemn and sacred ceremony as prescribed by the ancient *Vedas*."

Harshpat, the judge's son, was standing there with a basket full of rice puffs. The mother of the bride was also standing by her son.

The two brides and the two grooms, one after another, were now ready to start the process of legalizing their marriages: Seven rounds around the fire, seven steps near the fire, each step with a vow of the bride.

Suddenly the family priest of the judge stepped up to the altar and said, "This marriage is not authentic. A woman cannot be a priest."

Harshpat, the judge's son, grabbed the family priest by his hand and very politely escorted him from the altar.

"Please sit down here quietly, Pandit ji! Sit on this chair. That woman is Shashi's priest. Her name is Maitri and she is from Arya Samaj. She is following the standard ancient Vedic tradition. The Arya Samaj does not recognize your medieval view of such a ceremony. I know what I am talking about. You know my *nana* was a professional priest," said Harshpat in a tense voice.

Everybody began to look at the disgruntled *purohit*. He barely sat on the chair for a minute. Then he got up and quit the *mandap* (stage) shouting in Hindi, "I know Harshpat's *nana* was a *purohit*. But his *nani* didn't know Hindi, not Sanskrit either. How did she know that women *purohits* performed weddings in Vedic times? Ha, ha, ha! *Achha tamasha!*"

Indeed, some did consider it a "good show" as they laughed when he briskly disappeared. But around the *Vedika* (altar) the double wedding ceremony began very solemnly again, and Harshpat again picked up his basket of rice puffs.

When the ceremony was complete, the bride's mother and father blessed their daughter and son-in-law, all of them crying. Then both parents, with tears in their eyes, blessed Mussi and Saina and hugged them both. Saina broke down into tears and Mussi stood spellbound. He seemed to be in ecstasy. His impossible marriage had become a reality as if in a fairy story!

Then Pawan gave Mussi another surprise. "Ladies and gentlemen, as you know, Mussi is now a married man. He needs a regular, stable job, and I have arranged such a job for him. He is going to take care of the Pauri prison's men."

Mussi fell flat at the feet of the judge. The judge lifted him up and hugged him. Finally, Mussi mustered the courage to speak, just one sentence. "Wakil Sahab is the kindest man." Now all could see tears in his eyes.

Suddenly, the family priest returned and joined the crowd. He shouted loudly, "Sisters and brothers, Saina's marriage is not valid. She is still married to her previous husband. Did you hear me?"

Harshpat heard him and dragged him out. He said to the priest, "Pandit ji, don't shout and please listen! My father already went before the court with Saina and got her previous marriage annulled. So what's your complaint?"

"That priest didn't say the mantras of *kanya dan*. So both marriages are not legal," complained the sulking priest. "What a joke! She didn't even wear a veil to cover her face."

"Pandit ji, *kanya dan* means a gift of the girl. A girl is not a cow to be given as a gift in a *go dan* ceremony during the wedding. Tell me. Is there any *purush dan* in your ceremony where the groom is offered as a donation to the bride? Pandit ji, India will not be truly liberated until we treat men and women as equal partners. Women are going to behold a new dawn without any veil."

"Your dawn will be clouded. You will be a *vajrapat*, not a Harshpat!" Pandit ji had declared him a thunder-strike and not a joy-strike, the latter being the meaning of Harshpat's name.

"Pandit ji, priests are deadly social pests. Science education will sooner or later develop a pesticide to kill their reproduction of sickening rituals." Dr. Harshpat then left the priest standing there alone and joined the wedding

party to mingle and enjoy the sweets of the wedding celebration.

Chapter 9

A little after one p.m., the Sarola chef sent his assistant to announce that the wedding lunch was to begin at the front orchard's open area. All of the guests and locally invited friends went to the orchard to sit on the grass, the men's and women's rows separated. The food was served on leaf plates and without spoons or napkins. But drinking water was served in metal glasses.

Then the food, all vegetarian dishes, was served. Some guests from the plains expected *roti* and *puri* breads. They didn't know that in the Himalayas breads were eaten for dinner and rice for lunch. Today was in fact their first experience with many food items in Himalayan cuisine.

The Sarola himself came out dressed in his proper outfit, just a white *dhoti* covering him from his chest down to his knees, and walking bare-footed. His sacred thread was clearly visible around his neck. And, of course, a sandal paste mark on his forehead indicated that the first thing he did in the morning was take a bath followed by a short puja.

One by one, the Sarola served rice and *dal* to all the guests. Except for these two items, following tradition, all other items were served by volunteers. Then the Sarola sat in a corner with rice and *dal* on his leaf plate. The volunteers served him the rest of the food items, and he quickly finished his meal and sat on a rock watching the guests.

After all the guests finished lunch, they moved a few yards away to wash their hands and mouths in a spot established for that purpose. Some guests personally complimented the Sarola, who was still relaxing on the flat top of the rock. The first man, not a guest, was Swami Nirakaranand. They hugged each other. After a short conversation, the swami slowly walked away.

Dhirendra, the groom's father, then came to meet the Sarola. With folded palms, he said, "*Namaste.*" The Sarola reciprocated. Dhirendra said, "Thank you so much, Sarola ji. What a feast!"

The Sarola smiled with folded hands. They both sat on the rock.

"By the way, you look less like a Saryupari Brahmin than an Udupi Brahmin chef of Mysore." Dhirendra continued, "I studied there in my younger days. Our hostel's chef was an Udupi Brahmin, and he dressed almost like you are dressed now. He would serve classy south Indian dishes on plain fresh banana leaves. But your ghee-mixed fragrant basmati rice coupled with the whole *tor dal* is a first for me. Pawan ji told me he invited you not just because you are a Sarola Brahmin but because your culinary skills are unmatched."

"Your kind words are very important, not only for me but for my family, too. My wife and children think I must improve my cooking!" the Sarola responded, blinking his hazel eyes.

Dhirendra laughed and quoted a Hindi proverb: *ghar ki murghi dal barabar*, a house chicken is equal to beans. The proverb is a reference to considering a successful family member as very ordinary.

"I know. That is a common family convention. But let me express my personal feeling about basmati. I guess someday the world will appreciate this unique fragrant long rice."

"It's unaffordable. Even in the hills it is served only occasionally. For our daily rice, we eat ordinary kinds."

"We will miss your other delicious dishes, too. I would not like to miss your dishes too long!"

The Sarola didn't mention that the really delicious dish he missed was the Pahari mutton *biranji* (biryani).

"I saw Swami Nirakaranand just as he left you. He is a fascinating man. How did he take *sannyas*?" Dhirendra asked, emphasizing his interest with a smile.

Sarola ji told him more than he expected. "Sakar and I received our B.A. together. I know a lot about him."

Dhirendra looked overwhelmed. A college-educated cook!

The cook noticed his amazed eyes and responded, "Yes, we were class-fellows." After a few seconds' pause, he continued, "Like his brother Pawan, he also passed his LLB law degree and practiced law in Pauri, but just for one year. He met many sannyasis while he was there, and two influenced him the most. One was a lama and the other was a Vedanti. So, he left his successful law practice and took *sannyas* from them—getting clean-shaved, his head included, and wearing ochre robes. As a monk, he renounced all property claims. He became Swami Nirakaranand. His ashram was near Uttar Kashi on the bank of the Ganges. You might have heard the name of the yoga guru Swami Tirthanand, the Vedanti."

"No, I am not familiar with this name."

"Anyway, he trained Sakar not only in yoga but in social services. One social service was very unusual in those times. Due to the influence of Mahatma Gandhi, several volunteers were dedicated to helping the untouchables, known as the *dom* people. Sakar was interested in providing education for untouchable kids. So, he had a plan to move closer to Pauri or Srinagar where he could start a primary school. He thought the untouchable people would establish a good rapport with him and send their kids to his school. The Uttar Kashi ashram was well-funded by rich and religious families from the plains. The ashram was willing to provide funds to build a one-room school but no other regular expenses such as payment for a teacher. He might request you to help him. Can you help him?" The Sarola looked into Dhirendra's eyes.

"Yes, I can check with our local Arya Samaj."

"That will make Sakar very happy."

"But the Arya Samaj will do the *shuddhi* of those children if Sakar wants its help. You know the movement of 'purification' of the untouchables!"

"That might be difficult. I know what Sakar believes: it is not important what others think of you, only what you think of yourself matters. Moreover, he follows Mahatma Gandhi, who never considered *harijans* impure. The untouchables don't need purification, or *shuddhi*. They need education. He does not even call them *harijan* because he thinks our untouchables find it still discriminatory, and besides, just using a euphemism isn't helpful. Upper castes won't sit together with *harijans* to eat because, for them, a *harijan* is a *dom*," the sarola said.

"This word *dom* is certainly objectionable. One shouldn't use it privately or publicly. Bigotry is bigotry."

"You are right. If we cannot criticize our religion, then we don't have real religious freedom. Your help will be a positive statement against untouchability here."

"We will try to help him. Thanks for your recommendation."

Just before he left, Dhirendra touched the feet of this

learned man for he realized that the Sarola wasn't just a village cook.

Sarola ji had avoided conveying Sakar's other family facts. Sakar was Pawan's step-brother. Pawan's father had helped his brother's childless young widow, and at some point he fathered a child by her. He named him Sakar. The local traditional name for such a child was *bhaujeti ki santan*, the progeny of the sister-in-law born of her brother-in law.

He also didn't reveal that Pawan, as a lawyer, was conscious of the fact that this kind of progeny was considered legitimate but looked down upon as socially impure. So, he kept Sakar's share with him. The other nine shareholders easily believed that, though Sakar had renounced any ownership, he might need funds for philanthropy. But Pawan was also able to convince all the shareholders that he had to pay a lot of legal expenses out of his pocket to fight for the additional compensation. So, each shareholder got about two hundred rupees plus one hundred more. In those times this amount was enough to cover the school fees of a child up to high school. All the child had to do was walk to the nearby school, and the famous Christian school was almost next door.

After Dhirendra left, Sarola ji was completely surprised to see two women proceeding slowly toward him, both smiling. One was Chandrika, the bride's mother, and the other was the priest, Maitri, who had performed the two weddings.

After the exchange of *namaste* greetings, Chandrika handed over an envelope to the Sarola chef. "This is our token *dakshina* for your favor."

The Sarola hesitated to take it. But then Maitri intervened, "Sarola ji, please hold the envelope by its corner. You don't have to touch Chandrika's hand! Our ancient

Vedic tradition is different, but we know the Saryuparin Brahmin tradition."

The Sarola immediately touched the feet of both women. "Our ancient law-giver Manu has said, 'Deities rejoice where women are worshipped.' When my son received the sacred thread, I whispered the *gayatri* mantra in his ear, but I didn't forbid him to utter this Vedic mantra in the presence of women."

He didn't say that the Pahari Brahmins were also in the Vedic tradition. The Brahmins cooked various meats in the Vedic times, and the Pahari Brahmins continued that ancient tradition until the British times. Now they were forever free to enjoy good meat. He deliberately avoided debunking the Arya Samaj myth of the Vedic Brahmins' vegetarian cooking.

"The Sarolas utter the Vedic mantras loudly. Even the drummers and bagpipers hear them. We Sarolas are no dummies," he added and quietly accepted the envelope.

As the two women moved away, they saw Mussi running toward them. He had brought two sickles, one for each of them.

"This is to show you my appreciation for your favor." He handed the shining tools to them. Both thanked Mussi while continuing to walk and talk with him.

"Mussi! I have one question, if you don't mind," Maitri said.

"Sure. What is it, Panditani ji," Mussi responded very politely.

"I didn't see any of your relatives or Saina's. Any reason?"

"Our relatives wouldn't support our marriage. We were expecting Saina's brother Pran and his wife Rikhi. But they live in Haldwani and Rikhi is sick. Otherwise they wanted to attend our marriage."

"Tell anyone opposing your marriage: True marriage

is by consent, not by coercion. That is why I agreed to perform your marriage."

"Maitri ji, you are way ahead of our *parampara*. Your blessings will stand against all opposition."

Maitri thought of recommending that he join the Arya Samaj where he could find how many stupid *paramparas* (traditions) have been clipped. Instead, she took her sickle Mussi had gifted her in her hand and waved it around Chandrika's head.

Mussi laughed. Chandrika also laughed, but for different reasons. Maitri knew all about her background.

Chapter 10

When Swami Nirakaranand arrived at his ashram, he found a note on his door: *I will meet you tomorrow morning at your ashram to discuss a very serious matter. Sister Tara*

The swami looked puzzled as he unlocked the door. The door was little hard to open, and he kicked it with his canvass shoe. He went inside. First he drank a glass of Ganges water, and then he relaxed on his wooden bed. After a short nap, he took a bath and meditated.

The next morning Sister Tara knocked on his door a little before noon. The door was open as he had been expecting her. She touched his feet and the swami put his hand on her head to wish her well. He offered her a chair then went inside to get her a glass of water. He sat on the bench facing her.

"You look very disturbed and your eyes are red. Did you get enough sleep?"

"No, Swami ji. But I am very sorry to bother you. I was supposed to come here much earlier. But something unexpected happened. Your friend Swami Vedantanand has closed his ashram this morning. There is a notice on its front door: *Swami Vedantanand ka yah ashram band ho gaya.*"

"Where did he go? Any news?"

"I don't know where he went, but I have news I don't want to make public. I want to confide only in you because you are the one who introduced me to him." She finished the whole glass of water quickly. "I think I need some food in order to gather energy to give you the news. I haven't eaten breakfast this morning."

Swami Nirakaranand got up. "Let me bring some snacks."

He went inside and began to prepare *pakoras*. He remembered why and how he introduced her to his friend Swami Vedantanand, who subsequently accepted this American young woman, Terry Smith, as his disciple. Terry, a convert, became Tara.

She was from Chicago, and during her college years, Swami Vivekananda's historic lecture, which he delivered in Chicago, was her favorite. She was impressed by the Vedanta version of Hinduism, and after finishing college, she left for India and traveled all the way to Gaumukh, the source of the Ganges. On her return journey, near Uttar Kashi, she met Swami Nirakaranand. She wanted to be his disciple, but he was not a follower of Vedanta. Swami Titrthnand, a lama and not a Vedantist, had taught him yoga and told him that yoga's aim, according to Patañjali, was not the realization of Brahman, the absolute self of the Vedanta. The lama believed in the non-existence of self or *atman*. Because Terry was interested in Vedanta, the followers of which believe that all is Brahman, the absolute self, and there is no duality of individual self and absolute self, Swami Nirakaranand introduced her to his neighbor, Swami Vedantanand, who became her guru.

He was not a Himalayan yogi. His birth place was a small village near Patna in the Indo-Gangetic plains. Tara was more interested in a Himalayan yogi, but Swami Ni-

rakaranand convinced her that a yogi could be from anywhere. After all, he told her, Swami Vivekananda was not
a Himalayan yogi but he was a Hindu leader and someone Swami Vedantanand admired, until she told him that
Swami Vivekananda ate meat including beef. The reaction of Swami Vedantanand surprised her, "Proselytizing
for Hinduism and eating meat is not Hinduism."

When Tara had told Swami Nirakaranand about Vedantanand's comment, he said, "Swami Vedantanand has
a false understanding of Hinduism's history, but I agree
with him about Swami Vivekananda's proselytizing and
beef-eating. Big verbiage is garbage if not backed by performance. I heard that Vedantanand, like Swami Vivekananda, says in his *satsang* discourses, 'I am proud to be a
Hindu.' It doesn't occur to this ignorant swami to ask an
untouchable if he or she could say, 'I am proud to be a
Hindu.' This pride belongs to higher castes only. If you
question their shameful religious behavior they will defend it vigorously, and without guilt. The result is more
untouchables seeking conversion to other religions."

Nevertheless, Swami Vivekananda converted some
from the West. One of the well-known converts was Sister Nivedita, who represented a combination of attributes
that most impressed Swami Vedantanand. Swami Vivekananda's "mission" became sensationalized and so he
became famous, and now Swami Vedantanand was proud
that he, too, had a white disciple, Sister Tara. Nivedita
and Tara were not only white women but from the West
and with a Christian background. Many from the higher
castes considered such Christian converts as untouchables.

On the other hand, Swami Nirakaranand had observed,
especially in the Garhwal Himalayas, that many untouchables converted to Christianity and achieved higher status
than they had in Hinduism. To prove the sincerity of their

conversion they emulated many habits of their missionaries, such as eating the same meats that their missionaries ate.

He noticed that Tara likewise followed her Hindu missionary's diet. She became a complete vegetarian, which was an unspoken rebuke to local Brahmins who were not vegetarians. The absence of beef in their diet was enough for them to claim the honor of being Brahmins. Nevertheless, they wouldn't eat with her in their kitchen.

He knew that Vedantanand, a Brahmin, didn't behave like these phony Brahmins. Vedantanand would ask Tara, occasionally, to distribute the *prasad* food to his *satsang* attendees. Some attendees would accept the *prasad* and bow to it or put a bit of it on their heads but wouldn't eat it. They would throw it away after leaving the *satsang*. It wouldn't occur to them that they were throwing away the *Vedanta* that the swami had preached earlier: *sarvam khalvidam Brahma*—all this indeed is Brahma (absolute self).

Did any Indian ever practice the Vedanta? He thought that Swami Vedantanand should have answered this question before proselytizing for the fantastic *Vedanta*.

While recollecting these things, Swami Nirakaranand wondered what news Tara wanted to confide to him. Engrossed in his thoughts he spent a little more time in preparing hot *pakoras*. Finally, he brought two platefuls of *pakoras* and tea cups. The tea contained no water, just milk only. He placed the cups and plates on a small table between them.

"So kind of you, Swami ji. Shall we start?"

"Yes, I am sorry that it took me so long."

"No problem," she said, as she took a sip of tea. "Ah, this is all milk tea. Very good. I needed some strength."

Both began to eat hot *pakoras* while sipping the tea.

"Would you like to know why my eyes are red?"

"Yes, please."

"You are right that I couldn't get sleep in the Uttar Kashi Dharmashala."

"What? Why did you go there? Anything wrong with your rented room?" the swami asked, his concern evident in his voice.

"Let me finish these delicious *pakoras*, and I will tell you the news. I am really hungry." After she finished eating, she began to tell him the news he had been waiting for. "You know Swami Vedantanand holds weekly *satsang* sessions with devotional songs and sermons of Vedanta. When all attendees had left the ashram after the last session, he told me to wait. I waited. He said he had some food for me. He did have food, which we shared together. After we finished eating, he went alone in the kitchen to wash the plates, even when I had offered to wash them. After a few minutes he called to me from the kitchen, 'Come here! You can pack some snacks to take out with you.'

I went into the kitchen and he was standing there completely naked—"

Nirakaranand looked into her eyes. "In front of you?"

"—he asked me to undress. 'Let us two selves become one absolute self. You must realize what non-duality means in real life, Tara,' he said in a commanding voice, lust in his eyes," the blonde with her blue eyes said without blinking.

"Oh, no! He went totally insane," Nirakaranand said with his eyes open wide and both hands on his cheeks.

"When I refused, he stretched his arms and embraced me. Then he began to raise my ochre sari. He didn't know I had trained in self-defense. My father is a World War II veteran, and he taught me how to fend off an attacker. Pardon me for being so graphic, Swami ji!"

"That's all right. Say whatever you faced with this thug! He has stained the ochre robes of all monks." As he said this, he touched his ochre-shirt's sleeve. "Go ahead and tell me about this fake Vedantist."

"I grabbed his testicles until he fell down in excruciating pain. I kicked him. I kept kicking and kicking his testicles. That exacerbated his misery so much that he lost consciousness. I ran, not to my room but to the dharmashala. There, many women and men care for each other's safety. I feared that he might come to my room."

"But sometimes you hear bad news about what happens in dharmashalas, which are meant to be the rest houses for pilgrims. I would say they are still better than monasteries. In my opinion, the Buddha made a big mistake allowing monasteries with both monks and nuns. Whenever you have monks and nuns living in a monastery, you can expect exploitation of women. Our Garhwal Himalayas have the most revered temples, and so many pilgrims wish to visit, and poor pilgrims have to stay in the dharmashalas on their way. And some stupid men misbehave."

"You are right. I have heard how in some temples jogis raped joginis."

"Did you tell your story to the dharmashala people?

"You are the first person I am telling because I am leaving for America as Terry Smith. This is the last time you are seeing me in ochre dress. I don't want to make my reason public. My guess is that Swami Vedantanand has disappeared because he fears I will go public. I hope you don't make this news public, however. Now I have to go. Many thanks for the lunch."

"Contact me if you face any problems," Nirakaranand said. Then he folded his hands as he said, "Namaste."

She touched his feet.

He blessed her by putting his hand over her head as he

said, "*Śivāste panthānaḥ santu.*" It means: May your
paths be safe.

"I wish you great success in your school project," she
responded and quickly became invisible on the trail studded with coniferous trees.

Nirakaranand cried like a child. What if this sadist sadhu had raped her and made her pregnant! Such a thought
made him cry because of a bizarre possibility. He wondered if he himself was a child of rape. So far he had considered himself a "love child" born of the Hindu tradition
of levirate marriage. His father married his mother after
she became pregnant, polygamy accepted as normal here.
They died before he was ten-years old. He felt grateful to
his lawyer step-brother, Pawan, who always treated him
like a sibling and raised him with dignity.

Chapter 11

One month after her wedding, Saina was invited to attend the mock funeral rite of her father. Her brother Pran had returned to his village from Haldwani, a small town with small rolling hills joining the lower Himalayas with the Indo-Gangetic plains. This town's natural beauty was marred by mosquitoes, which sometimes caused a malaria epidemic. It was malaria of Haldwani that made Rikhi delirious almost every day. In that state, she would talk incoherently.

Without suspecting malaria as the cause, a Haldwani priest had performed a tantric exorcism on her. He told Pran that Rikhi was haunted, possessed by the spirit of his dead father. His father didn't die a natural death but because of an accident. He was buried under a landslide on his sacred journey to Mansarovar via the Mana Pass that divides India and Tibet a few miles north of the Badrinath temple. Since he didn't receive the proper funeral rites, the priest said he became a ghost, and the priest suggested a mock funeral rite to release the dead man's soul to heaven.

"This rite must be performed only at the dead man's ancestral shrine or *pitrikuṛa*," was the strong recommendation of the priest.

Saina and Mussi went to attend the rite for her dead father. A free lunch called the *Shraddha bhoj,* or honorific feast, followed the rite. Pran's family priest contradicted the Haldwani priest's recommendation. Instead he stressed the need for a *bali*, an animal sacrifice, to please Lord Narsing. "You and Rikhi went to Haldwani without paying a visit to that mighty god's shrine! So, she is suffering from His displeasure!" the priest warned Pran.

This priest, like other priests, knew the gastronomical benefits of small and big sacrifice. The sacrifice of a cock would be enough for a ghost. But for Lord Narsing only a ram is recommended! The priest convinced Pran that his recommendation was Vedic. Apparently Pran, like most Hindus, didn't know that the story of Lord Narsing (*Narasiṃha*), like Vedic temples, was non-existent in the Vedic scriptures.

With the help of Mussi, Pran was able to get a very fat ram. The animal was sacrificed in the *puja* at the local Vedic temple of Lord Narsing. In the entire tantric *puja* the priest never pronounced the lord's correct Sanskrit name, *Nṛsiṃha* or *Narasiṃha,* as if the Garhwali pronunciation would be no problem for the omniscient god!

Rikhi was served *prasad.* She couldn't eat it as she felt nauseated. Since the ram's steak was the sacred food or *prasad*, the priest allowed her to lick a little piece of it and give it to Pran. All other attendees were also given the same *prasad.*

The priest was given not only the steak but also the whole head as his *dakshina*, the traditional gift for priestly service in food and cash.

The *dakshina* cash was higher for Narsing Puja, much higher than for the exorcism. The former took more time, and to pass the time the priest recited the Puranic story of Vishnu's Man-Lion Avatar for the benefit of the children among the attendees. He said, "The children must know why this puja is helpful. Listen very carefully before the ram is sacrificed!"

Everybody became quiet. Sacrifice meant killing of a ram, an exciting event.

"Bhagban Bisnu becomes angry if you don't believe in him as God," the priest said, and he raised his index finger to warn the children. "The lord took the avatar of a lion and a man in one body. Thus he got the name Nar-Sing. 'Nar' means man and 'Sing' means lion. He haunted his devotee Parlad's father Hiranyakasyap. Hiranyakasyap had refused to accept Bisnu as God, but he failed to convince his own son Parlad not to believe in Bisnu. Parlad refused to abandon his faith, for which his father punished him now and then, and the torture of Parlad made Bisnu very angry. The lord tricked Hiranyakasyap. He disguised himself as part lion and part man, and with his mighty paws, he tore Hiranyakasyap's stomach and ate up all of his intestines."

The children looked awed. They didn't know why this pandit pronounced Vishnu as Bisnu, Hiranyakashipu as Hiranyakasyap, Prahalada as Parlad.

That's the way Pran had heard the same story when he was a child. He felt great relief after the ceremony, but Rikhi's condition didn't change even after a month.

Fortunately, Harshpat was visiting his parents and other relatives to celebrate his graduation with them and other Kotwals. Murti and Balram hosted a special evening feast in honor of his graduation. The surprise guest was Sakar, Swami Nirakaranand.

Sakar asked his nephew, "Dr. Harshpat, are you allowed now to treat anyone anywhere?"

"Yes, Chacha ji. Last week, for example I gave quinine to Saina aunty's sister-in-law. Her malaria was caused by Haldwani's mosquitoes, not by ghostly haunting. She is improving and now has no more episodes of delirium."

"What episodes?"

"Whenever she had a high temperature, her voice would be hoarse, somewhat like a male voice. She won't remember what she said. I don't want to go in detail, but Pran chacha thought it was his dead father's voice. I don't understand how his dead father could ask for his proper funeral rite."

"How about Lord Narasiṃha's displeasure?"

Harshpat laughed. "Chacha ji, I know they sacrificed a he-goat."

"Pran is naive. He was duped by his family priest who told him how angry Lord Vishnu could be."

"Pran chacha would have known the Vishnu story since his childhood!"

"A very scary story for the children! God could behave like our man-eating tigers!"

"Yes, God is the biggest cannibal. Only the doctors can scare Him!"

They laughed in unison.

"Doctor," the swami said, "If Pran had any common sense he should have asked the priest: Why is it that the Man-Lion avatar of Vishnu haunts Hindus but not Africans? Africa has far more lions than India."

"Not only Africa, but in fact no other part of the world is under the authority of Vishnu's avatars! But if Pran is a believer then he is a believer. Common sense has nothing to do with belief," Harshpat said with a laugh.

"This is why I want to educate children not to believe in Hindu pagan practices. Would you like to support me in my endeavor? I mean, suppose I want to start a primary school for untouchable children. Would you treat them and their parents just like you treated Rikhi without any *puja*?" asked the swami.

"As a doctor I have taken an oath to treat any sick person, and there is no *puja* element to consider."

"What oath?" the swami asked.

"Actually, I took two oaths, one loudly and one with a whisper. The loud one was an English translation of the ancient Greek Hippocratic Oath of doctors. The whisper I added on my own."

"I never heard anything like the 'whisper oath' of doctors." The swami looked curious.

"Chacha ji, I decided on my own to use a Sanskrit oath for doctors. Actually, you know it by heart!"

"Sanskritic Oath for doctors! What's that?"

"*Sarve bhavantu sukhinaḥ, sarve santu nirāmayāḥ.*"

"Of course, the ancient medical wish of all doctors: 'May all be healed, may all be without ailments!' You can add its other half, too: 'May all look to their well-being, let no one be a victim of pain.'" But then he retracted his suggestion. "I think the shorter the better. The first line you quoted is enough, Doctor! No discrimination against anyone anywhere. And unlike the Greek oath, the Sanskrit oath is secular."

"That's right. The ancient Greeks had gods like Apollo, by whom the physicians used to swear that oath. But these days no Greek gods are mentioned in the Hippocratic Oath. Look at its simple English version, which also is secular. The original Greek oath may have been authored by a vegetarian like Pythagoras. That oath does not imply worship of Greek gods as a means of relief from pain."

"True. Today Greeks don't worship their ancient gods, and in ancient times they believed their angry gods were pleased by animal sacrifices. Like the Greek oath, the Sanskritic wish has no indication of any animal sacrifice for warding off sickness."

"Chacha ji, we need more hospitals, not houses of

gods. In a hospital, nobody will stop you from praying while you get medical treatment. Nobody is sacrificed in a hospital, not even a murderer."

They stopped talking when they saw Balram coming toward them. "Dinner is ready," Balram announced.

At the dinner Mussi sat beside the swami. "This is a meatless biryani because you are our most revered guest today. Last time I had meat biryani was at the Narsing Puja of Rikhi."

"Yes, I heard you brought that ram. You and that priest wanted to eat mutton biryani. Isn't that the real reason?" the swami said, his expression indicating his unease.

"No, Swami ji! You have been misinformed." Mussi spoke very softly. "I don't want Balram ji to hear me, but it was his brother-in-law, Maheep bhai, who arranged for the ram, not I. Maheep bhai killed the ram at the puja. I didn't enjoy how he severed his head with three or four strikes of his blunt *khunkhri*. I did remind him that he was expected to kill only in self-defense. His answer was that he was defending Rikhi from Lord Narsing's sickness-inducing wrath."

"Now, Mussi, if you didn't enjoy that senseless slaughter, then why did you eat the biryani?"

"To be honest with you, I didn't want to face the wrath of Lord Narsing."

"I am telling you, and you tell Maheep, that Narsing is a fake god. Don't do such a cruel and stupid thing again."

"I am afraid Murti didi might hate me for that. After all, Maheep ji is her brother."

"All right. He will get his lesson. You don't worry. Let's enjoy this meatless biryani Murti has made."

At the end of the meal, Mussi whispered into the swami's ear.

"Oh, no! And here I am planning a school for our local untouchable children!"

The swami stood up and abruptly walked away.

Chapter 12

Bhagbati arrived in Delhi four days ago to attend the inauguration of Indian independence on August fifteenth of 1947. He was given one week's leave to represent his Sanatan School at the independence celebration in New Delhi. He stayed with a relative, Shankar Sharma, in Ghaziabad, a town near New Delhi. As he was about to enter the house, a bullet passed over his head, slightly grazing the skin of his skull. The relative took him to his family doctor, who took care of the minor scratch. It was not clear who tried to kill Bhagbati, but there Hindu-Muslim riots had occurred in Ghaziabad before and after Independence Day.

"I am going to kill a few Muslims," said his enraged relative, Shankar. "Why are they here if they believe in Jinnah's partition of India? My father rightly believes that Hindustan means the country of Hindus."

Bhagbati knew that his own father, like many Hindu Mahasabha members, also believed so. He wanted to say to his father, "India does not mean a Hindu's backyard, but a land where the river Sindhu emerges from the Himalayas."

But he rather preferred a behavioral explanation. "Shankar!" he said, "The religious basis of India's partition could be worse as time goes on. It could make many Hindus more Hindu and many Muslims more Muslim, altering their utopian dreams into dystopian nightmares. Two behavioral negatives don't make one positive. Religious euphoria is like dropping an atom bomb on democracy." He took a long breath and then continued, "This partition is a vestige of our primitive ancestral past. Our human ancestors have preserved the behavior of monkeys, our very close cousins. We have seen groups of monkeys fighting each other over the occupation of a garden full of fruits. They become very violent and try to hurt their opponents."

"So, Jinnah wanted the garden to be divided?" Shankar remarked.

"Yes, other leaders yielded to Jinnah's demand for partitioning India." Bhagbati continued, "Sardar Patel agreed to recognize Pakistan even before Nehru and Gandhi. Apparently, the Indian leaders didn't consult each other ahead of time, and the people were not consulted either. The majority of Muslims were not consulted as to whether they agreed to be out of India simply because their religion is Islam. Indian Islam is not a foreign religion for all religions become regional and so India's Islam is Indian Islam. Indian Muslims are Indians. They are just like you and me."

"If that were so, then why do we have such unbelievable chaos? Muslims are Muslims and Hindus are Hindus, people belonging to two civilizations that are poles apart."

"No, we are not poles apart. Here in India we developed an integrated civilization. But the integration of two different civilizations is a continuous process. And we have integrated yet a third component into Indian civilization, Western civilization from the British. English rule introduced us to the ways of the West. An example is that educated Indians use English, a Western language. Have we not become Indian English?"

"Anything we have in common with the English could work against us now. Jinnah couldn't speak Urdu, which will be used as the main language in Pakistan. His medium to legalize the partition of India was English." Shankar paused to see how Bhagbati would react. But Bhagbati remained quiet, his smile intact.

Shankar inserted a question for Bhagbati. "Do you consider the English-given hockey a symbol of integration of the three civilizations?"

Bhagbati didn't expect this question, which he thought was frivolous. He laughed while saying, "Yes."

"It's not a laughing matter. We used to have Hindus and Muslims on our field hockey teams before. Now Indians and Pakistanis will play the same game against each other. Each team will try hard to score a goal against the goal of the opposite team, an eye for an eye!"

"I doubt field hockey matches will allow the opponents to hurt each other. It won't be like an Indian killing a Pakistani and vice versa. That is not going to be the goal of any international game such as hockey. The goal of that kind of game is international good will and international integration."

"I don't think so. International sports create more hatred and less goodwill. The losers would like to obliterate not only the entire winning team but even hurt their country, if not by their actions then by their words. You will believe when you watch bloody riots at international games. In the future, more and more police will have to patrol these games to control any riots." Shankar added his forecast with his index finger raised.

"Anyway, that's really beside my point. But how do you know the shot at me was from a police patrol or from a gang of fanatics?" Bhagbati asked.

"It is hard to be sure, but I have seen police officers patrolling the entire area. The officers did fire shots to scare the rioters, who also used guns. It's not easy to distinguish a rioter from the innocent passerby. Only the animals—the dogs, cats, cows, and donkeys—are considered as innocent passersby. Only humans had no freedom. The curfews were for humans, not for animals. I don't think Hindus and Muslims feel they are the members of an integrated civilization. Can't they learn from the street animals how to live together?"

Bhagbati remained silent.

The two relatives decided to stay in Ghaziabad.

The inauguration was held at midnight. Since Bhagbati was a son of a Brahmin Sanskrit scholar, he clearly understood why midnight was selected. Midnight was considered the astrologically auspicious time, the *shubh muhurt,* to start free India.

Shankar criticized Prime Minister Jawahar Lal Nehru. "Do you know, Bhagbati," he asked, "that Nehru never believed that the stars were responsible for the freedom of India?"

Bhagbati defended the first prime minister of India. "Jawaharlal Nehru is a lonely atheist whose voice of reason had no value for his colleagues. I know how they convinced him that this *muhurt* would safeguard India's future. I doubt that any *muhurt* would foster communal harmony."

Shankar and his family members were all awake in their Ghaziabad home with Bhagbati as midnight approached. Nobody was talking. The radio was on.

Suddenly they heard Nehru's voice at the new nation's parliament:

"Long years ago we made a tryst with destiny, and now the time comes when we shall redeem our pledge, not wholly or in full measure, but very substantially. At the stroke of the midnight hour, when the world sleeps, India will awake to life and freedom. A moment comes, which comes but rarely in history, when we step out from the old to the new, when an age ends, and when the soul of a nation, long suppressed, finds utterance…"

After Nehru's speech, Shankar's wife Ranjana served a plateful of *pakoras*. Not just any *pakoras* are considered auspicious, but only *pakoras* made with the black beans of *urad*.

Sweet milk tea, which was introduced by the British rulers, accompanied the *pakoras*. Then an assortment of Indian sweets followed.

Bhagbati looked happy. He thanked Ranjana for her treats.

"Thanks to Pandit Nehru who inaugurated free India not by Sanskrit mantras but by his English speech," Ranjana said with a smile.

"Yes, Ranjana! I, too, am impressed by his speech," Bhagbati echoed. "It appears that Nehru's midnight freedom speech has become the lamp to lead the subjugated people to the gate of the biggest democracy of the world."

Ranjana added her own words of appreciation for this unusual speech. "Also, Nehru's first Independence Day speech speaks more than what it speaks. Nehru chose English for this speech, the language of those who had subjugated India. He didn't choose his native language Hindi or Urdu. India's first Independence Day speech in English by Nehru at midnight implies that India will wake up in the daylight of Western values. Our democracy is only one example."

But Shankar did not look as if he were impressed.

"You don't look very happy with Pandit Nehru's speech, Shankar!" Bhagbati said.

"I am concerned about this midnight speech of freedom. Great oratory can hide great lies even in broad day-light."

"What do you mean?"

"The riots."

Right now, the immediate reaction to be seen was if Nehru's captivating speech could stop the local riots. The leaders were not prepared to handle this unprecedented carnage. Some leaders spent more time invoking gods and goddesses before they came to hear Nehru than they did controlling the continuous riots. Bhagbati was aware of the reports of refugee trains coming from Pakistan littered with mutilated bodies: penises cut off, eyes gouged out, rods inserted in women's genitalia, breasts bloodied with wounds, heads severed from torsos.

Those gathered for this celebration had no way of knowing that a few days later Pakistan would also complain about trains full of dead bodies coming from India. Brutality seemed to reign in both new nations. Nor was this expected that many refugees on either side would tell how Muslims saved Hindus and Sikhs and how Hindus saved Muslims from this shameful carnage, but those stories would be told as well.

Bhagbati was aware that a few college-educated men and women born into Hindu and Muslim families refused to believe in "divine words." Maybe, he thought, a few atheists will ultimately prevail and eliminate the most common cause of hate—religion. Although the masses believed that the lord knows all languages of all lands, he knew there were no words of God. He knew God lived in an unknown and inaccessible fantasy land, without any knowledge of any language.

Shankar, Ranjana, and Bhagbati began to joke about prayers. "Suppose Sanskrit is the divine language. Then why no mention of it or the *Vedas* in other 'divine books,' such as the Bible and Quran?" Shankar queried Bhagbati.

"God must be ignorant and maybe non-existent. Or maybe God exists but has not acquired any language yet. That's why He didn't know how to give orders to the perpetrators to stop killing the very beings He had created. Or maybe He was giving commands in old Sanskrit or Hebrew or Arabic," Bhagbati replied.

"Then God should have learned Hindi or Urdu," Shankar commented.

"No. God won't speak these ordinary languages— languages below His dignity," Ranjana added, a joke.

Their ridicule of religions lightened up their mood, and they finally went to sleep.

Chapter 13

The next morning, Bhagbati got up out of his bed and saw the first light of the day, the light of first freedom. After breakfast, he mustered the courage to return to Hardwar despite the warning of Shankar and Ranjana. Instead of the train he took a bus.

On the bus, he couldn't find a way to inform his father that he was headed to Hardwar, a place not only safer but holier than Delhi. Bhagbati remembered how his father had thanked God for saving him when he heard about his scratch by a bullet. He had asked Bhagbati to ignore the Congress Party and return to the Hindu Mahasabha. Bhagbati said no. To him, being part of the Hindu Mahasabha meant supporting the Bhagavad Gita's justification of honor killing. Arjuna, as advised by Krishna, saved his honor by killing his own relatives and friends. Otherwise he would have been considered a coward.

But Bhagbati thought otherwise. Religious justification of honor killing was inhuman. The Hindus and Muslims—the same people, like relatives and friends—murdering each other failed to understand that they engaged in the most dishonorable and despicable acts during India-Pakistan partition. They failed to understand that they were born in a land where ancient thinkers like

Brihaspati and Buddha never believed in the lie that some human words are divine. In fact, many college-educated morons still believed that their scriptures were God's words, and Bhagbati thought of many Hindu Mahasabha members who were college educated as just that, morons. Some of them hated what they termed the words of atheism attributed to Brihaspati and Buddha.

Interestingly, Bhagbati saw a man entering the bus and moving toward him. Before the man sat beside him, he spat out through the window of the bus. A few drops of the man's saliva fell on Bhagbati's face. Bhagbati wiped his face with his bare hand. He could see a chewed red lump of *pan* that the man had spat settling down on the muddy street.

Just as Bhagbati wanted to say, "The *pan*-chewers will make the free India a filthy India," the man introduced himself very politely. He was a newspaper reporter.

Bhagbati's attitude changed instantly. They started chatting.

The first topic was the riots. A few minutes later, Bhagbati asked the reporter a couple of questions. "What do you think of Nehru's Freedom Speech? Will it foster communal harmony?"

"That I don't know. But I am sure, Nehru's speech—not begging the blessings of God or gods and goddesses, not favoring any religion—will inspire future democracies. His speech subtly implied no mixture of church and state."

"No inspiration for Pakistan, though," Bhagbati said with a sigh. "There were celebrations throughout Pakistan, with praise of God for creating a new nation."

But the reporter corrected him, "Not true. For example, those who were in Balochistan were disgusted to be a part of Islamic Pakistan."

"And you must have heard a lot about Abdul Gaffar

Khan, better known as the Frontier Gandhi!" Bhagbati remarked.

"Of course, Abdul Gaffar Khan, too, wants an independent Pakhtunistan for his Pathan people. Yes, the Pathans are not happy about their forced inclusion in Pakistan. The happiest region is the Pakistani Punjab. More prayers were offered there than in other regions of Pakistan. Ironically, the Punjabis suffered the worst by partition. The Indian Puanjab had the same fate. No prayers saved the murdered Muslims and Hindus."

"I agree with you. That's why I have lost faith in the prayers of Hindus and Muslims."

"Never in human history has religion caused such mass hysteria. The unfortunate thing is that future generations may not remember this deadly disease. Some will keep claiming their religion as a religion of healing, thus fighting for the preservation of this deadly disease," the reporter predicted.

"It's strange human behavior. Devout people will desperately look for ways to eradicate even a minor disease, but they will enthusiastically preserve this killer disease, religion. However, I think, eventually, future generations will be intelligent enough to find religion of no value to them," Bhagbati said optimistically.

Along the route, these two fellows saw people gathering and shouting the praises of Mahatma Gandhi and Nehru. The reporter remarked, "Some historical facts are hitting my memory as I hear these men being praised. You remember, Hitler invaded Poland after he had signed a peace pact with British Prime Minister Chamberlain. The Big War started and Britain faced its certain destruction. In desperation Churchill sought help of the United States of America. He never anticipated that for such help President Roosevelt would add another condition to US participation in the Second World War: Britain must give

India her independence. The president insisted on his condition, but India didn't get her freedom at midnight under Churchill's watch. Churchill lied. He tried to ignore his promise given to the American president. But thanks to Prime Minister Atlee, who ignored his predecessor's lie."

"True. The masses believe that the Congress Party achieved India's independence from the British Raj under the leadership of Mahatma Gandhi and Nehru. Even the role of India's military in Britain's victory in World War II was not understood, let alone the role of President Franklin Roosevelt."

As soon as the bus entered Meerut, rioters stopped it. The reporter ran away, and somehow, Bhagbati, too, escaped and ran to the nearby police office. The officers were frantically helping the local victims, including the refugees. A police truck full of refugees was ready to move to Hardwar. Bhagbati, luckily, got a ride in that truck.

As the truck neared the next UP town, Muzaffar Nagar, two parties of rioters blocked the road. The six police officers sitting in the truck began to fire in their direction and the rioters dispersed without incident. The truck moved ahead quietly.

When Bhagbati and the others reached Hardwar, the refugees joined another group of refugees in a big temple where they were served free food and given shelter. Bhagbati refused to eat even though the temple host tried to convince him that the food was *prasad* for all visitors, not just for refugees.

He asked the host how the temple was able to provide free meals, and the host named several very rich religious funders. The temple was part of a Gurukul-type school where poor children got free education. Some of the refugees had children with them, and their children played football in the school's playground after the meal. The temple had also made arrangements for temporary accommodations.

That revelation inspired Bhagbati to have his own school for poor children in Dehradun. He began to make mental notes. His school should provide not only free education but also free healthy lunches and exercise such as yoga postures and breathing. Because religious hatred and its consequences continued, however, no prayers of any religion would be offered in his imagined school. He would, rather, like to lay down the foundations of rationalism for his school's students. Religion had been a pest for long time in humanity's garden, and its eradication would only be achieved by applying the right pesticide, which must be rational thinking.

He remembered how two parents objected to their children's participation in his Sanatan School's prayer that was offered before the first class in the morning. The prayer ended with the Sanskrit words *tasmai devāya namaḥ*, salutation to that God. The parents were Jains, and like Buddhists, didn't believe in God.

The headmaster dropped the prayer. He was aware of how religion-based schools try to ram their prayers down the throats of students. This headmaster didn't want to continue that tradition. Bhagbati was also grateful to the headmaster because he was kind enough to employ not only him but also Uttara. It became possible because of his father's influence. The headmaster was a Hindu Mahasabha member, but because he had a daughter of his own, he allowed coeducation, believing his daughter was equal to boys. Unlike Bhagbati's father he did not believe in the view of Manusmriti: A woman gets her salvation by serving her spouse.

Bhagbati knew very well how his father treated his mother. She was always submissive to him.

Bhagbati appreciated the headmaster for another reason. At the investiture of Bhagbati's sacred thread, his father whispered the sacred Vedic *gayatri* mantra in his right ear. Just after the mantra he added that Bhagbati was forbidden to utter the mantra in the presence of women and untouchables. The headmaster actually uttered many Vedic mantras, including the *gayatri,* in the school prayer, which were repeated by both boys and girls after him.

Bhagbati understood very clearly that eventually he would have to leave this school if he was to have his own dream school.

How would he realize that dream became his challenge? Before he left the temple, he thanked the host. "Thank God, not me!" The host said very humbly.

Bhagbati didn't want to ask a question, but he did, "Why thank God? For refugees fleeing from their birthplace?"

"Well, all this chaos and suffering is because of their own karma," responded the host.

"I don't believe in karma," Bhagbati said with a faint smile.

"You don't have to believe in karma. You feel the effects of karma because karma is a fact," the temple man said.

Bhagbati momentarily closed his eyes as if he was trying to internalize what this meant. Then he said with a nod, "I understand. *Achha, namaste*," he said very politely and slowly walked away.

Chapter 14

When Bhagbati returned to Dehradun in the evening, he was surprised to find his father-in-law in his home. He bowed and touched Pawan's feet.

"Now I have two reasons to be happy to return. You are here, Baba ji, and I am feeling great relief to be out of Delhi's heat."

"Baba came here to celebrate India's Independence Day at the Indian Military Academy. And also to meet Mahant ji of Guru Ram Rai Darbar," Uttara said to Bhagbati.

"Mahant ji?" Bhagbati asked her, his tone reflecting his confusion.

"New Mahant ji. Did you know he is our relative?" Uttara looked into Bhagbati's eyes.

"Ours too!" Bhagbati smiled. "All Pahari Brahmins are relatives. Isn't that a well-known fact, Baba ji?" Bhagbati asked Pawan.

"That's right," Pawan replied.

"What is interesting is that a Brahmin sits at the top of a Sikh branch! What if Guru Ram Rai had not sought peace with the Mughal emperor Aurangzeb?" Bhagbati asked Pawan, looking at him curiously.

"Then he could have been the Eighth Sikh Guru, and then there would have been no chance for our relative!" Pawan responded.

They all laughed.

"We are proud to be related to him. There is news that he wants to open several new schools," Bhagbati commented.

"Baba wants funds for Sakar Chacha's school. He has a meeting tomorrow morning with Mahant ji," Uttara said.

"What is the current progress of his school, Baba ji?" Bhagbati asked Pawan.

"That's a long story, Bhagbati. We will discuss that later. First, you rest. Take a bath and have good sleep after dinner."

സ്ഥ

The following morning, after breakfast, they started the discussion. Bhagbati was flabbergasted to know that Sakar was now well-respected as Swami Nirakaranand and had already laid down his school's foundation.

"How did Chacha ji get funds for his project?" Bhagabati looked excited as he put this question to his father-in-law.

"Why don't you come along with me and we will talk about it on our way. I don't want to be late. Mahant ji is very particular about being on time."

In about twenty-five minutes Pawan and Bhagbati started walking, looking for a *tanga*. They saw a *tangawala* and waved for him. The *tangawala* stopped, and the two men climbed into the horse carriage and sat in the back seat with their backs toward the driver. The driver turned the carriage around and proceeded toward the road to Guru Ram Rai Darbar.

Pawan started with the talk of funds. "You wanted to know how Sakar managed to get funds. That's a secret and we will talk about it later. But I am more interested in Mahant ji's help."

"If he is willing to help you, then Sakar Chacha ji will have to name his school after Guru Ram Rai. I heard that Mahant ji intends to associate the name of Guru Ram Rai with all the schools he will build," Bhagbati said.

"Sakar has already given the school a name, and I doubt he would change it. But I still want to talk to Mahant ji. He is our relative and so maybe he will let Sakar keep his name," Pawan said, and he blinked his eyes.

"What name has Sakar Chacha ji chosen?"

"Asim School," Pawan said. "You are a Sanskrit scholar's son. Do you know its meaning?"

"Yes, the term means 'borderless school,' and you want to add a hearing allusion: 'Non-Seam School.' Right?"

"That's it: a seamless school. Brilliant! Sakar believes that his little school should embrace the whole world. No borders of religion, caste, nationality, country, gender. No discrimination of any sort," Pawan explained.

"That's what I told my father. He starts his puja with the *Prithivi* mantra, which means the planet earth is our motherland: *Prithivi Mata*. To that he adds *vasudhaiva kutumbakam*. If he really meant the Hindu ideal, 'world alone is the family,' then why can't he eat with the untouchables? Why can't he invite Christians and Muslims to dine with him in his home? Aren't they our family members? I have asked Baba these questions several times. Every time he would get mad at me...I am so delighted to hear about the Asim School. Baba ji, you need not meet with Mahant ji. I have a strong hunch he would insist on the name Guru ji."

"That makes sense. After all he is the head of Guru

Ram Rai Darbar. I understand your point. But it would be inappropriate for me to cancel our meeting now. We will keep our options open."

As their horse carriage neared Ghanta Ghar, a police officer stopped them.

"I want to check you and your tanga for weapons," the officer said in a stiff voice.

"What for?" Pawan also asked with a tone of authority. "I am a lawyer. I must know the reason."

"I am sorry, sir! I am just doing my duty. The police have to protect all citizens. There are rumors that more trains from Pakistan are arriving in Delhi and other places, trains full of dead bodies."

"These are not rumors. I witnessed them when I was in Ghaziabad. But we have no weapons. We are going to pay our respects to the Mahant ji of Guru Ram Rai Darbar. He is our relative."

"So you must be Garhwali Brahmins. I am a Garhwali, too. My name is Autar Singh Panwar," the officer greeted them with folded palms. "Sir ji, the local Muslims are scared. We are doing our best to avoid any riots in our peaceful town. I suggest you don't go through the Ghanta Ghar Chauraha. It's getting overcrowded now. Just take that road, *Tangawale!*" the officer told the driver while pointing toward the other road.

"*Wo to bahut lamba rasta hai, Sahab!*" the *tangawala* said. "That's too long a road, sir!"

"*Lamba to hai. Lekin is wakt wo sahi hai,*" the officer advised. "Indeed it's long, but at this time it is safe."

The *tangawala* understood that it was an order, though a very polite order. The *tangawala* was not even a Pahari. He was a Muslim. Why buy trouble with a Rajput officer? He quietly turned the *tanga* around and proceeded as directed.

The *tanga* safely arrived at the Darbar, but an hour

late. A man greeted Pawan and Bhagwati at the entrance. "I am Pawan Kotwal, and this is my son-in-law, Bhagvati Prasad Pokhriyal. We have a meeting with Mahant ji."

"Oh, yes. He was waiting for you, but he left just a few minutes ago. He has gone to check a site for a new Guru Ram Rai School. Can you come tomorrow in the evening?"

"I am not sure, but convey my *pranam* to Mahant ji. Thanks."

They returned home by the same *tanga*. Uttara was surprised to see them back so late.

"You look depressed, Baba! What happened?"

"First, we need tea and snacks. Then we will explain," Pawan replied.

They went inside. Uttara quickly prepared tea and brought some *parathas* and chutney with Dehradun's *bal* sweets. Then Pawan told her how the meeting failed.

"Baba ji, don't call it a failure. Maybe it's a good thing that you didn't see the Mahant ji. What if he would have been willing to provide funding but only if the name were changed to Guru ji? And then it would be more embarrassing for you if Sakar Chacha ji sticks to his chosen name."

"You are right. I know Sakar has a secret helper."

"Can we ask who he is?" Uttara asked, curiosity apparent in her tone.

Bhagwati added, "Yes, Baba ji. Let us know who this helper is!"

"I am that helper," Pawan said. He paused while looking at their confused faces. "Uttara, you know the government gave the Kotwals a big compensation to build the bus route through our forest. I kept Sakar's share aside."

"So you want to use that share for Chacha's school. I get it," Uttara said, nodding her head.

"But with that money he can barely complete the two-room school. He needs money for at least one teacher."

"First let him complete his school building. He should attach two latrines, too. One for girls and one for boys. Then we will look for teacher's compensation later."

"That sounds good to me. You know more about schools than I do. I will tell Sakar what you have suggested."

There was a knock at the door. The postman was waiting outside. Uttara opened the door. The mailman handed over a telegram and quickly left.

Uttara opened the telegram. "Oh, no! Baba, my mama ji fell from a cliff. He is in coma."

"Mama ji? You mean your mother's brother Ram Char?"

"Yes." Uttara exhaled a long sigh.

"I will leave tomorrow morning," Pawan said as he placed his hand gently on Uttara's shoulder.

The next morning, they all left together for Pauri.

Chapter 15

The death of Ram Char united Pawan's entire family, including Swami Nirakaranand, who performed the cremation rites on the bank of Alaknanda near the Srinagar town of Garhwal. After the funeral, the swami returned to his Uttar Kashi ashram. For more than a month he was very depressed, but not due to the death of Pawan's brother-in-law. His school's construction near his village was at a standstill. Even though he was a swami, he occasionally behaved as his original self, Sakar Kotwal. His guru, whom he addressed as Lama Guru Bhotia, had told him repeatedly to remember the last words of the Buddha: Keep striving without negligence.

"No divine power from the sky comes to help you, only you alone can help you. However, there are opportunities flying around you. All you have to do is light your lamp and stretch your hands, not to pray but to grab those opportunities in the light," the guru had told him.

The lama was right, but only partially. Swami Nirakaranand modified his guru's advice. No man can succeed by taking shelter in himself. His success becomes possible because of social sheltering, with the assistance of those around him. The man who thinks that he can see enough in the light of his own lamp is mistaken. Soon he will realize that he can see far and wide by virtue of what he thought of as social lighting, what is learned by virtue of positive interactions with others.

His modification made sense to him when he received a check for $1,000 from Terry Smith in the mail. He felt as if this gift came via divine power. He gave five rupees to the mailman, the amount almost half the monthly salary of the mailman.

And for the swami, one thousand dollars were like one thousand luminous lamps lighting the path for his forthcoming school children. Gone was the swami's depression. He felt so elated that he shouted in Hindi, "*Sākshar sansār, saksham sansār,*" literate world, strong world. Terry, former Sister Tara, attached a note that said this money she had collected from several charity groups was meant for his school. She thanked him for his kindness. That note made him more convinced that one cannot alone light his own lamp with his own hand. His lamp is a product of several invisible hands.

"Thanks to those kind people I will never know," he murmured as he read that note.

๛๛๛

The following day the swami left for Pauri to meet Pawan.

Pawan and Nanda greeted Sakar. After tea and snacks, Nanda asked him if he had seen his school.

"No, bhabhi. What is there to see! The construction is not moving anywhere. But it will now."

"How?" Nanda smiled with a confused look on her face.

Sakar told Nanda and Pawan how he received $1,000 from Terry. Both showed their surprise and delight.

"Tomorrow morning you can show me where you plan to have two latrines," Pawan said.

"Yes, that shouldn't be any problem. The site should be close to the school. You know how children suddenly feel pressure!"

They all laughed.

The next morning Pawan and Sakar sat together for a breakfast of parathas and asparagus patties with pickles, courtesy of Nanda.

"How did you get this kathal pickle, bhabhi?" Sakar asked his sister-in-law. He knew that the jackfruit pickle was impossible to get in Pauri's bazaar.

"Uttara and Bhagwati gave it to your bhai ji."

"Naturally, jackfruit trees are as popular as lychee trees in Dehradun."

After breakfast Pawan and Sakar proceeded to the school. Sakar was speechless for a while. He had difficult time stopping his tears. The two-room school was already complete. The school construction had already begun under Pawan's supervision.

"I had no knowledge of it," Sakar said as he fell at his brother's feet. Pawan lifted him up and hugged him while crying.

When Sakar composed himself, he asked Pawan, "Bhai ji, you certainly surprised me, but where did you get the money to finish it?"

"From your account."

"What account?"

Then Pawan disclosed how he used Sakar's share of the family money to finish his dream project.

"Now we need to find a teacher, Bhai ji. I think I have enough money for a teacher's salary."

"Definitely! Let us meet Uttara and Bhagbati. They know better than we do about this matter."

"How soon can we meet them?"

"How about next week?"

Sakar nodded. After checking the spacious rooms, he showed the construction workers two sites for the two latrines, one on the right side for boys and another on the left side for the girls. The water for all purposes was easily available from the adjacent creek.

Chapter 16

On a Saturday evening, Pawan and Sakar knocked on the door of Uttara's house in Dehradun. Pawan had already informed her by letter of the purpose for his trip with Sakar.

Bhagbati opened the door and touched their feet in respect. Then Uttara did likewise.

Bhagbati was not following his father's path anymore. Nevertheless, he respected his father as a good Sanskrit scholar. He instructed Bhagbati in many aspects of Sanskrit poetics, including one property of language: semantic multiplicity. "Every sentence has many-sidedness regarding meaning." That was his father's advice. Bhagbati was always conscious of it while dealing with serious transactions.

Today at breakfast he observed his father-in-law using multiplicity of meaning: pretense. As a lawyer, Pawan was accustomed to using pretense to win his argument. By contrast, Bhagbati was aware that Sakar would not use this kind of linguistic property. Sakar was a monk who believed in straight and honest talk. To him, if somebody claimed he was being honest with you, that also meant the speaker was dishonest at other times, including with you, and by extension might be "pretend-ing" to be honest even now.

Pretense could be non-verbal as well, and Pawan was accustomed to using it. His favorite pretense was in hunt-ing when facing a tiger. He would remain nonchalant, pretending that he was not concerned at all about the presence of the tiger when in fact he was very much con-cerned about the beast.

"Uttara! Your stuffed *gahath* parathas remind me of bhabhi's cooking. So delicious! How did you get *gahath* beans here?" Sakar had expressed his appreciation and asked without pretending.

Uttara smiled. "That's why Baba and I slipped out when you were busy with your yoga exercises and medi-tation. We purchased them right here in a Dharampur shop. Ma loved Pahari *gahath* and *tor dal*."

Bhagbati, while enjoying the spicy paratha stuffed with mashed horse gram beans (*gahath*), added his ap-preciation. "I wish I could eat dishes of Ma ji here in Dehradun every day. I ate more whenever she served basmati with whole *tor*."

"I, too. Nanda is the greatest cook," Pawan added. "You should visit us more often, Bhagbati."

Bhagbati was not sure if Pawan was pretending.

But then Sakar interjected, "We want you to visit us as soon as possible and have a look at our school. It's ready. We had better look for a teacher. The last time we spoke on the matter you said that you and Uttara can help us find one."

"Yes, we will," Bhagbati said with a jerky nod and stretched smile.

"Your teacher candidate must understand what our school is about, Bhagbati," Sakar said.

"I don't know much about your goals, but certainly the teacher must follow them," Bhagbati replied.

"Ours is a borderless school: Asim School. This name implies that the school is not limited to geographical or national borders. My name is Sakar for our relatives, but elsewhere I am Swami Nirakaranand. So the teacher might make children religious in order to impress a swami like me. But we want no borders of religion, caste, and gender."

"Chacha ji, our school started with a prayer. I always resented it. But I was an employee of the school."

"Let me tell you how I started resenting prayers. I was a boy scout. All boy scouts had to salute and say loudly, 'I will serve my country, God, and the king.' Have you heard these vows of boy scouts during British rule?"

Bhagbati responded quickly, "I was never a boy scout, but I have heard those pledges: *Mai desh, Mahesh, aur naresh kī sewā karūngā*."

"Yes, we used Hindi as well as English," Sakar said. "These vows are borders. They limit the human capacity to do good to all irrespective of their country, religion, and ruler."

"I agree with you, Chacha ji," Bhagbati said with a glimmer in his eyes.

"I also agree," Uttara echoed her husband.

"Then both of you can explain these basics to the teacher candidate," Pawan said. "Sakar is interested in real atoms, not in imaginary *atman*."

"Bhai ji is right. I have no desire to promote Hinduism and declare myself a leader of Hinduism. Nobody can be a leader of a religion. Our religion is not even one religion. One preacher says something, and another says just the opposite. Do you think that my grandma would have believed a Vedic view that this cosmos evolved out of nothing? She thought Lord Krishna created the cosmos as the *Bhagavad Gita* claims. Many gullible devotees like my dadi seriously believed that a man could create the universe. Was there really a man in the beginning of this cosmos? Dadi didn't know that even cockroaches were born before humans."

They all laughed.

"That's true. Dadi always believed Krishna created the cosmos with his Maya. Krishna didn't even know much about our earth. Did Krishna mention anywhere that Europe or America existed? I doubt Krishna knew that humans had already created pyramids before he was created."

They all laughed again.

After finishing the tea and toast breakfast, both brothers decided to meet a lawyer friend in Dalanwala, a very posh colony of Dehradun.

"Don't wait for us, Uttara. Jogindar will not let us go without lunch," Pawan said.

"But what if he is not home?" Uttara asked.

"Then we will return immediately," Pawan replied.

"I hope you don't try to meet Mahant ji again. He may not be there," she said.

"Sakar is not interested in receiving funds from religious organizations. I had suggested to him to approach Dhirendra and Chandrika for Arya Samaj support, but Sakar would not want to change the name of his school to DAV School. Your Dharma Samaj is in the same category," Pawan said.

"Dharma Samaj and Arya Samaj are not the same religion. One is idolatrous and the other is opposed to idolatry. That was my point. As you said, Hinduism is not one religion. It's just a cover term for indigenous religions," Sakar interjected with a laugh.

"I agree with Chacha ji," Bhagabati added without laughing. "My father doesn't recognize Arya Samaj as Hinduism. He is a very strict Sanatana Dharma Brahmin.

Sanatana Dharma is the *only* eternal religion according to him."

"There you go. Everybody thinks his religion is eternal, but if a religion is 'eternal' then what is the need for creating a new religion to oppose the preceding religion! And then the new religion's followers don't like any opposition and so they deny others the same process that made their religion possible. They call their opponents blasphemers. They forget that they too are blasphemers because they opposed the preceding religion," Pawan retorted.

Everybody was silent. After all, this last conclusion was a judge's statement.

The judge broke the silence. "Enough of religion." He knew that Sakar was a swami and that meant some sort of religious talk, most of it frivolous. "Now let us go, Sakar!" Pawan said as he got up.

After the two brothers left, Bhagbati and Uttara engaged in very serious discussion in the kitchen as they began work on their lunch project. Bhagbati peeled onions and garlic cloves, shedding tears as he cut the onions. As Uttara mixed masalas she sneezed twice.

"Let's wait a little bit to talk," Uttara suggested. Bhagbati washed his face, and then both entered the sitting room.

"What do you think of Chacha's school?" Uttara asked Bhagbati when they were comfortably seated.

"I think his school is very close to my own dream school. I hope I am able to get funds."

"That's the biggest problem. Fantasy Land has everything except funds."

They both laughed.

Then they discussed Sakar's request for a teacher, including funds to support his or her salary. They did not realize they had spent more than two hours on this matter until they heard a knock on the door.

Uttara opened the door. The two brothers were back.

"So Uncle Jogindar was not home." Uttara looked into her father's eyes.

"You guessed correctly, beti," Sakar responded. "But in a way, that was good. Nobody was there except their chaukidar, who told us that he had gone to Guru Ram Rai Darbar to plan the next Flag Fair. I didn't know that he is a supporter of the Darbar."

"All Sikhs of Dehradun support the Darbar. Sikhs from other parts of the country come to attend the *Jhanda Mela* and offer money to help the Darbar," Bhagbati said.

"This is a sea change. Guru Ram Rai was disqualified for the honor of Eighth Guru. Now any Sikh who visits Dehradun pays respect to Guru Ram Rai Darbar," remarked Sakar.

"And the local Hindus honored the guru by calling their town Dera Dun, Valley of the Guru's Homestead," Bhagbati added.

"Talking of sea change, Mahant ji heads the Darbar and this Himalayan Brahmin is a vegetarian! How many Pahari Brahmins have the guts not to devour animals?"

At this remark by Pawan everybody laughed except Pawan himself.

"Baba, that reminds me. We need to go to the kitchen. We are going to make biryani," Uttara said with excitement.

"I hope it's not the Pahari type!" Uttara's swami uncle joked, and they all laughed.

"Well, my husband still follows one of his father's ideals: Be kind to all beings, not just to your dogs and cats."

At two, the standard time, lunch was ready. The time was too late by British standards, as was the standard dinner time for Indians. Many Indians developed a taste for the British habit of toast and tea, but not for the British time to have it, even in the Dehra Dun-Mussorie area, a bastion of English culture.

♋♋

The next morning for breakfast Uttara served not only toast and tea but also some pastries and fruits.

"Indians should eat fruits at every meal," Sakar said appreciatively while chewing a fresh guava with gusto.

"And add salads also," Pawan commented.

"We developed these dietary habits because we owned orchards and a big forest, Baba. From our forests we got free fruits like *kaphal,* raspberries, wild pears, and figs. Remember how Ma used to scold us when we would eat fresh pea pods and leaves and leave very little for her to cook? Ma wanted to change our bad habits."

"It was not your fault, Uttara. You children got those bad habits from me and Sakar! Prachi and Harshpat recommend these bad habits to their *desi* patients. Good doctors!" Pawan said.

"That's true. I was not a good role model. I loved to eat raw food," Sakar commented.

Finally, when the breakfast was over, the two brothers began to pack their stuff.

"We better leave," Pawan said to Bhagbati.

Uttara overheard and came out from the kitchen where she was doing the dishes.

"Baba, it's too early. I am going to fix a few potato parathas for your lunch. And you know you may have to wait at the bus station for an hour for the bus rarely runs on time, the driver waiting and waiting for more passengers."

"I know. We will buy tickets and just walk around and

digest your heavy breakfast," Pawan replied.

Sakar hung his big handbag around his shoulder and talked to Bhagbati with a very affectionate look and a smile on his face. "Beta, both of you keep looking for the teacher. That's the big task for you now."

"Chacha ji, we have found two teachers already." Bhagbati had wanted to surprise him.

"Who are they?" Sakar asked, widening his eyes.

"You are talking to them," Bhagbati said, adding to Sakar's surprise. "Uttara, you explain to Chacha ji."

"Chacha ji, in your absence yesterday, we discussed your teacher search. Bhagbati's dream of having a school is very much like yours, and we both reached a conclusion. He and I will leave Dehradun to become teachers at Asim School."

Pawan blinked at Uttara with a mysterious smile, and she reciprocated. His pretense was working.

But Sakar's eyes were closed. Tears flowed from them. Then he wiped his tears and hugged Bhagbati and Uttara. "You are my dearest friends, children."

"Then let's go inside. What's the hurry to leave? You can take the second bus, which is scheduled to leave at noon."

"I am not going by the noon-time bus," Sakar said, moving his gaze from Uttara to Pawan.

Pawan blinked. "Yes, that's an odd time to leave."

Uttara understood the meaning of the lawyer's blink, a sort of leading question as she said, "Why don't you wait until tomorrow, Chacha ji? Bhagbati and I are interested to know how you want to start Asim School."

Sakar moved his eyes toward Pawan. "Bhai ji! Is that all right with you?" Sakar kept looking at Pawan.

Pawan paused for a moment and then smiled. "Yes. Let's celebrate. Uttara! Can you cook *mitha bhat* for lunch? That will make our celebration a sacred ceremony."

"Not only the sacred sweet rice but whole *tor dal* and *basmati bhat* as well," she said, and she held Sakar's hand in hers. "We now have the whole day to discuss your school, Chacha ji."

Chapter 17

After lunch Pawan took a nap. Out in the sitting room, Sakar was visiting with Bhagbati and Uttara.

"That was a great lunch," Sakar said, "but you added too many raisins to the sweet rice. Shredded coconut and saffron made it too elegant. The Pahari *ghee* is the best grease to fry the rice of *mitha bhat*. And I am happy that you both have continued eating salad and fruit with lunch."

"And with dinner too," Bhagbati commented.

"I am planning to raise fruits and vegetables all around the Asim School's lot," Sakar said.

"What kind of fruits and vegetables, Chacha ji?" Bhagbati asked.

"The easiest ones: apples, peaches, pears, French beans, *sem*, Pahari peppers. And definitely both kinds of apricots."

"My preference would be for the almond-type apricots because children can eat not only the pulp but the seeds, too. I have been told by Dr. Harshpat that these almond-type apricot seeds are actually nuts, as good as almonds in terms of their nutritional value," Uttara interjected.

"Children need a nutritious diet, and they should be taught how to grow food."

"Yes, I am always in favor of utilitarian gardening. So, I would like to teach children as you suggest. Don't waste your back or front yard on ornamental plants. Grow these fruits and vegetables instead. They all have flowers and fragrance, and your yard will not only be very beautiful but fruitful."

"Not only backyards but roads can provide free food. Use every roadside area to grow apples, which as you said are the easiest fruit to grow. Sell the apples fresh. If too many are left unsold, make their *murabba*. This jam is good to spread over bread," Bhagbati suggested.

"Excellent idea, Bhagbati! Yes, we can do that, and the government can do that, too. The whole country must ratchet up utilitarian gardening. India needs food desperately now, and as the population of India will increase with every tomorrow, every today will become a greater nightmare," Sakar said in enthusiastic support of Bhagbati's idea.

"I overheard you talking. No nap for me, I guess," Pawan said as he entered the sitting room. "Speaking of children from impoverished families: when they are born, their parents have high hopes for them just like the parents of any child. But they have to go through traumas, the parents as well as the children. It's my own estimate that ten percent of children grow up to be adults with socially unacceptable lives: either beggars or criminals or both. Among the two, criminals are worse. And if one is in both careers, then he or she is the worst of our human lot."

"Did you say ten percent are criminals?" Bhagbati asked.

"Yes, ten percent at least," Pawan replied. "As a matter of fact that percentage goes even higher as the population increases. Population growth creates joblessness and joblessness exacerbates criminality. The nation is forced to spend money to build more jails, money that could have gone for more hospitals."

"Are you sure, Baba ji, that ten percent of the population is criminal? How did you arrive at that percentage?"

"By surveying the prison inmates and their outside criminal connections," he quickly replied.

Then he added further to completely convince Bhagbati, "Don't forget the crooks whose criminal acts go undetected and unreported. I know many men, some of them my relatives, who should have been in jail for wife beating. They beat their wives and use them as labor for a wife is the cheapest form of labor. And that labor includes child bearing. Look at Bansi Lal. I overheard that he often slapped his wife. If he didn't like his wife then why did he have eight children? Shouldn't he be put in jail? Jail or no jail, parents learn from their children what they don't want to learn."

"And children learn from their parents what they should never have learned," Bhagbati said with a polite smile. He was thinking of his father's Brahmin fanaticism. He never thought of marrying an untouchable girl, even if she were a local Christian girl whose untouchable parents or grandparents converted to Christianity and got an opportunity to educate their children and enable them to stand on their own feet.

"Anyway, two sons of Bansi Lal were arrested for armed robbery. They never shot anyone, just pointed their gun at them and threatened to kill them—"

"How did they get the gun, Baba ji?"

"They used their father's gun, Bhagbati," Pawan replied. "Retired World War Pahari soldiers can keep a licensed gun, as you know. He would scare his boys with his gun, pretending to shoot at them. Occasionally he would also insult them in public, assault them verbally or even physically. Digam and Sagar, those two sons of Bansi, couldn't find jobs and so started stealing, first from their own relatives and later from big shops. They were not born thieves. Their birthdays were celebrated with the Ganesh Puja, but Puja helps only the freeloading priest who performs it. Our Christian principal used to say in English, 'Lord God helps.' Today I would have told him in English, 'Except in our justice system, where neither Lord God nor Lord Ganesh helps sinners.' As Sakar said once, 'Honest confession is the last best chance for a crook's nirvana.' At last, those two criminals, I mean Digam and Sagar, confessed and they will be released soon."

Bhagbati laughed along with Sakar and Uttara.

Bhagbati also confessed, "Baba ji! Why is God called Lord?"

"I had no idea until I learned it in my Christian school. The principal taught us in Bible class: 'God told our first ancestors Adam and Eve that He was their lord.' The principal never told us that some Christian scholars have already established how God was created much later by the descendants of Adam and Eve!"

"Maybe the principal didn't know that fact."

"Perhaps, but remember, missionaries fight for faith, not for fact. Had I told our principal what I just said, he would have whipped me with his baton. Forget Christ's sermons on non-violence!"

Bhagbati laughed at Pawan's response as he nodded his head. "My father, too, behaves like missionaries," Bhagbati commented.

Pawan listened to Bhagbati's comment with a poker face. After a moment of silence, he continued, "You see how children are influenced by their parents' behavior. Sakar is a swami. He is in a position to counsel the parents of his school children to be good role models for their sons and daughters."

"Bhai ji, you too can counsel them. You are the professional counselor," Sakar responded.

"Let me wash my face," Pawan said and he left for the washroom. As he walked away, he thought about role models. He washed his face and then looked at himself in the mirror.

He blurted out, "You should never elect politicians who have a half dozen children and claim to know how to improve the economy and health of the nation. They don't realize they are the worst role models for parents."

In the sitting room, Sakar was pacing around Bhagbati and Uttara. He felt elated as he picked up a metal plate from the table, which he began to bang with a spoon. At the same time, he was gathering his thoughts for what he would say to his free teachers, now sitting quietly and enjoying his elation.

After a while Sakar sat down and placed the plate and spoon aside. He turned his eyes affectionately toward Uttara and Bhagbati. "You both will have paid jobs in Asim School. I cannot pay much, but enough for your daily needs."

"Chacha ji, we will not ask for any money unless we are desperate for cash. Uttara and I have decided to live in your guest room and walk to Asim School. We will not be a burden on Baba and Ma. Baba has already told me that we can grow fruits and vegetables to sell at the Pauri bazaar. You will be leasing your garden to us for our business for free. Baba ji says part of the huge garden area and the house is your share. But let me ask you a question if you don't mind," Bhagbati said.

"Sure," Sakar replied.

"How did you get money to pay us?"

"I really don't have much money. But for at least one year I will have no problem."

"No, no. I mean how were you able to receive funding to pay a teacher?"

"That's a long story, son. I will pay first and explain later," Sakar responded with a smile.

Pawan came back quickly and interjected, "I heard you, Sakar! Never mind paying them. Just tell them to be good teachers!"

Bhagbati and Uttara laughed.

"Don't laugh, my children! I want to tell you how important it is to be a knowledgeable teacher," Pawan said without laughing with them.

Bhagbati stopped laughing and requested, "Baba ji, let us know your thoughts, please. I am excited."

"My first requirement is that teachers must have correct information about what they are going to teach. When I was in the seventh class, I was slapped by my English teacher for my mispronunciation. One long chapter in our textbook was on Cervantes' novel *Don Quixote*. The teacher corrected my pronunciation *daun kwikjaut*. 'Say *kwikzaut*!' he scolded. As you know many of us pronounce *z* as *j*. I tried twice. Then he slapped me, saying, 'What's wrong with you, stupid!' I felt humiliated, but I was helpless to complain against this English teacher. He was my uncle, husband of my father's cousin! I was not his first student to be humiliated like this. It was his annual ritual to diminish his students."

Bhagbati laughed.

"But wait for the more interesting part of the story. Much later, in my law school there was a Spanish-speaking lawyer who came to give us a talk. I told him this story. You know what he said! 'Cervantes would have fainted if he had heard his character's name pronounced by your English teacher.' He told me that in

Spanish it was pronounced as *Don Kikhote*. The *kh* as in the Urdu word *khush* or as the *h* the English word happy, and the last vowel *e* is pronounced as the *a* in the Indian English word *major*."

"What? My teacher didn't know this either!" Bhagbati remarked with a surprised look in his eyes.

"Well, you can say that it happens with foreign names. But what about Indian names? In Hindi they say and write Ravindranath for Rabindranath Tagore. And most Punjabi speakers pronounce and write his name as Ravindar Nath, as if Tagore was born in Punjab! Why can't they listen to the Bengali pronunciation? This is the problem with Indians. They don't pay attention to the native pronunciation of our own great leaders. Most Indians write Subhas Chandra Bose's name as Subhash Chandra Bose. It's a pity."

"Baba ji, I agree with you. It's a shame," Bhagbati said, echoing Pawan's frustration.

Sakar interjected, "Bhagbati and Uttara, you are going to be the first teachers of Asim School. I know you cannot know every subject, and that's understandable. You should teach the students what you know. But don't claim to know what you don't know. The main thing is to achieve our goals."

"How do we define achievement, Chacha ji?" Bhagbati asked.

"Achievement's formula is 'one plus infinity.'"

"I don't understand. Chacha ji, you are a *sadhu* and so use *sadhukkari* speech. I mean, sadhus mix up several languages in their sermons. Saint Kabir is a classic example." Bhagbati turned his gaze on Uttara to check her reaction. Uttara smiled.

"Mine is not really a mysterious kind of speech like Kabir's," Sakar said. "Let me give you a couple of examples. Bhagbati! Are you going to tell your students that ancient Indians had airplanes?"

"No, absolutely not," Bhagbati quickly replied.

"Why not? Many highly educated Indians claim that," Sakar argued.

"But there is no proof for their claim, Chacha ji."

"You are a Sanskrit scholar's son and you must have read Kalidasa's play *Shākuntalam*. In that play King Dushyanta travels by a plane between earth and heaven—"

"Your speech is clear to me," Bhagbati said with a smile. Uttara laughed.

"Now, if you and Uttara teach that the plane of Kalidasa is a joke, then that's one step achieved! After that, there are countless myths to be debunked. That's what I mean by 'one plus infinity.' And here is one more to add to the infinite number of myths, Uttara. Are you going to tell your girls that your mother and Murti bhabhi are beautiful because they are *gori*?"

"No, Chacha. There is no proof that white skin is superior."

"And yet many women worship goddesses and most goddesses are pictured as *gori*. Strangely, the black and brown devotees of these religions are the majority population of India. And those very women are responsible for the lucrative market of skin-whitening concoctions!"

"I know, and they also worship Ganesha, whose elephant head is white. Have you ever seen a white elephant, Chacha ji?"

"Not in our Himalayas where Ganapati was created. Only Lord Shiva would know how he located that kind of white-looking baby *gaja*. And so quickly!"

"Maybe your hunter father would know better than Ganesha's father. Have you seen any white baby elephant in our Himalayas, Baba ji?"

They all laughed.

"It's very hard to convince believers that the Sanskrit *Purana* scriptures are mythological works," Bhagbati added.

Then Uttara added her own commentary related to Shiva mythology. "You know the Ganga dropped to the earth from Lord Shiva's head, and so we keep a bottle of *Ganga jal*. They say Ganga's water is white and Yamuna's black. We have never drank a drop of Yamuna, and yet both rivers originate right here, from the same Garhwal Himalayas. Thousands of pilgrims take bottles of Ganga water from here every year. Did you ever see a bottle of *Yamuna jal* in our Kotwal families, Chacha?"

Sakar laughed. "The Kotwals need a better cleanser," he said after a pause. "All their filth goes first in the Chandrabhaga, which meets Alaknanda, which meets the Ganga at Dev Prayag. And then a bottle of *Ganga jal* from that confluence becomes holy for them. My Ganga water is from Uttar Kashi and tastes so good because it is free from the Kotwal colony's filth."

They all laughed.

Then Sakar continued the topic of debunking myths. "I am confident you will not give false information to your students," he said, moving his index finger back and forth horizontally. "You will not teach students that the Ganga was really brought to India from heaven by King Bhagiratha, no matter how incredible a mountaineer he might have been."

Pawan showed his appreciation by clapping. "And don't worry that believers' feelings will be hurt. Reforms cannot take place without hurting believers' feelings," he commented.

"Baba, you are a lawyer. Lawyers are accustomed to hurting their opponents' feelings." A devilish laugh escaped her mouth.

"Keep debunking those countless myths," the swami said. "For now, we have already covered a range of avoidable topics. We will cover more when you begin the job!"

Chapter 18

The Parent-Teacher-Founder meeting took place on the covered front porch of Asim School on July 1, 1948, one week before the school's opening. The meeting started with Sakar's greeting: *"Namaste"*

The crowd, all males except Uttara, responded, *"Namaste, Swami ji."*

Then he said loudly, *"Inquilab* (this revolution)."

The crowd responded, *"Zindabad* (long live)."

Then he uttered, *"Gandhivad* (Gandhism)."

The crowd roared back, *"Zindabad."*

Then he gave a speech in which he talked about how the school would be run. At the end of his speech he asked if there were any questions. Not a single man asked him a question. Some of them began to leave, saying, *"Bhaut dhanyabad, Swami ji!* (Many thanks, Swami ji)."

Sakar interrupted their exit, saying, *"*Don't leave. In a few minutes, Nanda bhabhi and Murti bhabhi are bringing *mithai* to celebrate." He didn't disclose that it was *mitha bhat.*

Nobody left, and some began to ask questions. One was: "Why is this school's room called *Terry Kaksha*? Is it the same as *Teri Kaksha* in Hindi?"

"Yes, it means 'your class' in Hindi," the swami replied, "but it is named after Sister Tara whose original American name is Terry. She supported this school with one thousand dollars American money, about four thousand rupees."

A loud applause followed. Some had their palms on their cheeks with wide open eyes. Some began to whisper among themselves.

After a pause, the swami said, "Please continue with your questions."

A man stood up. "My name is Badri Datt Bughana. I will contribute my money."

Another man stood up. "I am Tota Ram Khanduri. I too will give."

The swami thanked these men and replied, "Whoever wants to donate can pledge by raising their hands."

Another man raised his hand and said, "My name is Radha Ballabh Pant. My *sala* has invited your first-class students to have free snacks in his shop, any Sunday, at his Pauri Sweet House." There was a big applause and laughter. A few more hands were raised and other kinds of offers made. Sakar thanked all those gathered and requested that they meet him later. A round of applause followed.

Another question came from the audience. "It's wonderful that this school has two toilets, one for boys and one for girls. Do you have any *jamadar* from Pauri to clean them up?"

"Yes, we have two *jamadars*. I am glad to introduce them right now: Bhagbati Prasad Pokriyal and Uttara Pokhriyal will clean the toilets as needed regularly. And Sakar Kotwal will do the same, but occasionally."

The crowd began to react with whispers. Then a man got up and said, "If you three Brahmins can clean up then I can also clean up. I am a Rajput. My name is Param Singh Rawat."

"Of course, Rawat is Sanskrit *Rajaputra*. It means 'prince' and that's how the word Rajput is derived. If princely people can clean latrines, then we fulfill the dream of Gandhi ji. Thanks, Param, for your courage."

Another man got up and said, "I am not a Rajput. My name is Lachchhu, Lachchhu Auji. Please don't use the Gandhi word 'harijan' for us. Use 'silpkar' instead. We are artisans. I am auji, the tailor. And I will clean up latrines."

"I, too, will clean up," echoed another man.

Many other hands went up.

The swami said, "We will assign the days for all of you volunteers. We also need a volunteer to teach our students how to grow vegetables and fruits around the campus of this school, and only those flowers that are good to eat."

One man got up. "My name is Rabi. I will do that job. I was Rai Bahadur Sahab's gardener. He believed in that kind of gardening, a useful plantation. I mean fruits and vegetables—"

One man interrupted, "But Rai Bahadur Sahab loved to grow roses."

"That's true. I grew white, pink, and yellow roses. He loved to eat *gulab pakoras*. And rosy patties. Everything made with rose petals!"

There was a big laughter. The swami thanked him by leading a round of applause.

A man stood up and said, "I have a question, Swami ji! You said that the school will operate under Gandhian ideals. Are you going to ask children to pray with the shlokas of the *Gita*? Our Christian school of Pauri starts with Bible class."

Right then, Mussi and Saina arrived at the porch. At a corner, they began to set out the food they had brought with them.

"Thanks, Mussi and Saina, for the food!" To these words of the swami the audience added a round of applause.

"Now, back to your question," the swami said. "Will the school start with a *Bhagavad Gita* recital? No. No prayers of any religion, including the *Gita* verses—"

A man interrupted, "But the *Gita* was a favorite book of Gandhi ji. He translated it for those who don't understand Sanskrit."

"No great person is perfect. Gandhi ji never believed in the caste system, but the *Gita* reinforces it. He never believed in any human's sinful birth, but the *Gita* says there are some *pāpa yoni* people, like women. Harshpat and Prachi are doctors. Both have convinced me that no person has a 'sinful birth.' They also didn't share the *Gita*'s concern regarding *Varna Saṃkara* children."

Sakar remembered Prachi's warning: *The Bhagavad Gita's* misogyny and fears of miscegenation must be treated as ancient scriptural xenophobic diseases that infect humanity.

Sakar continued, "All human children belong to one human family. That's what India's motto has been: *Vasudhaiva Kuṭumbakam*, the world alone is the family. Gandhi ji believed in that motto. That's why we need a borderless school where church and education will be kept separate. However, any student is free to pray, but silently. We are not a missionary school."

Only one applause interrupted his speech. Lachchhu clapped his hands.

The swami continued, "But we will teach yoga. Dr. Harshpat and Dr. Prachi have volunteered to come here for one week every year. They will teach students yoga as exercise, not as religion."

"Why not you? You are a swami!" Lachchhu asked.

"I may teach yoga, but my fear is that the children are

likely to feel that I am teaching it like other swamis. Swamis teach yoga with their colorful religious robes and hairstyles. Yoga has no colors, no borders, no religions, no beards, no hairstyles," the swami replied while placing his hand over his clean-shaven head. "I call it the lama haircut, but don't tell my lama guru!"

He was interrupted by a burst of laughter from the audience. He resumed his speech. "To say that yoga came from a god is just a myth, not a fact. The fact is that ancient Indians developed yoga as exercise to achieve and maintain good health. Then they gradually added to it some philosophy whose roots were in a godless *Sāṃkhya* thought. Did you know that the first atheist of the world was Acharya Brihaspati, who might have lived before Buddha?"

As the Hindi proverb goes, Sakar was playing the lute Vina in front of water buffalos, the attendees. They did not seem to know this story for none responded.

He wanted to explain the reference, but the entry of Mussi and Saina distracted him. He greeted them with a smile. Saina had a bucketful of leaf plates and leaf cups. She emptied the bucket and leaves on a small table. Mussi had two big pots. He put them on the bench attached to the table and then walked toward the creek with the bucket in his hand. After a few minutes, he returned with fresh water.

Then Saina opened the pots and looked at Sakar. "The food is still warm, Sakar ji," she said.

Sakar announced to the audience, "Let us celebrate this meeting with the food Saina and Mussi have brought. Let's give them a big round of applause!"

The audience clapped loudly. Soon a line was formed. The artisan Lachchhu was first in the line. He picked up a leaf plate, and with a ladle, he scooped up some food from the two containers. There was a line behind Lachchhu but nobody came forward when they saw the food on his leaf plate: *Mitha bhat* and *biryani.*

Sakar looked depressed. The Brahmins and Rajput waiting in the line wouldn't eat this cooked food because Lachchhu, an untouchable, had touched it. Some began to drop out of the line and slip out of the meeting. But then Saina quickly served the two dishes to Bhagbati and Mussi. They understood her strategy and immediately started eating. Sakar joined them.

Param Singh turned around and noticed them eating the food with Lachchhu. He returned to the food table and addressed the crowd. "If these three can eat with Lachchhu, why can't we? Remember our national hero Chandra Singh Garhwali? He and his wife joined Gandhi ji and lived in his ashram by invitation. He followed all the rules there. He cleaned the toilets of harijans. He cooked and shared food with them. What's wrong with us?" Param Singh began to eat.

Param's short speech inspired Sakar. "Let me explain why the other room will be named Chandra Kaksha. The name is to honor Chandra Singh Garhwali. Chandra barely went beyond a primary education, but in spite of his very poor education he became a soldier in the Garhwal Rifles. In 1930, he was ordered by the British to fire at hundreds of freedom fighters assembled at Peshawar. Except a few, they were Muslim Pathans. By Chandra's command, not a single shot was fired at the increasing and protesting crowd. He was impeached and imprisoned for life. But a few years later he received his freedom with the help of Makundi Lal, an Oxford-educated barrister from Garhwal. That's when Chandra Singh and his wife Bhagirathi joined the Gandhi ashram. After leaving the ashram he became an activist. Like Gandhi, he was opposed to the caste system that was not challenged in the *Bhagavad Gita* by the Brahmins who were its authors writing in the guise of Krishna. He dropped the Rajput caste name, Singh, of his children. I have shortened his name further to show that this school belongs to the whole world, just like Chandra, which means 'moon.' Unlike Gandhi, Chandra became an atheist. I am proud of what Chandra taught, not by his education but by his action."

"Swami ji! How wonderful!" Param Singh interjected while eating. "I thought it meant the moonshine class room. But thanks, you made it clear that you meant Chandra Singh Garhwali."

"Don't thank me. It was Pawan bhai ji's idea," Sakar revealed. "Actually I had thought of calling that room *Barrister Lal Kaksha*. Barrister Makundi Lal married an English lady who adopted India as her country. Mixed marriage is a powerhouse for cultural integration and tolerance. Doesn't this illustrious couple represent our school's ideal of no borders?"

There was big applause, but Saina didn't clap. She just wiped her tears with the corner of her sari.

The three men who expressed their desire to help the school with funding came forward to eat. They all told Sakar that they personally knew Chandra Singh Garhwali. "No Pahari ever took so much risk to free India as Bhandari ji, Chandra Garhwali's original name," said one of them as he picked up a leaf plate.

A couple of men who had slipped out came back, all drenched because of the monsoon season was upon them, and a torrent fell from the sky.

"It's nice you came back," Param Singh complimented one of them.

"I forgot my umbrella," the man said, "but it's very windy anyway. I saw some umbrellas destroyed by the wind."

"The winds will stop, but it's really raining heavily.

Why don't you eat in the meantime? You will like the biryani. There is no meat in it, though," Param said with a laugh.

"No, I am not like you who would eat with that *dom*," the man responded.

Param Singh grabbed the man by his neck. "You *Puran-panthi*, India became a slave because of people like you. Now India is free. Leave this country if you don't believe in the equality of all Indians!" He dragged the man out into the heavy storm. The other man came out and shoved Param Singh.

"I am proud of our *Purana* scriptures. What right do you have to force him share food with that *dom*?" the man shouted at Param Singh.

Param Singh caught this man by his arm and dragged him in front of the artisan, who immediately held Param's hands in his hands and said, "Bhai ji, please stop."

"Do you know what he said of you just now? He would not eat with you because you are an untouchable." Param looked at Lachchhu momentarily and then turned to the man who had insulted the artisan. "Just apologize to him and promise you will never use the word *dom*."

"No need to apologize. I know him. He is Pandit Bharat Ram ji," Lachchhu says. He then addressed the pandit, "Pandit ji, this food is cooked by Brahmins." He turned to Saina who was eating *mitha bhat*. "Saina ji, could you give him some *mitha bhat*. That's our sacred food."

Saina brought a plateful and handed it to the pandit, who put some grains on his head to show respect. "Now, that's enough. No need to eat and no need to apologize," Lachchhu said with a conciliatory smile. The pandit quickly ran out with the plate and without uttering a word. His mouth was too busy with the *mitha bhat*.

"Catch up to the other man. Share some with him!" Param yelled at him.

എൻഈൻ

When everybody was gone, Saina and Mussi swept the yard and the rooms of the school. Saina looked at the wall where, on a big rock slab, the name *Teri Kaksha* was engraved. After cleaning that room she came out into the yard and asked Sakar, "Bhai ji! Why didn't you name that room *Sister Tara Kaksha?*"

Suddenly his face looked filled with sadness. "You look sad, Sakar Bhaiya. Why?" Saina asked.

The swami remained silent, but his silence turned into tears. "That's all right, Bhai ji! You don't have to tell me anything about that name."

However, the swami felt that he must say something. "Saina, when Terry decided to return to her country, she wanted to go by the name she used before leaving for India."

"That makes sense, to keep one's original name. I still like to address you as *Sakar Bhaiya*. You should keep that name. It is much better than Swami Nirakaranand!"

The swami smiled and said, "I will think about that, Saina."

The swami had not revealed to anyone other than his nephew, Dr. Harshpat, why Terry left India. Harshpat shocked his swami uncle when he called Terry's abuser a sociopath rather than a swami.

Sakar recollected Harshpat's behavioral explanation: "A sociopath is that person who shows himself what he is not. Swami Vedantanand is a sociopath. His crying is false, just a show to seek kind feelings from others. Some gullible people continue to believe him, but others hate him behind his back. He actually has no conscience. He doesn't hesitate to lie and blame others, and he has no sense of guilt or remorse for his hurtful lies. If ever exposed, Swami Vedantanand is likely to defame Terry by claiming she tried to seduce him. To make matters worse, he will keep denying that he has a serious behavioral sickness."

Sakar didn't mention a word to Saina about what this sociopath swami did to Terry. He only said, "Thanks to you and Mussi for your help," and went out to clean the latrines.

The following week the school opened on time, as required by the district school board. There were more students than expected, twenty-one in all, and amazingly, nine students were girls!

Chapter 19

A sim School functioned according to plan. Sakar himself taught yoga once a week, and the land around the school was used for gardening. Every week every child was required to plant something under the guidance of Rabi, the gardener of Rai Bahadur Sahab. Parents were required to pack any uncooked snack they could afford for their child. During half-time every student would munch roasted *bhatt*, soya bean, seeds provided free by Bhagbati and Uttara, which were grown only in certain areas of the Himalayas.

In the month of October came *Dipavali*, the festival of lights. A picnic was already planned for the day before the festival began. In this region, *Dipavali*, known also as *bagwali*, was celebrated for four days.

The Kandolia forest at the top of Pauri was chosen for the celebration. This forest had a small flat area reserved for such activities like the boy scout parade, *kabaddi*, *gulli-danda*, and other outdoor games for school children. Sometimes, high ranking visitors were given rousing welcome parties here. Some organizers still remembered how one British governor was honored with an evening party in this forest by the local World War II veterans. That celebration ended with many inebriated men, courtesy of the governor who provided free Three-X rum. The English governor himself looked dazed, but maybe by the gorgeous moon-lit view of the Himalayan Chaukhamba Range, the divider of India and Tibet, rather than the flow of the powerful rum.

Parents were free to accompany their children to this picnic celebration. The invitation from Kundan, Radha Ballabh's brother-in-law, to have free snacks in his sweet shop was used as an incentive. Beside fireworks, sweets have been the traditional symbol of the *Dipavali* festival.

Surprisingly, only five fathers joined the picnic party, Lachchhu (with his son) and Param Singh (with his daughter) included.

No member of the party had problem reaching Pauri. They all rested at the bus stand and partook of snacks. After a short rest, they took the trail to Kandolia, walking until they reached the wilderness. To the south was the dense Adhwani Jungle, and at the base of the mountain was a dry creek. The absence of water did not discourage the growth of villages scattered along both banks. Each village had another natural source for fresh water. The big advantage to living in the area was farming and easy access to Pauri, not to mention the access to wood from the Adhwani forest. Some of the school kids wanted to go to this forest, but Sakar told them that the sweet shop would close early because of the *Dipavali* starting the next day and so instead they found the small playground. Boys played football and *kabaddi*. Girls played *kho kho* and hide-and-seek.

After about two hours, Sakar announced. "It is three. Are you ready for the sweet house snacks?"

He was answered with a resounding, "Yes!"

The trip down the mountain was fast, about forty minutes, and at the sweet shop they were greeted by Kundan in Hindi, "*Ao baccho! Sab bench me baith jao.*

(Come in children! All sit on the bench)." There were four big benches, and the children occupied three. All the adults occupied the small portable chairs.

The shop's waiter began to serve sweets and *namkeens*, salty snacks, on leaf cups and plates. A father went inside to talk to Kundan.

That father was quite clear in what he told him. Kundan came out and asked Lachchhu to sit down with his son Kusla on the steps. They both sat on a step and the waiter served them all the snacks and sweets. Kusla began to cry and refused to eat. Lachchhu tried to console him and wiped his tears.

"I want to sit with my friends," Kusla wailed.

Then Binti, Param Singh's daughter, got up with her snacks and sweets, ran to the steps, and sat beside Kusla. "*Bhaiya, ab khao na!* (Brother, won't you eat now!)." Kusla stopped wailing and began to eat. Param Singh, too, got up and sat beside his daughter. Sakar, Bhagbati, and Uttara followed Param Singh's example.

"*Shabash*, Kusla. You did what Gandhi ji taught us," Sakar said to Kusla, caressing his head. Then he looked in the direction of other kids and said loudly, "Children, come down here to sit with Kusla and Binti!" All the kids came down and occupied the steps. Now all the children looked happy as they finished their snacks and sweets.

☙◦❧

Two days after this picnic, Sakar received totally unexpected news. Kundan's sweet shop was burned down. The police didn't suspect arson. Fireworks from *Dipavali* were blamed. But Sakar was befuddled.

Then, on the fourth night of *Dipavali*, Asim School, which was closed for the holidays, was destroyed by fire.

Sakar, Bhagbati, and Uttara were completely distraught. They knew it was arson.

Sakar was devastated. The following morning when he woke up, he decided to make alterations to his torn dreams. After breakfast, he went to Pauri to visit his brother's favorite tailor. The tailor, known as Aladin, was shocked when Sakar gave him an order for three pairs of white *khadi* clothes for himself.

One week later, Sakar went out to take bath in the Chandrabhaga. After his bath, he put on a new white outfit: a pajama, a kurta shirt, and a Gandhi topi. Then he burned his ochre clothes in a ritual cremation of his old self then carefully doused the fire with water.

Bhagbati and Uttara were in shock when they met him in the front yard. "Chacha ji! What happened? What took you so long?" Bhagbati asked.

Sakar responded, "Yes, I waited so long, for years, but now I am what I am. I am born again as Sakar Kotwal." He was smiling. When nobody reacted, Sakar said, "I will explain later, Bhagbati. Let's eat bhabhi's parathas first."

Uttara began to sob and covered her eyes with her palms.

Sakar went inside and met Nanda. She couldn't utter a word as if passing through an episode of amnesia. Suddenly, she screamed, "Sakar!" Then she hugged him.

"I understand, bhabhi. You have been waiting for me. I am hungry. I need big parathas to celebrate my conversion."

At the end of their breakfast, Nanda said, "You burned your swami clothes, just like those men burned the school."

"What men?" Sakar asked with a puzzled expression on his face.

"Your brother suspects Param and Kundan."

"No, bhabhi. Forget them. I will tell bhai ji. Suppose

they burned the school in retaliation, they will only deny it, or they will blame each other. We blame them, and they blame me for arranging that picnic. The blame game doesn't solve problems, only exacerbates them. That's what my lama guru taught me. The lama advised, 'Tell the blind blamer that it was your fault, not his, and thus you open up his eyes and very likely with favorable looks.' Mahatma Gandhi has taught us: an eye for eye will make us blind. I have decided now to work at the famous Gandhi Ashram of Wardha."

"When did you decide, Chacha?" Uttara asked with great curiosity.

"After this reckless destruction, Beti. I will talk to you later about what I have planned."

Chapter 20

"Am I smelling very special flavors?" Pawan said to Nanda as he entered the front door.

This was a special Saturday evening dinner. Nanda had prepared patties of tender *lingura* ferns in addition to the *jhirna* (asparagus) curry and *puris* (fried puffed bread).

"You are smelling your favorite foods: *lingura* and *jhirna*."

"Did you go to our forest for them?" Pawan asked Nanda.

"Saina and Ghosa brought them in the afternoon."

"Ghosa who?"

"I am glad you asked. She is pregnant and craving *lingura* and *jhirna*. Saina took her into the forest and they collected a lot. They wanted to share her story and their vegetables with us. The story is actually meant for you."

"I can't wait to eat these vegetable! Then you can tell me her story," Pawan said as he moved away to change.

Ghosa's story wasn't unusual. She became a *jogini*, not that she wanted to be one. She came to Srinagar and joined the community of *jogis* and *joginis*, more than one hundred monks and nuns. The local temple head, the *Mahant*, headed this community. He was a distant relative of the Kotwals. One day Ghosa told Mahant ji that she was raped by a *jogi*. Mahant ji immediately summoned that monk. Instead of meeting the Mahant, the monk disappeared. That's when Mahant ji advised her to go immediately to Pauri and meet Pawan for legal advice. He had already told Ghosa how Pawan and his family members helped Saina.

Ghosa was married when she was seventeen years old. After nineteen years of marriage she remained childless. She wanted to adopt a boy, but when her husband, Bihari, checked with his parents, they scolded her for her proposal. They told her that an adopted child from any caste would be a *bastard*, not a real member of their family, as far as they were concerned. But Ghosa challenged their attitude and decided to adopt an orphan. Their xenophobia deepened when they found the boy she wanted to adopt was from a Rajput caste.

Ghosa's parents and her husband's parents were Brahmins.

One day Ghosa's sister-in-law, the wife of her husband's brother, secretly told her that Bihari was being pressed by his parents to marry a younger woman. That's when Ghosa left her home and became a nun, a *jogini*. Within a year, a fellow monk victimized her.

Before Ghosa told her the entire story, Nanda said she suspected that Ghosa might have befriended the jogi with no intention of seduction, but her courtesy was costly. As they say in Garhwali: *jyaũ jyaũ jogi taĩ jaga dyā tyaũ tyaũ mais hoṇu tayār* (on and on, give space to a monk, on and on, he is ready to be your husband).

But Ghosa insisted that was not the case. It was rape.

Ghosa made it clear to Nanda that she was not there to seek help to abort the baby from her two doctor children. Saina, too, advised her against any attempt to abort the baby. In fact, Saina was willing to adopt Ghosa's child to free Ghosa to continue her *sannyas* (renunciation) as a *jogini*.

"Ghosa wanted some legal action," Nanda said to Pawan after she told him about Ghosa's visit.

"What we will do first is report this to the police and find that jogi," Pawan said.

"And then put him in jail?"

"Not necessarily. There are several options. My preference would be force him to marry her to raise the baby together."

With Pawan's help, a search warrant was issued. Two days later a dead body was found at Dev Prayag near the confluence of the Ganga and Alaknanda—the jogi's body. Apparently, he atoned for his sin by drowning himself in one of the holiest confluences.

The district police office informed Mahant ji. The news made Mahant ji very sad. He had expected to follow Pawan's idea, but now the jogi was dead. His death convinced Pawan and Mahant ji that the jogi was the father of the baby.

A few days later, Pawan and Mahant ji had a secret meeting at the Srinagar's Shiva temple. "Every baby of the world needs to be raised by two parents, a father and a mother, because they brought the child in the world," was the firm opinion expressed by Mahant ji. Pawan told him that Mussi and Saina were willing to adopt the baby and let Ghosa continue her life as a nun. Mahant ji was against such adoption because Ghosa was the real mother of the baby and must be responsible for raising her baby. "Raising your child is superior to your renunciation," the Mahant told Pawan emphatically. Pawan thought of his own father, who could have abandoned Sakar but did not.

He was also aware of the fact that Mahant ji was an authority on Hindu scriptures. Otherwise, he would not have been appointed as the head of an important temple.

Yet he didn't want to impose the decision of a male, the Mahant, on a woman victimized by another male who belonged to the monastery. Pawan told the Mahant of his concern, and both agreed to talk to Pandit Vishweshar Dobhal, a priest with some authority.

"Yes, *niyoga* is a standard procedure to procure a child. The scriptures consider it a proper solution to have an heir. But it is to be used with the agreement of the husband who allows his wife to sleep with another man. Bihari never allowed Ghosa to sleep with that jogi. The baby was conceived by virtue of rape. We cannot force a man to accept this kind of fatherhood."

Pawan understood the pandit's opinion from a legal point of view. The *niyoga* surrogate fatherhood was a mutual agreement between two males and a woman. These were not Ghosa's circumstances.

Nanda was disappointed when Pawan told her what the Mahant and the pandit said. She decided to take the matter into her own hands.

The following day she went to meet Ghosa and Saina. Her plan impressed the two women. Mussi agreed to accompany the three women to confront Bihari at his home. They were confident that the planned confrontation would result in what they wanted because Bihari was still unmarried. No parents were willing to offer their daughter's hand to him, which was very humiliating for him and for his parents.

Bihari was totally stunned to see Ghosa alone. "Go away, you fake jogini!" he shouted.

But Ghosa kept her cool. "I have come here to fulfill your desire," she responded. "Just give me some time to tell you why I am here."

Bihari nodded as he gave her a spiteful look. "Just explain in two minutes, and quietly. I don't want my parents to come out and stone you."

"Yes, just two minutes, and then I will go away."

First she quickly explained to him what *niyoga* meant.

"I know what *niyog* is," he yelled at her.

"You can accept me and my child using *niyog* as your basis."

"Nobody would call your act *niyog*."

Then he saw Nanda, Saina, and Mussi coming toward him.

First Mussi came near him and said, "*Namaste*." Then he spoke out loudly and boldly. "Bihari bhaiya, we have checked with our Mahant ji and Pandit ji. It is up to you to accept Ghosa's proposal. Otherwise, she has another plan for you."

"What plan?" he asked Mussi angrily and without greeting him.

"I will prove," Ghosa answered, "that it was me, not you, who deserved a second marriage. You were trying to take advantage of the stupid Hindu tradition that a woman can't remarry. You will not get another woman, but even if you get an offer, I am going to tell her parents and others that you are impotent."

When Bihari saw Ghosa turn her back to him, he requested that all of them come inside. They all accepted his request.

അഃഃ

After her return to her home, Nanda told Pawan how her plan had worked out so well. Bihari accepted Ghosa and her baby under the interpretation of the *niyoga* tradition.

"Your recommendation of *niyoga* is one hundred percent coercion, an example of non-violent rape, and must be stopped, Nanda!" Pawan responded.

"And how about violent rape? Would you instead support Saina's choice in such circumstances?"

Pawan laughed and held Nanda tightly in his arms.

Then they moved to their sleeping room and sat on their bed. Pawan remarked to Nanda, "I hope Sakar is not interested in any joginis. His lama guru would know how Buddha started the culture of the bhikkhu and bhikkhuni, what we call the *jogi* and *jogini* here. I suspect this Buddhist tradition was the model for the Christian tradition of monks and nuns. A culture of monks and nuns develops into secret sacred prostitution."

"I know the easiest way of covering up sins is to put on religious clothing and to carry a sacred book. Even a religious mark such as a *tilak* on your forehead is good enough to hide your sin. But even a married man, religious or not religious, can desire a woman who is not his wife," Nanda commented.

They covered themselves with a quilt and lay on the bed. Nanda was expecting some response from Pawan. Pawan remained unmoved. She inquired, "Why are you quiet?"

"Your comment made me think of my father," Pawan whispered.

"I don't care about your family history so long you are not interested in any other woman," Nanda said, and she put her head on Pawan's chest.

Chapter 21

November fourteenth, the birthday of Jawaharlal Nehru, was going to be celebrated at the Congress Party's headquarters in Pauri. Sakar had been invited by a friend, a prominent member of the local Congress Party, to be a speaker at the celebration. He declined the invitation. Instead he requested the friend to announce there that he was leaving for Gandhi's ashram that morning.

This friend was familiar with Sakar's opinion about Gandhi and Nehru. He had enjoyed discussing these two charismatic political leaders with Sakar on several occasions. The friend knew that Sakar still behaved like a swami, that he could talk about the various philosophical and religious beliefs of these two leaders and, more importantly, their differences. Nehru was not that interested in the prayers that could be heard in Gandhi's ashrams. Gandhi believed in one God, not in the polytheistic Hindu paganism. But democracy *is* a form of political paganism, many different political parties, their leaders, and symbols. Gandhi was determined to have political paganism in India. Monotheism in the political sense was dictatorship, quite the opposite of pluralism, the hallmark of democracy. Gandhi practiced a little bit of yoga, too. The

proponents of yoga believe in pluralistic selves, not in
one Supreme Self (no *Yogasutra* aphorism of Patañjali
mentions a Creator God or *Paramatma*). Gandhi followed
monotheism, the earliest foundations of which were laid
in the Middle East.

The friend thought that Sakar might like to throw
some light on other questions he had raised. Why didn't
Gandhi, a lawyer, argue in favor of godless Buddhism,
the least irrational religion in the world? Why did a lawyer like Gandhi attempt to prove the existence of a non-
existent God? Why didn't he think like Nehru, who was
fully aware of the irrationality of religions? Nehru firmly
believed that a country's progress would be faster under a
secular democracy. Sakar had a special admiration for
Nehru because he didn't believe in the religious tradition
of having many children. Why was Mahatma Gandhi late
in his observance of celibacy?

Sakar knew celibacy was not fun. His own married father went to the other extreme. He had sex with the widow of another man and then felt compelled to marry her
after she became pregnant with a child named Sakar. But
he had no economic complaint against his father. A family of four, it could be argued, is almost celibacy, but a
family of twelve is lunacy. He was thinking of the ancient
blessing given to the new bride to be a mother of ten
children, or *Dashaputrī bhava*. Such a blessing crossed
the limits of lunacy!

The friend was disappointed by Sakar's refusal to
speak at Nehru's birthday celebration. On that morning,
when Sakar left his house, he was overwhelmed to see
the Kotwal children and adults waiting in the front yard
to give him an emotional farewell.

Murti handed him a bottle of *murabba* jam and a bottle of chutney made with the fresh leaves of *dhaniya* (co-
riander). Balram brought a packet of *bal* and *singori*

sweets for him. Nanda packed a bundle of *bhari rotis* (stuffed fried flat bread).

Sakar addressed them: "Now that you have brought so much of food, my problem is how I am going to finish all this by myself!"

"No problem, really! You will finish it," Nanda interrupted him with a funny smile, an odd expression on her face.

Pawan placed a *tilak* mark on Sakar's head. Sakar touched his brother's feet. Then he touched the feet of all the elders. Pawan requested of Sakar, "*Wardha se chitthi jaldi bhejna* (Send a letter from Wardha soon)."

Sakar left his residence with his brother, Saina, and Mussi.

He was surprised to see a small crowd at the Pauri bus stand. They were singing a song. The song's refrain contained the words *Gandhi Baba.*

A man greeted him with a garland, which he put on his neck. He asked Sakar, "Which Gandhians inspired you most?"

"Before I answer your question, I want to say a word. The song that praises Gandhi ji as a *baba* is not Gandhian. The name *Mahatma* for him is enough. Gandhi ji never considered himself a religious leader. Our secular democratic country doesn't need to be guided by any religious individual like a baba or pope. That said, these are the two top disciples of Gandhi ji who inspired me: Kaka Kalelkar and Vinoba Bhave."

"My favorites, too. I hope you meet them. Best wishes!" the man responded.

Another man came with a khadi shawl and presented it to him. "This shawl is our town's gift for you. Its wool is local. We hope you will become a top Gandhian from our region."

"*Bahut bahut dhanyavad.* But I am not going to be

what you are expecting. I am hoping that someday there
will be renowned Pahari Gandhians."

The bus was delayed for about half hour because of a
mechanical problem, and while they waited, the audience
wanted Sakar to give a talk about his reasons for taking
this unexpected turn in his life. He agreed, but he suggested a question-and-answer style talk.

A man said, "You are dressed in white khadi topi, pa-
jama, and kurta. It's clear you are now a sevak of the
Wardha ashram, not a swami of an Uttarkashi Ashram.
Were you influenced by Gandhi ji, who was a *sadhu* in-
side and a *sevak* outside? He remained a servant of India
until he was assassinated. Other leaders became rulers.
They were influenced more by the British rulers than by
Indian Sevak Gandhi."

Some among those gathered laughed.

Sakar also laughed and then responded, "I was really
influenced by Saina, wife of our family friend Musa
Singh—"

There was some laughter. Sakar heard a few whispers
about the word 'Musa!'

"Yes, Mussi's wife Saina. She wanted me to be me,
myself, Sakar Kotwal, and not Swami Nirakaranand. My
lama guru taught me not to believe in something like *self*.
There is no *atman*, he taught me. You are just a life and
you will be nothing at the end. So, help others if you live.
Even after death, your dead body should be useful. Let it
be used as food for other animals as they do in Tibet. I
realize now that my body, like any being's, will be reduced into nothingness forever. Then why do I need special clothing and a special hairstyle to qualify for heaven?
'There is no heaven up there, nor its God either,' my two
family doctors, Prachi and Harshpat, told me. 'Chacha,
this earth is the place where you live, call it heaven or
hell,' Prachi told me. Doctors are trained specialists in

life and death, not the untrained authors of the various scriptures."

Unexpectedly, the bus conductor announced that the bus was about to leave.

At the end of his talk, Sakar paid tribute to Nehru. "Let us salute Prime Minister Nehru on his birthday. Nehru was born a Brahmin, but he grew up without Brahmanism. Nehru means integration of us all." Then he folded his palms and said loudly, "*Achchha, ap sabko bahut dhanyavad. Al bida! Namaskar.*"

Sakar was greeted by Bhagbati and Uttara inside the bus. The couple was clothed in khadi: Bhagbati like Sakar and Uttara in khadi sari and blouse. "What are you doing here?" asked the stunned Sakar.

"We are going with you, Chacha ji!"

"Yes, we are going with you, Chacha," Uttara echoed her husband's words. Sakar sat down beside the couple. "We have been brooding and brooding over the loss of our school," Uttara continued. So, Dr. Harshpat gave us some very timely advice: 'Whining about a problem causes depression; finding the solution of that problem removes depression.' We followed this advice. Our solution is to join you."

Sakar's eyes became teary as he sat down beside the couple.

The crowd, waving the tricolor flag of India, shouted, "*Gandhivad, zindabad,*" over and over until the bus left.

c/ɔc/ɔ

After a week Sakar sent a short letter to Pawan to inform him of his safe arrival. Three weeks later Uttara also wrote her parents a letter:

Baba and Ma,

Pranam. We all are doing well here at the ashram as Sakar Chacha has informed you in his letter. Each of us has been assigned a work schedule that includes cleaning the toilets. I have been assigned some cooking. One of our best friends is a young man from south India. We communicate with him in English. I never expected an atheist in a Gandhi ashram. He told us, "God loves nuts. Hindus worship God with nuts, senseless and senseful nuts." At first we thought he meant the almonds and cashews we offer in puja, but when he laughed, we too laughed. He really meant it. We never saw him participating in the ashram's prayers. Nor does he eat the bland Gandhian food. He joked, "I believe in my hot pickles, not in your cold Badri Narayan." There is always a different bottle of the hottest achar hidden in his khadi kurta pocket. He adds that pickle to the ashram cuisine. He told us that, in his south Indian home, when his father returned from his office every evening first thing he would inquire was what his mother cooked in chilies for dinner. But our friend is more stimulated by Gandhian political action, which he thinks is unprecedented in human history.

We also have a Gujarati friend who has promised us a meeting with Kaka Kalelkar and Vinoba Bhave. Like them, he is a graduate of the M.S. University of Baroda, and he has connection with them through that institution. He joined the ashram just a few days after the assassination of Gandhi ji. He told us that even now many Indians feel that Gandhi ji should not have given any monetary aid to Pakistan. They want to decimate Pakistan. They don't realize that even kind words are free insurance for good will. Ramnik bhai strongly believes that no country has the right to destroy any part of our Mother Earth. Nations are artificial, but people are natural and earth is natural. We must help the people. And our holiest land is in Pakistan, the land where the earliest Vedic verses were born, recited, and sung. Only an idiot would demand decimation of any holy place. Gandhi ji was trying to teach that ideal by including the prayers of all the major religions of the world.

And guess what! Ramnik bhai has a connection with our Badrinath temple, too. He has visited it three times and wants to visit again. He told us that his parents had great faith in Badri Narayan, but not in our Himalayan food, which Badri Narayan loves most. There is always a sugar packet in Ramnik's kurta pocket, and he sprinkles sugar over every food item. He says that all Gujarati food dishes, except water, are actually sweets! Even the pickles are sweets! Our south Indian friend hates not only Gujarati pickles but even other dishes. But he confessed that taste buds have their own biases.

So, we have two friends who have opposite tastes, and yet they are here together as Gandhians. We are amazed how Gandhi ji could convert diverse characters without conversion! We three—Sakar and Bhagbati and myself—are also in the process of conversion, and I will write about that soon. Pranam.

Chapter 22

That promised "soon" of Uttara's letter became a victim of procrastination, which became a concern for Nanda and Pawan. Their worry was exacerbated by no letters from Sakar and Bhagbati.

A couple of months later, out of desperation, Pawan left for Wardha. The trio was not there. Somehow, he was able to meet a man at the ashram who was Ramnik's friend. He gave Pawan an Ahmedabad address of the trio without explaining the reason they moved there. Pawan was under the impression that the address must be close to the Gandhi ashram at Sabarmati.

But Pawan located their residence, not in the ashram, but in a posh house of their own. How could they afford this kind of house in this huge industrial city of India, and in one of its above average colony?

They greeted him. All of them went inside and sat down on a rug. Uttara quickly got up and went in the kitchen.

Pawan kept looking on the long hairy top knot (lock of hair called *shikha*) that Sakar and Bhagbati had grown in the middle of their heads. Customarily, that top knot has been an indicator of a male Brahmin. Pawan and Sakar had dropped their top- knots after high school. But why did he become a disciple of a Buddhist lama guru and shave his head completely in the first place? The Brahmins, including the neighboring Muslims, hated the *nastika* (atheist) Buddha. Why did Sakar change his mind and his hair again? Pawan thought perhaps that Sakar wanted to be the truly original Sakar, a Brahmin boy. He and Bhagbati did look like Brahmin boys right down to the typical outfit: a *kurta* shirt and a *dhoti*. The only normal person, he thought, was Uttara, who always wore a sari after marriage. Before marriage she used to wear a kurta and shalwar in the Punjabi style.

Uttara quickly brought Gujarati snacks and *shrikhand*. "Baba," she said, breaking the silence, "enjoy this Gujarati *bhusa* and *lassi*!"

"You mean these foods are Gujarati garbage?"

"No, Baba. This all is so tasty that you will want a second helping."

"Then why are you calling it *bhusa*?"

"Actually, the Gujarati word is *bhusu* and it means snacks. But the same word is *bhusa* in Hindi and does mean garbage."

"I understand now."

Then Sakar opened the discourse. "Bhai ji, you must be wondering how we ended up here. We made it a point not to mention our whereabouts at least for a year. But our work here began to reward us so unbelievably quickly, Bhai ji. We have been burden on you. Your favors to us are so many, but then it is not necessary to describe them in your presence. Ramnik bhai arranged work for us here. So we have now become independent."

"What's your line of work, Sakar?"

"I am going to tell you the entire details. Ramnik bhai is a very kind Gujarati. By nature he looks like a born Gandhian. He found out that the ashram job was taking a toll upon Uttara's health."

"Yes, Baba, Chacha is right. He was very much concerned about me. He didn't want to disclose my condition
to you. You understand why!"

"I do," Pawan said. "Then what happened?"

"Bhagbati sought a solution. He asked Ramnik bhai if
he could help us. We told him what we are and what we
did before coming to Wardha. He promised to help us
out. One evening he came to meet us. The moment he
entered my room, he touched Chacha's feet and said with
respect, 'Swami ji, Pranam!' Chacha looked speechless.
He was unable to figure out what Bhagbati had told
Ramnik bhai about our background."

"Bhai ji, when he saw that I remained quiet, he began
to talk to Bhagbati. He said, 'Bhagbati, you wanted me to
help you out. You all are going out to Ahmedabad as a
team for a good paying job, a very respected job. I have
arranged everything for your team.' We all became
speechless. He noticed our behavior and he kept looking
at all of us with a very sweet smile. Then he continued.
'Swami ji, Bhagbati told me that your horoscope names
are not Kotwal and Pokhriyal, but Sharma. In Gujarat nobody would take Kotwal as a serious name for a pandit.'
So I am now Pandit Sakar Sharma."

"Chacha ji forgot to tell you that his first name was
very good, but not my first name. Ramnik bhai told me
that in Gujarat I better pronounce my name correctly:
Bhagvati Prasad," Bhagbati said with a smile.

Pawan, too, couldn't resist laughing. After he stopped
laughing, he asked Sakar, "So how is this name change
related to your work?"

Sakar explained, "We are now a puja team. I am a pujari and Bhagbati and Uttara are my assistants, thanks to
Bhagbati's father, who taught him how our rituals are
performed. My name, Swami Nirakaranand, made it clear
to Ramnik that I was familiar with our Hindu shastras. He

came from a business background and was well-connected with several Gujarati businessmen, who were impressed and arranged this puja job we now have."

"Chacha ji forgot to tell how Ramnik encouraged us." Bhagbati looked very eager to give Pawan more juicy details. "Gujaratis are a most religious people. Gujarat has the highest population of vegetarians in the world. Although Gujarat is a coastal region, only some small communities are associated with fishing. They sell their catch to the fish-eating communities of the coast. Once the Gujaratis find that you are Brahmin, pandits from Badri Narayan of the high Himalaya, then all pandits of India are literally lower than you! I will show you a lake near Ahmedabad dedicated to one of the Garhwali pandits who came to that city long ago to perform big pujas. That pandit must be related to you. Gujaratis honored the Garhwali pandit as the highest holy pujari. You may expect that honor someday."

Uttara reminded them, "Don't forget Ramnik bhai's comment of appreciation. Even a mule from Badrinath would be considered holy in Gujarat—"

Pawan interjected with a smile, "I understand clearly. He has already found three holy mules!"

They all laughed.

Then Uttara explained further, "Ramnik bhai told us that many rich Gujaratis support the Swami Narayan religious organization of Gujarat. I had no knowledge of this organization. We were surprised that the founding swami of this organization was also from U.P. and established himself here as a great saint. Then Ramnik bhai put us on a higher pedestal. The founder was from the U.P. plains, whereas we were from the U.P. Himalaya. All we have to do is tell the Gujaratis that Himalayan Badri Narayan is much higher than their coastal Swami Narayan!"

Pawan laughed again and said, "So you three are now doing pujas for money. Puja business is run by fraudulent knowledge, by *thug vidya*. Can you prove that God sits in Badrinath? The Gujaratis should know that Himalayan Brahmins are not vegetarians. They sacrifice animals in their temples and here they are fooling simple devout Gujaratis. We Paharis think that our Himalayas are *Dev Bhumi*, the land of gods. Indeed it is *the* land of gods— the more gods the more sacred slaughter of animals, and so the more free sacred meat. Such animal slaughter is uncommon in other religions."

"But the ancient poet Kalidasa called the Himalayas the 'godly soul,'" Bhagbati replied.

"It makes sense for him to say so," Pawan explained. "Kalidasa was a Himalayan himself, and so proud of his birthplace, as is apparent in the many Himalayan characters and places in his works. You said Ramnik has visited Badrinath three times. Hasn't he noticed that Garhwal is the most backward part of not just India but the world? What did Badri Narayan do for the Pahari people? And I am sure you do those pujas starting with Lord Ganesh. The lord was created by Parvati in our Himalayas. Why couldn't Kalidasa ask the lord to improve his native region first?"

They all laughed at Pawan's lecture on divine exposure. They didn't dare try to outargue a lawyer and hunter and so preferred to remain silent. He looked like he was contemplating why these three Brahmins engaged in exploiting Gujarat's extreme religiosity. He found only a simple answer, which looked like a revelation to him: Religion is driven by economic engine.

Uttara found a genuine pretext to stop her father's ridicule of religious acts. She said, "Let me bring the famous Gujarati *masala chai*, Baba."

"You mean *chai* with spicy *chhaunka*?" Pawan quipped.

Now they all laughed. "No, Baba! It's a special spicy tea, but it's not a curried tea, just delicious spices."

Chapter 23

Pawan returned to Pauri. At the Pauri bus stand he met Pandit Bharat Ram. They greeted each other, but Pawan was not interested in engaging the pandit in longer conversation. He felt relief when Bharat Ram gave an excuse to leave him quickly. The excuse was that Pandit Bharat Ram was going to perform *graha puja* for a client at night.

On his way to his home, Pawan began to ponder the excuse of planet worship, or *graha puja,* as an act of priestly trickery to earn free food and some cash. He knew that the "week system" of dividing a month was not Vedic but Greco-Roman. As soon as that system reached India in ancient times, pandits like Bharat Ram quickly adopted this system in order to milk it: the priests attached inappropriate Vedic mantras to worship the seven planets of the week, Sunday to Saturday. To milk this system even more, they added two more imaginary planets, Rahu and Ketu. They convinced the despondent devotees that their adverse fate would change by worshiping the nine planets. The worshipper was required to offer every planet its favorite food as a gift. For example, Saturn, or Shani, loved black beans, matching the complexion of the dark planet. The sun needed white rice, matching the planet's bright light. On top of that, each planet needed some cash with its food gift.

Whatever the priest wants in his diet became easily available without expending any effort in its production! And with the free food, he gets free cash, the *dakshina*! And the free meal for him after he finishes the ritual and declares it *graha shanti* or planetary peace! This ritual should not be called *graha shanti* but *pandit shanti*, Pawan thought: peace with the pandit. The ancient Greeks and Romans would have been shocked to know how their gift of weekdays to India generated gifts for her freeloading priests!

Pawan was disturbed by these thoughts as he reached his home. Should he tell Nanda that his own brother and son-in-law were earning their livelihood by this priestly thuggery? And his daughter was an accessory to it!

When he reached home, it was already dark. He found Nanda very much depressed. He made her more depressed when he told her how those three had changed their worldview.

"Sakar is under the influence of his lama guru's worldview, but he keeps changing his worldview. I understand that a person's view of the world is tied to that person's security," Pawan commented.

"What do you mean?" Nanda asked in a confused tone.

"Everyone has his own worldview and justifies it. But then everybody, at least thrice in life, replaces the old one by a new worldview and justifies it in turn. Those three mules adopted the ashram's view and justified it. Soon they replaced it with the priestly view, which they justify now. Sakar should have taken law practice seriously."

After Nanda heard all the details, she lamented, "Someday, soon, Sakar may die of big heart attack like my father, whose greed led him from teaching to regular indulgence in those rituals and sacred feasts. Lots of time for worship means no time for exercise. Otherwise his school job was an honest way to earn a living. He taught his classes while walking, which is certainly good exercise."

"Don't worry! You will see him changing his worldview again. Uttara has changed her lifestyle. She has almost forgotten to cook our north Indian food. She loves the free Gujarati Puja food! Thanks to *grah puja* here or there," Pawan said with a laugh. Nanda didn't laugh. She nodded, an expression of loss in her eyes.

ಲಲ

A month later, Nanda suggested she and Pawan take a trip to meet Harshpat or Prachi. But Pawan's court load was getting heavier, which made a long trip impossible. Nanda was fortunate enough to have a friend like Murti who had always been enthusiastic to take short trips with her. Murti suggested a trip to Hardwar, the closest town, which divided the plains from the Garhwal Himalayas. Their trip's pretext was the forthcoming *Maha Shiva Ratri* celebration at Har ki Pauri.

A bath at any point on the Ganges was considered holy, but the holiest place to bathe was Har ki Pauri, which means Hara's footrest, a particular spot along the Ganga. Hara was Lord Shiva's name, and thus this town was known in the scriptures as Hardwar, Hara's door. Hardwar was also called Haridwar now, courtesy of Vishnu's devotees. No animal sacrifice took place here, and no indulging in alcohol, meat, or fishing. So, there was no free meat available here unlike in many higher Himalayan temples.

Traditionally, no animal sacrifice was allowed in Shiva's temples, but Shiva's wife or his assistant, Lord

Bhairava, could be offered lots of animal slaughter. From Hardwar and over the entire Indo-Gangetic plains animal sacrifice would be considered sin in most temples, with some exceptions like Kali's temples on the eastern end of the Ganga. Even some eastern swamis of the Ramakrishna order would eat meat, just like the Pahari priests from the northern Himalayan region of the Ganga and its tributaries!

Nanda had no interest in indulging in alcohol, meat, or fish. But Murti, like other Paharis, had no objection to meat or fish, if available, even in Hardwar. Lately, she was missing game meat because its provider, Pawan, had abandoned hunting. Every Saturday, however Balram, would bring home fresh goat meat from Pauri's butcher shop, the owner of which was named Hussain, a Muslim. Hindus would not share their food with any Muslim or Christian, but they would buy uncooked food products no matter the caste or religion of the seller. However, some Hindus knew that Muslims cooked the tastiest food, including meat. Balram was one of them and ate with Hussain, especially mutton. But in taste, meat-lovers rated bazaar mutton lower than game meat.

Murti didn't mind abstaining from meat for a few days.

Nanda had relatives in Hardwar. Pawan contacted them and made the bus arrangement for Nanda and Murti.

At Hardwar, the relatives gladly welcomed the two ladies and agreed to take them to the service worshiping Shiva's *linga* at Har ki Pauri on the evening of the Maha Shiva Ratri. On their way to Har ki Pauri, they saw crowds of devotees, including a group of naked saints (*naga sadhu*) chanting the Shiva mantra *om namaḥ shivāya* (Om, bow to Shiva). Some of them looked high due to smoking *bhang* (cannabis). They were mispronouncing the Shiva mantra as *om namo sibāy*.

Before the *linga puja,* many of the attendees went for
a holy dip at Har ki Pauri. Murti and Nanda had clothes
in their bags to change into, and so they took a couple of
dips in the clothes they were wearing. Nanda enjoyed
bathing near the bank, but then moved a little further into
the river where the water was deep and forceful. With
some hesitation, and after Nanda's encouraging words,
Murti tried to reach Nanda. The currents of the Ganga
swept her under. Fortunately, a man jumped into the river
and quickly got hold of Murti. She was traumatized for
about ten minutes after she left the water.

As Nanda helped her change her clothes, she apologized for encouraging her to go further into the river.
"Are you feeling ready for the puja?" she asked the shiv-
ering Murti. It was still the month of February and the
Ganges water was cold, but not as cold as in Dev Prayag,
which was further up from Hardwar.

"Yes, I am ready to join the puja, Didi!" Murti responded.

The *linga puja* was done very elaborately by the priest
and men and women offering flowers over the *linga.*
Then came the auspicious time of midnight. The *arti,*
with burning candles on a silver plate and accompanied
by a devotional song, was offered to the *linga.* Murti was
in tears when she heard this line: "Lord Shiva removes
miseries of the devotees in a second."

After the *arti* the two female hosts of Nanda and Murti
suggested that it was time to go back to their place and
rest. As the four women stepped onto the street, they saw
three *sadhu*-looking men following them. One of them
bowed to Murti and began to drag her aside. The remaining rogues dragged the two other women to the other side
of the street. The untouched woman ran and yelled for
help. Several men immediately got hold of the three
thugs. More people came to help. The three rogues were

beaten by the crowd and had lots of bruises on their bodies. They were left lying on a corner moaning.

Murti was shaken so much that Nanda had to calm her down. "Murti, we both made a mistake."

"What mistake, didi?"

"It's not a mistake really. I meant we should never forget to stick a small sickle in our waistband. You understand what I mean?"

"I do, and I will remember your advice, Didi."

"I would have taught a hard lesson to that sister fucker that would last his lifetime. He smelled *bhang*, and that bothered me more than the actual attack!"

They both laughed. The other two women didn't laugh because they had no idea why Nanda and Murti were laughing.

Chapter 24

Two days later, Nanda and Murti took the bus early in the morning to Kirti Nagar, situated on the bank of Alaknanda. The bus stopped for lunch at Dev Prayag. These two women had parathas and pickles with them for lunch, which they had already eaten in the bus, and so they used the lunchtime stop to collect some holy *Ganga jal* in their empty pickle bottle at the confluence of Alaknanda and Ganga, which was not far from the bus stop. They walked to the spot where these two rivers meet and filled the bottle with the holy water.

When they came up, the bus driver told them that the bus had some mechanical problem, which meant about a one hour delay. But the bus had more serious problems, and so another bus was arranged. This one was at a bus stop across the Ganges. All of the passengers walked across the Ganga to where the bus was waiting to switch to the Alaknanda route.

Their bus moved on to Kirti Nagar, and from Kirti Nagar they had to walk to Srinagar over an iron suspension bridge (*jhula pul*). After the bridge, the bus stand of Srinagar was more than a mile walk along the river. They were exhausted by the time they arrived at the station, only to find out that their bus to Pauri left half an hour ago and no bus was scheduled for Pauri after sundown. They had already lost two hours.

"Didi, there is a solution. Let's go to Dang."

"Dang? Do you know anyone in that village?" Nanda looked surprised at Murti's suggestion.

"My father had two sisters, Naumi and Sampatti. Naumi lives in Dang. She and pupha ji must be alone, for their son has a job in Meerut."

"I didn't know your father had two sisters. Sure, let's go meet your puphu ji."

While walking to the village, however, they grew even more tired. The walk was full of big rocks, or *dangs,* as the name of the village suggested. But the view of the gentle river Alaknanda below and of the mountains all around was far more peaceful than that of Hardwar. They lay down on a rock to take their rest.

When they awoke, they didn't realize that they had slept for more than an hour, and it was already dark. They got up and began to walk up the trail, but in the dark, they took a wrong turn and found themselves on a very rocky trail. Murti bumped into a rock and fell into the ditch below. While Nanda tried to lift her up, her handbag slipped and rolled down the embankment with a crackling sound. The bag had a bottle of Ganges water from Har ki Pauri. But Murti was able to get up and walk.

Nanda shouted for help. A woman from a nearby house heard her cry. She came out and guided them to the right house.

Murti gave Aunt Naumi a surprise when she knocked on the main door of her house. Her husband opened the door. When Naumi heard Murti's voice, she immediately came to the door.

After the usual exchange of greetings, Naumi's daughter Sohini and her husband Girijesh came to the door to greet them. They all went inside the house and sat on a *dari* rug.

"I am so happy to see you both. When did you come here?" Murti asked Sohini.

"We came here three days before Shiva Ratri, Didi. My husband got an extended leave because of Shiva Ratri. We are leaving the day after tomorrow," Sohini answered her cousin, Murti, very affectionately. "We were supposed to leave two days ago, but this is *bater* hunting season. My husband was lucky. This morning he went up the hill and found a crowd of *baters*. He shot six of them. So you will have a grand meat curry tonight!"

For a moment Murti's eyes grew bright when she heard the news of quail curry, but the brightness faded instantly. "I love meat, especially game meat, but not to-night. We were at Har ki Pauri worshiping Shiv ji. And Nanda didi is vegetarian. Jeth ji was a good hunter. He used to provide us all sorts of game meats. But recently their family abandoned all meat."

"Murti is right. My husband was addicted to hunting, mainly wild animals for meat."

"Very strange! Brahmin vegetarians in our region!" quipped Girijesh.

"There are some exceptions, but they don't count." Murti was thinking of Nanda's parents.

"Well, the Ghildyals consider themselves higher Brahmins, and so they don't kill, but they eat meat be-cause the animal was killed by someone else!"

They all laughed.

"By the way, my name is Girijesh, a name of God Shiva. I shouldn't eat any meat either. Right, papa ji?' He looked toward his father-in-law.

"Yes," Sohini's father answered.

Then Murti told them how the thugs attacked them af-ter the puja in Hardwar. "Shiv ji saved us. It's true.

Bhagban Shankar removes all troubles."

Girijesh interjected, "Very strange that Shiva ji didn't know of your forthcoming attack, which he should have removed before it happened! Maybe the devotees offered him too much *bhang* and he forgot."

Nobody laughed, and so the topic of conversation changed. Sohini was afraid that Girijesh might tell more Shiva jokes, which he did not consider jokes but commonsense questions. He did have a few questions for these two devotees. Why does God Shiva's consort Kali love animal sacrifice in her temples here but not in Hardwar? If Shiva is a universal god, then why is He not known in the countries of Middle East, Europe, Africa, and America?

Sohini was anticipating such questions from Girijesh, and so, before he could say a word, she asked Girijesh to help her pluck the quails. The couple walked toward the kitchen.

Then came dinner time. Sohini served the food she had just cooked, and Murti and Nanda started eating.

Her puphu kept insisting, "Murti! You know you and I were not born as Ghildyals. You can taste just one piece of *bater*. Here, taste this little piece. Just this piece only."

Murti knew that traditionally an aunt was always considered equal to one's mother. "All right Puphu ji!"

She tasted that piece and reacted immediately. "Sohini cooked it as good as Nanda didi. Didi, you should also try just one piece."

"Yes, beti, just try one piece," Murti's aunt affectionately requested of Nanda. Naumi put a piece on Nanda's thali.

Nanda knew that quail soup is considered superior to chicken or wild fowl soup in this region, and so she agreed. "Puphu ji, I am moved by your affection." Nanda began to chew a bite. "Oh, what a strong flavor! You can give me some soup."

Naumi began to pour some quail soup on a *katora*, a metal bowl, and offered it to Nanda. Nanda's eyes brightened when she saw that the soup contained lots of pieces of quail, more pieces than Murti got in her bowl!

After Nanda finished eating, she said, "The soup of this meat was beyond me, Sohini. I have no regret for losing that bottle of *Ganga jal*."

"What *Ganga jal*?" Girijesh inquired.

Nanda told him how she fell and the bottle of the Ganges water broke.

Girijesh quipped, "I am happy you liked my hunt's results. And forget about that bottle. For Paharis a bottle of cheap liquor is more desirable. Take a bottle of *koda daru*!" Girijesh laughed.

After a pause, he remarked, "I don't drink holy water because of all the feces of our villages and towns that enter the river down there. But I don't tell devotees from the plains!"

"Murti, don't tell my husband," Nanda interjected. "He might go to hunt *baters*!"

Murti smiled as she nodded her agreement, but after a minute she said, "Didi, I am confused between Kali and Parvati. Shiva ji knows that Kali sucks blood. Ma Parvati is Pahari. She rides her lion. I think, like all Pahari women, Ma Parvati must be eating meat. Do you believe that Ma would feed grass to her lion?"

Both women laughed.

After a pause Nanda responded, "I believe, like any good husband, Shiva ji helps Parvati to feed the lion. A lion is a lion and will always roar like a lion, and it will always eat like a lion, too. Nobody feels pity for the lion's poor prey."

"Are we really returning from our holy pilgrimage from Hardwar?"

They laughed again.

The next afternoon, Nanda and Murti took a bus and safely reached home.

Chapter 25

Three weeks after their trip to Hardwar, Nanda had the opportunity for a short trip to the village of Badur, a half day's walk from Pauri. The occasion was the forthcoming wedding of her mausi's daughter, Mohini. Since Pawan had to be out of town during the wedding, Murti agreed to accompany Nanda.

The two women received bad news upon their arrival at Badur. A tiger had killed the *godan* cow (cow gift) two days before the wedding. It was decided that the wedding could go ahead as planned but without the gift of a cow to the new couple from the bride's father, although this breach of the *godan* custom was considered very inauspicious. The sacrificial ram reserved for the god Nagraja to ensure a happy married life for the bride and groom was still safe.

Recently several other tiger attacks on cattle had taken place due to Badur's location near a dense forest and a big creek. The villagers found out from Nanda how good Pawan was at hunting tigers.

A month after Nanda's return from Badur, her mausi's son Nabal appeared at the office of Pawan in the afternoon. It was Christmas Eve. Nabal looked nervous. He told Pawan that the villagers were desperate to get him to

Badur because a tiger killed a she-buffalo two days before, and Pawan asked him if some remains of the buffalo
were still uneaten. Nabal told Pawan that almost a half of
the beast was still there. Pawan told him to keep an eye
on the remains and prepare a *machan* on the nearest tree.
Eventually, the tiger would come back to eat the rest of
the dead animal.

Nabal returned to Badur in the evening. The next
evening, Pawan came to Badur and stayed at the home of
Nanda's mausi. The next morning, he examined the *machan*. After a light dinner, he took a glass of *chai*, went
out to check the *machan*, and sat down there.

Around ten p.m, the villagers ran toward the *machan*
as they heard a series of gunshots. The tiger was lying
dead beside the buffalo's remains. It was considered
something of a miraculous event, and so a celebration
was in order.

The following evening Nabal and his parents threw a
party. They invited the head of the village *panchayat* with
a few other members and the village priest. The *panchayat* head immediately arranged to slaughter a sheep and
prepared meat *biranji* (biryani). Since it was prepared to
honor Pawan, he joined the celebration. He was moved
when all the *panchayat* members requested that he stay
until the end of the celebration. The panchayat members
were, like him, part-time village-level judges and the
most esteemed citizens of the village.

The other important member of the village, the priest,
was absent on purpose. The celebration was supposed to
start with his *puja* of Lord Ganesha.

The *panchayat* head explained the reason for the absence of the priest. "We wanted to start the celebration
with a short *puja*," he said apologetically. "Our village
pandit ji refused to do *puja* for us. He complained that no
tiger should be killed because that animal is Mata Parva-

ti's symbol. He wanted us to offer the dead buffalo immediately to our *dom* caste people for their meat. I refused because what was forbidden meat for higher castes must be forbidden to low castes, too."

Pawan had a good laugh. He was aware of the conventional ignorance that was hard to change, but he was still hopeful that keen observation could improve it. Someone from this audience, he thought, might tell the priest to be a good observer.

He got up so that all could hear his explanation. He looked around and said, "How did your pandit confuse a tiger with a lion? Hasn't he seen the pictures of Mata Parvati riding a lion? The male lion has a mane, which makes him look big. Male tigers have no mane and are larger and faster than the male lion. Lions of our Himalayas are extinct, except one, which Parvati owns. We have been worshiping Mata Parvati for so long, and yet, let me confess, I haven't seen that lion with her or without her. Has anyone here?"

The audience responded with laughter.

Pawan wanted to mention one more difference, the stripes on the tiger skin. But he saw the volunteers starting to serve leaf plates for dinner. He sat down quietly as the first plate was placed in front of him.

The main course was mutton biryani. Pawan didn't want to offend his hosts, since the party was to honor him, and moreover, he was sitting beside the *panchayat* head, who functioned like a chief judge in local disputes. They became friends instantly, and without any barriers, in spite of the fact that Pawan was a law graduate, a professional lawyer, and a court-appointed judge and the *panchayat* head didn't have education beyond middle school. In some villages, the *panchayat* heads were completely illiterate.

Pawan ate everything and thanked the chief as he appreciated how great that biryani tasted. He said to the man, "It's good that your priest didn't show up for the Ganesh *Puja*. This great *biranji* would not have made sense for Lord Ganesh."

"I don't understand!" the chief said, confusion in his tone.

"Ganesh ji is an elephant. Right?"

"Only his head."

"Right, but he eats with his mouth like all creatures, and elephants don't eat meat," Pawan said as he smiled and patted the chief on his shoulder.

The chief laughed. "I understand your joke. But you are right. What's the fun in inviting Ganesh ji if we want to have *biranji*!"

"As a rule, don't give Ganesh ji a chance to sulk by ending his worship with your non-vegetarian food!"

They both laughed.

ᘓᘐᘓᘐ

However, on his way home, Pawan began to appreciate the priest's stand. He realized that the *panchayat* chief was also under the influence of ignorance caused by inconsistent traditions. The untouchable people could not afford *biranji* (biryani), and the buffalo biryani was possible for them to enjoy had they been given the dead beast immediately.

Pawan was aware of the age-old traditions. A cow's meat was forbidden because she gave milk. A she-buffalo's meat was forbidden because she gave milk. A she-goat, too, gave milk, but her meat was very popular even at the temples. The people of Badur continued to practise this lopsided tradition.

Pawan wondered how the Badur people would have reacted had he tried to convince them that, as early as

Vedic times, Indians enjoyed beef. He momentarily cringed at this thought. Had he said that in his little speech there would have been shouts against him. There would have been more shouts had he said, like an Arya Samajist, that the Vedic people refrained from meats! He remembered how an Arya Samaj preacher in Pauri was stoned when he said that. He also remembered how Bhagbati had problems convincing his father that ancient Vedic priests were not vegetarians, beef their favorite food to celebrate a marriage.

Pawan was very happy that he got a chance to enjoy his favorite food, biryani. Why shouldn't he eat it secretly! So what if Nanda found out!

When he left the bus road and descended the trail to his village, he saw a few Tibetan herders camping with their sheep across the creek. He knew that these traders used sheep for wool. But sheep meat, like any other meat, was not forbidden in their diet. His information was based on Sakar's lama guru, a strict vegetarian. Buddhists were not supposed to kill animals for food. Killing meant non-observation of *ahiṃsa*, "non-violence." Monks or nuns could accept any food, including meat, in *bhiksha*, but they were expected to discard that meat later without the knowledge of the person who gave it as part of the alms or *bhiksha*. Their refusal to accept meat as alms would be deemed discourtesy, hence an act of *ahiṃsa*.

These Buddhist herders did kill sheep for meat. But they were householders, not monks or nuns. Pawan had heard from Sakar that his lama guru strongly opposed these herders' eating a yak that died of deliberate slow starvation, its meat considered "non-violent meat." In Sakar's opinion, non-violent meat didn't violate the Buddhist hallmark principle of *ahiṃsa*.

Then a thought hit Pawan in a flash. Obtaining non-violent meat by starving the animal was like non-violent rape. His father might have done that, had non-consensual sex that produced Sakar. Who knows what happened! He cringed and tried to forget about it quickly.

Another question began to bother him. Why couldn't the Badur people, the untouchable people, eat the meat of that buffalo? They didn't kill it, the tiger did. They could have used the Buddhist principle. No, he thought. Even such a liberal Buddhism was not the right fit here in these hills. Nor was the Arya Samaj. The Paharis, like the ancient Vedic people, believed in killing animals for food, believed in non-consensual killing.

In the evening, Nanda was flabbergasted to see Pawan returning with a happy expression on his face and no sign of fatigue. He told her all about the event. Then Nanda surprised him when she said, "Sure, Lachchhu and his relatives would have enjoyed buffalo *biranji*!"

"How about tiger biryani? That tiger's meat went to waste."

Nanda laughed. She thought that it was opportune time to tell her own secret: the quail meat she had eaten on her return from Har ki Pauri. "How about *bater biranji*?"

"How did you think of *bater biranji*?"

Nanda finally narrated the quail story. Pawan enjoyed it.

Chapter 26

Two days later, when Pawan entered his office, he found a letter from Harshpat among his mail. He opened the letter and limped to his chair when he saw a photo with this caption: *Harshpat and future wife Marci*.

The letter from Harshpat was like a *vajrapat* (lightning strike).

Baba and Ma,
Pranam.
Unfortunately, the Brahmin girls you have recommended for me so far never went to college. So, I have been ignoring your judgments.

But, great news: I have found a girl. She was three years junior to me in medical school. Her name is Marci. A month ago, she and I proposed to each other. As you must have noticed, Marci doesn't sound like a Brahmin name. Marci's forefathers were scavengers in Bihar and later converted to Christianity with lots of tribal people. Now she has gone through one more conversion, mainly because her family still suffered the stigma of untouchability. I understand, with her background, disgruntled local Brahmin girls' parents will spread many rumors.

But ignore the age-old tendency to rumor. "Rumorology" is governed by the "law of irrelevance," the need to talk about things that do not matter. The fact is that she does not believe in religion and caste anymore. So, we are going to be married by a judge, not by a Brahmin or Christian priest. The wedding will take place on the last Sunday of next month, in Lucknow. Baba, you must validate our marriage. You are a judge, too!

Eagerly waiting for your blessings,
Harsh

Note: I am enclosing a letter and photo for Sakar Chacha and company. Please forward this letter to them immediately. I will contact Prachi and Sashi myself right now. More information later.

Then he read the letter for Sakar.

Chacha!

Pranam. Exciting news. Marci and I are engaged. A photo of us together is attached here for you, Uttara, and Bhagbati. You three must attend our court wedding on the last Sunday next month.

Marci comes from a Christian background, but she is a strong atheist. She does believe in Eve and Adam as our first ancestors. According to her belief, our God was created in the Middle East by humans ages and ages after Adam and Eve had many generations.

Sorry! No puja, no mantras, no gifts. Just your blessings at the ceremony.

Yours,
Harsh

Pawan forwarded this letter to Sakar by express mail right away. He included his own note to Sakar in which he expressed his opinion: *Since Harshpat is stubborn, he will marry Marci, no matter what anyone says. My major concern is how their children will be accepted in our society if they are not pure Brahmins. Harshpat is clearly violating our parampara. It looks like we are left with no choice, except to give our blessing. What do you think?*

The *parampara,* or tradition, that Pawan was alluding to was simply *Brahmins married Brahmins.* This old tradition guaranteed pure Brahmin progeny.

When Pawan came home in the evening, he found Nanda in the kitchen. He told her that he had an important letter from Harshpat. She requested him to read it to her as she was in the middle of cooking. He read it aloud. Nanda stopped and took the dish out of the oven. Both made their way to the sitting room.

Nanda was in shock. Both were silent. For them Prachi's mother-in-law from an untouchable background was nothing compared to this. Chandrika was at least an Arya Samaj woman and married to a Brahmin. A Christian girl, though atheist, was still a Christian girl, and what could they make of her coming from that kind of ancestry! They remained quiet for a while.

Then Nanda got up and said, "Let us go eat."

"I am not hungry."

"It's your favorite food—basmati and whole *urad dal*."

"That food we eat when celebrating a marriage."

"We eat it at least once a week. So, forget about marriage."

"You are right. I will eat. It's an education. We learn from our children what we never wanted to. Education is worth celebrating."

While eating, they began to talk about this marriage. "Should we tell other Kotwals about this?" Nanda asked. "Or should only we two share this news as a family secret?"

"Yes, we two only."

❧❧❧

Two weeks later, Pawan received a letter from Sakar by express mail. It was for Harshpat, and Sakar wanted it to be forwarded to him. Before forwarding it, Pawan took it home. Nanda looked surprised to see his happy face.

"You look happy. Any news?' Nanda asked him with a smile.

"I have received a very inspiring letter from Sakar."

"Why don't you read it to me aloud before I go in the kitchen? I have something on the oven."

"You are cooking something *swadishth*, and I can't wait to taste it. Why don't you finish the kitchen work? Then I will read it while eating." Pawan always considered Nanda's dishes salubrious (*swadishth*.)

Nanda agreed as she nodded her head.

At dinner, Pawan read the letter.

Dear Harshpat,
Bahut Badhai, Beta. Your marriage is inspirational. Barrister Makundi Lal was my inspiration for Asim School. He married an English lady, a Christian. You, too, have broken barriers. In every puja, I tell the attendees that India's best ideal has been vasudhaiva kutumabkam. This ideal was like a medicine to treat our social sickness of narrowness. So far Indians have failed to take this medicine. But you did not, Dr. Harshpat! We hope someday you will have children who will challenge Indian bigotry of miscegenation. Treat the Bhagavad Gita's "varnsaṃkara anxiety." I like Marci's comments on Adam and Eve.
Unfortunately, because of our puja plans at that time, we three will not be able to attend the wedding. If we

miss a puja, we may lose our clients. You can write us back at our new Ahmedabad address written on the back of this letter.

We bless you as two bricks to build a new India, an integrated and stronger India.

Love,
Chacha

Nanda, like her husband, was moved by the contents of the Sakar's letter. Their closest family members supported their son's marriage.

The next day Pawan went to Pauri and mailed the letter to Harshpat.

Harshpat was also moved by his uncle's letter. He immediately wrote back:

Chacha!
I am delighted by your letter and thank you for bolstering our confidence in our marriage. I told Marci that you liked her beliefs in Eve and Adam. She questions if speechless Adam and Eve were really able to understand Godspeak.

She knows that God was created a few thousand years ago by literate, but irrational, male Homo sapiens who believed Eve was created out of Adam's body. As a female doctor, she would welcome the news of the first man delivering a baby out of his body. I told her that your lama guru, too, considered such a funny creation of God a joke.

We will miss you three very much. Baba says no Kotwals except you, Papa, and Ma will know about our wedding. I guarantee the Kotwal tribe will find out sooner or later!

Eager to meet you with Marci for your blessings,
Harsh

A footnote:

Missing worship is not harmful but missing medicine is. Grandma used to be mad at me if I missed a laddu at the Ganesh Puja. Instead of cursing, she could have given me a laddu later. I am learning from Marci a lot about action-communication with patients. If a patient missed a dose of medicine, the doctor could say to the patient, "You are sloppy. Don't miss any dose." Instead, the doctor should say, "Don't miss any dose." Just eliminate the irrelevant part, "You are sloppy," and keep the action part: "Don't miss any dose." Your goal must be appropriate action, not a counter-productive antagonization.

Sakar was struck most by the footnote. That's what his lama guru also taught him. Humiliation was not a remedy. It caused pain (*dukkha*). A humiliated person was likely to ignore even good advice from the humiliator. Indeed, humiliation was counter-productive. He was happy that he didn't say any humiliating word against Harshpat's wish to marry Marci. Adults should not be advised who they could or could not love and marry. He didn't like Pawan's opinion. He felt good about his reply to Pawan:

Don't say to Harshpat something like this: "Though you are violating our parampara, marry her because you are stubborn." Instead, keep the action part: "Yes, marry her." And eliminate the junk part. If Harshpat is stubborn, he will marry her anyway, as you say, but he may not be on speaking terms with you later if you add junk such as: "You are violating our tradition and you are stubborn." Here I am following my guru's instruction: All traditions are subject to change. Respect the person most who rises against his or her odds."

Sakar was perturbed by Pawan's concern regarding not having pure Brahmin grandchildren. He thought of himself as not being a pure Brahmin child, and yet all Kotwals, including Pawan, accepted him as if he was a legitimate Kotwal Brahmin child. They never clearly told him how his birth took place. What if he was a rape child? If Pawan knew that he was a rape child, then he was very liberal and gracious to accept a rape child as his legitimate stepbrother. Then why was this liberal lawyer upholding this ignoble tradition of miscegeny in his son's case?

Chapter 27

One afternoon, Ramnik made a surprise visit to Sakar, Bhagbati, and Uttara at their Ahmedabad home.

"Namaste!" Bhagbati greeted him in Gujarati, "*Maja ma chho?* (Are you fine?)"

Uttara heard their exchange from the kitchen and came out to give him a warm welcome. "Let's go inside," she requested.

They all sat in the sitting room. Ramnik commented, "You have first-class furniture. I am impressed."

"So, what is the reason for this happy surprise?" Bhagbati asked.

"First I wanted to tell you that I am now back to my family business in Ahmedabad. Second, I have a proposal for Pandit ji. Is he sleeping?"

"No, no. Chacha has very little time to sleep. He is out helping a *mota seth* plan his daughter's forthcoming wedding," Uttara replied. "Let me bring tea." She moved to the kitchen.

"Who is this big businessman?" Ramnik asked Bhagbati.

"Jiva bhai Jhaveri, the gem dealer."

"I know him very well. He is our family friend."

"What a small world!"

"Not really. We business people run a big world," Ramnik said with a laugh.

"So what's your proposal?"

"Yes, it's a great proposal. Let's talk about it over the tea."

In a few minutes, Uttara brought *masala chai* and snacks.

Ramnik turned his gaze to Uttara. "I was telling Bhagbati that I have a great proposal for Pandit ji," he said. "I am going to use his sannyas name: Swami Nirakaranand. We all must request that he write his autobiography, the life story of a swami priest."

"Your proposal is sure worth considering, but I doubt he will have time to write a book, any book. His *puja* work is brisk. He is so busy that he wanted to attend our brother's wedding next month but can't. It's so depressing." Uttara looked sad.

Ramnik put his hand on her shoulder and said, "That's really too bad that he has no time for such a rare event. I have some suggestions to help him, Uttara ben!"

"Like what?" Uttara asked with excitement.

"For making his biography a possibility. One of my friends here is very good at writing. He lives now in Ahmedabad. Why don't you two tell him the life and work of Swami Nirakaranand reborn as Pandit Sharma? I will introduce him to you. He was educated in the best English schools and colleges of Bombay. One of his ghost stories is under consideration for a Hindi film. Like any average Bombay native, he speaks four languages: Hindi, Gujarati, Marathi, and English."

"What's his name?"

"His name might discourage you. Anyway, his name will not appear in the biography."

"But why not?" Bhagbati looked troubled.

"He will tell you that his name is little funny. Swanil Trivedi."

Bhagbati laughed, "Bothered by 'Swanil'? I understand he is not good wind.'"

"No. 'Swanil' is perfect but 'Trivedi' is not. He has no knowledge of the three Vedas that his name suggests."

They all laughed.

"Ramnik bhai, your suggestion is exciting. We need Swanil's writing skills in English or Hindi, not in Vedic or Sanskrit," said Bhagbati with a smile, and then he turned his eyes toward Uttara. "What do you say, Uttara? You know Chacha ji far better than I. Do you think he would like to make his life public?"

"Sure, there is nothing to hide in his life story." Then she paused for a few moments. "This evening," she said, "we will talk him into it and get his permission to start this project."

"I will arrange a meeting with Swanil and you can both talk to Swami ji," Ramnik said.

In the evening, Uttara and Bhagbati did talk to Sakar. "Give me some time to think it over. Maybe, just one night," Sakar responded.

During the breakfast with Uttara and Bhagbati the next morning, however, he remained quiet, troubled. How were his parents married while his mother was already pregnant? He had been successfully avoiding this question most of his life. But now this question of his life story being told for public consumption had arisen. He could have rejected this proposal, but he was fully aware of the extent of Ramnik's favor: complete financial security, and not his alone but for his niece and her husband, too.

છ૭છ૭

Two weeks later, they met at Ramnik's house. There

was nobody in the house except Swanil and Ramnik. The two very religious Gujarati men touched the feet of Sakar—aka Swami Nirakaranand, aka Pandit Sharma. "Swami ji, I am here for your blessings. It's my good fortune that I am meeting a saint from the Badri Narayan area. Ramnik bhai has already told me so much about you."

After the usual exchange of courtesies, it was agreed upon that Swanil would write Sakar's biography.

Swanil told Sakar, "Swami ji, I am proud to write about your life. I promise to start the work as soon as I have some sessions with Uttara and Bhagbati. Then I will submit an outline with some short samples, most probably by the end of next month. Then, with your approval, I will proceed with the book. I will know my schedule by then and will check with you for a convenient time."

"That sounds good," Sakar agreed. "I will be really busy the whole next month. So that gives you more time to prepare short samples," Sakar said while nodding his head.

Swanil, too, agreed. "I have one condition. My name Swanil Trivedi should not be anywhere in the book."

"Not even thanks in the preface?" Sakar asked with a smile.

"No thanks, and no payment," he said seriously. Then he joked, "Pandit ji, I don't believe in God. But I do believe in ghosts. I will write anonymously. I am a ghost for you."

They all laughed.

Swanil then repeated his offer: "The final manuscript will be my tribute to you, Swami ji. All I need is your blessings."

Sakar couldn't say a word. But his teary eyes did tell a lot.

"I hope to produce a biography as exciting as *Autobi-*

ography of a Yogi by Swami Yogananda."

Sakar looked a little startled. "Who is this Yogananda? Where is he from?" He asked Swanil with a sincere expression.

"He doesn't live in India. He is not a Himalayan yogi, but he claims to have a connection with an ancient yogi from the Himalayas, most likely your region, I guess. One day he left India and went to America. Now he is well known there. His books are selling like hot potato pakoras."

"That's wonderful." Sakar commented. "Our region has attracted so many saints, mainly because of the origin of the two holiest rivers: Ganga and Yamuna."

"That's true. The Nobel Laureate Tagore has exclusively mentioned these two rivers in his *Jana gana mana* song. What an honor!"

"Indeed a great honor," Sakar concurred.

"I will focus on you as a real native Himalayan yogi, Swami ji. That's an edge for you over other yogis. I hope you prove that by living a long life. Some famous swamis have claimed to practice authentic yoga. They couldn't even reach the age of sixty. There goes their claim! Staunch believers would always defend their early deaths by saying it was because God wanted them to join Him soon. I don't believe in God jokes! Even my grandmother lived to be eighty-one and knew nothing about yoga. She was illiterate. Her family name, Mrs. Trivedi, was as false as God! I don't think God wanted my grandparents with Him soon for they celebrated their *shasthi purti* marriage. That sixtieth marriage anniversary was witnessed by their six children and nineteen grandchildren."

Sakar reacted with a faint smile. Then he breathed a long sigh. He shouldn't have abandoned his idea of utilitarian gardening, he thought.

Chapter 28

The morning weather in Lucknow on the wedding day was great, sunshine with a cool breeze. But only a few attended the wedding of Harshpat and Marci in a Lucknow court. Marci's parents, Mr. and Mrs. Jacob, sat with Harshpat's parents. The males wore Western clothing—pants, and shirts. The ladies wore Indian saris and blouses. There was no sign that anyone was uncomfortable with this court marriage. Prachi and her husband Sashi were seated in the front as they were to be witnesses.

Then a private photographer entered and sat beside Marci's father. After mutual greetings, he commented, "You all seem to be very liberal in-laws. I feel honored to take pictures of such progressive parents. I am saying this because recently a boy and a girl got married, and I took their photos. The boy was Muslim and the girl Christian. Their parents were opposed to their marriage. The mothers were troubled more than the fathers, but none of the parents attended their marriage."

"Obviously, they faced the two walls of their respective religions blocking their rational path."

"Not two but four walls. One was Rajput Muslim and the other was an untouchable Christian. The fathers cared for caste only, but the mothers cared for caste as well as for religion. They even fussed about dress codes!"

"Adam and Eve were so lucky. They didn't have to encounter any mother-in-law myths. No problems regarding dress for Adam and Eve either. You would have loved to take their photos," Mr. Jacob commented, and then he laughed.

It was clear that the photographer didn't share Mr. Jacob's joke. He had just a dry smile.

Mr. Jacob quickly stopped laughing. "Oh, I want to tell you about our marriage-related differences. Harshpat told us that Pahari marriage ceremony is always celebrated with bagpipes and dhol-damau drums. Your photos would have been even better if we had the players of those instruments here."

The photographer looked startled. "I thought it was always celebrated with shahnai and drums just like here in Lucknow. Let us check with the Kotwals."

Pawan and Nanda frequently looked toward the court entrance. Each time, they would mumble inaudibly but their expressions indicated slight impatience. Mr. Jacob asked Pawan, "Everything looks fine there at the entrance?"

"Oh, yes, yes. I was just hoping the ceremony could wait a few more minutes."

"Any reason?" Mr. Jacob asked Pawan.

Before Pawan could reply, the judge entered the courthouse in his black robes. All other attendees stood up and then sat after he occupied his chair. Then he started the ceremony. It was very simple and took about ten minutes. At the end, the judge congratulated the bride and groom. He thanked all the attendees and told them, "Now you can celebrate. Best wishes!"

As soon as the judge left the court room through the back door, the attendees hugged the bride and bridegroom and blessed them. Shashi and Prachi signed the marriage certificate the court clerk had prepared. Then all of them heard sounds of bagpipe and drums outside. All of them moved outside and stood stunned at the court entrance.

"What?" Harshpat shouted with joy. "Chacha! Bhagbati! Uttara!" He ran out like a baby and touched Sakar's feet. Sakar blessed him and hugged him. Then Bhagbati and Uttara hugged them. Uttara, sobbing with joy, covered her eyes with both palms. Pawan and Nanda joined them.

Sakar couldn't wait to meet the bride. He went straight to Marci, taking Harshpat along with him. Sakar blessed her with his hands on her head. She looked a little shy. She wondered who this man in khadi dhoti-kurta-topi was until Harshpat smiled and said, "I know you didn't recognize my chacha ji, Marci."

Marci touched Sakar's feet and cried.

"Chacha ji, let me introduce you to Marci's parents," Harshpat said, and he took his uncle ahead. Simultaneously, Harshpat signaled to Bhagbati and Uttara to join him as well. He introduced his uncle to the Jacobs.

After the exchange of greetings, Mr. Jacob said, "We thought you couldn't attend the wedding, Sakar ji." He was going to say more, but he saw Uttara and Bhagbati moving toward him. No sooner had Sakar introduced them than the young couple touched the feet of the Jacobs. They looked moved by Uttara and Bhagbati's gestures of respect.

Then Sakar moved toward the musicians, behind whom Ramnik bhai was standing, enjoying the music. He brought him back to Harshpat and introduced him. Then he informed him, "This great friend, Ramnik bhai, arranged our surprise visit with the help of my other friend Jhaveri ji. They have connections all over India, Lucknow included. And your parents arranged the team of the Pahari musicians. Prachi and Sashi arranged their Lucknow trip."

Harshpat, his eyes turned toward the musicians as he pretended to be enjoying their music, was speechless.

"Doctor," Sakar said to Harshpat. "Let me tell the Jacobs all that Ramnik bhai has been doing behind the scene." They both took Ramnik to the Jacobs.

After a proper introduction, Sakar put his hand on Ramnik's shoulder as they faced Mr. Jacob. "Jacob ji, without Ramnik bhai this occasion would have been a phantom for me, Bhagbati, and Uttara. He is the power that made it real for us. You ask Bhagbati and Uttara." Mr. Jacob hugged Ramnik.

"Are you enjoying the Pahari music, Jacob ji?" Ramnik asked.

"Very much."

"Thanks to Harshpat's parents. They arranged this Pahari group of musicians.""

"The group may be Pahari, but the music is not quite Pahari. I guess our photographer, too, is aware of that. That's why he is paying so much attention to them. Picture after picture!" Marci's father said as he looked toward the musicians, saluting them.

Then Ramnik addressed Mrs. Jacob. "Please make this announcement to all."

He handed a note to her, which she read: *Let us move our party to the hotel lounge. We have three cars that will arrive at the gate any moment.* At the end of the note the hotel's name was written in big letters.

Mrs. Jacob expressed surprise by folding her palms over her lips. A party celebration arranged by Ramnik bhai in that hotel! She thought that Harshpat's parents believed in a simple marriage and a celebration in a simple restaurant. She was so spellbound that she quietly gave the note to her husband. Mr. Jacob understood and read the note loudly to the audience.

Harshpat was not ready for this hotel surprise either. "That hotel is really great, Ramnik bhai ji!" he complimented. "It serves first-class wines and meat dishes. My father-in-law will love this hotel. He is a meataholic!"

Ramnik had a good laugh then reacted with his own joke. "We wanted to take good care of your *sasur sahab*'s sophisticated taste. I had the impression that you were planning to take us all to the Hazrat Ganj's Chat House where no reservations are needed."

"That's right. We all wanted very simple celebration—a *chat* party!"

The party, which was pre-arranged by Jhaveri's Lucknow friends, was not actually in any hotel but in the famous Dilkusha Gardens, which were full of non-native trees and flowers. All the attendees assembled there under a canopy in front of the *Dilkusha Kothi*, a palace of the late Nawab of Lucknow.

When all were seated, Ramnik announced, "We just wanted to surprise you and let you know we are pleased by the openness of this marriage. Sakar ji believes openness, open borders, integration and not discrimination, is the way to world peace. So here we are under the open sky sitting in the center of Lucknow's symbol of natural and cultural integration, the integration of civilizations—"

Everybody stood up while applauding.

"Now the celebration begins," Ramnik said. From behind the palace a band of musicians appeared, marching toward the canopy. It was not the Pahari team of musicians but a band with English flavor: trumpets, drums, clarinets, etc. But it was headed by a shahnai player and a dholak drummer. All stood up and looked toward the approaching musicians.

When, finally, the party was over, and without a single meat dish, not a single bottle of alcohol, which is very unlike a Pahari party, the attendees took a tour of the old Nawab palace.

ॐॐॐ

The following evening, Sakar, Bhagbati, and Uttara, who were staying with Pawan and Nanda, had a long chat. The next morning all of them had to leave Lucknow.

At the end of the chat Pawan said to Sakar, "Ramnik told me about your biography project. He was excited. He really adores you. But I wanted you to be a little cautious. I mean about the man who is going to write your biography."

Sakar could read in his brother's eyes that Pawan was a little uncomfortable.

"I see a problem. Swanil seems to be a professional ghost writer. There is a serious problem if he wants to write a true biography. He would like to see his ghost writing becoming famous. You are a religious man from the Himalayas, which he knows very well, and so you are definitely expected to be a man of *siddhis* such as levitation, future prediction, fulfilling a devotee's incredible wish, God realization, etc."

He offered an analogy to Swanil's goals, religious authors. "The authors of those books lie. They tell an incredible birth story of their religion's founder, but how in the world did some non-existent entity such as God the King of Heaven contact the founder? Maybe some astronomers will expose their heaven." He once even joked to with Dr. Subrahmanyan Chandrasekhar of the University of Chicago, asking if he really believed in the heaven of Lord Indra. The astronomer was born in Punjab where a boy in every mile was named after Indra, popularly pronounced and written in Punjab as *Indar*.

Pawan's astronomer joke lightened Sakar's mood and he laughed along with his brother.

Sakar guessed that Pawan was also bothered by his birth history and that was the real problem he dared not name. But how would the biographer know if he was born out of love or rape? What if he asked more questions about the circumstances of his birth? He thought, "My mother didn't make any protest against the rape and instead accepted marriage to my father. Could she have adopted Saina's strategy? No, my mother must have been timid, not brave like Nanda bhabhi."

This question, what the biographer might have found out, disturbed Sakar so much that he lost several hours of sleep in Lucknow. His eyes were red, which everyone noticed the next morning. After breakfast everyone left for the Charbagh train station.

Chapter 29

After his return from Lucknow, Sakar was surprised to receive an outline from Swanil with several short samples of the proposed biography. He was not very keen to read it, but he decided to read it before Bhagbati and Uttara. After all it was his biography in question.

He sat down on the *dari* rug and began to read the first short sample.

Sakar, or Swami Nirakaranand, descended from a line of yogi saints. His first guru, Swami Tirthanand, initiated him into sannyas at Uttarkashi. Swami Tirthanand was also initiated at Uttarkashi by his guru, Swami Buddhanand, who lived in a cave on the Ganga bank of Gangotri. Swami Buddhanand was initiated by Yogi Ananda. Yogi Ananda looked to be forty years old but was actually born around 1526 AD. He had witnessed India's Battle of Babur and Ibrahim Lodi. Babur decimated Lodi's army with the miraculous fire power of artillery that he had brought from his native Uzbekistan. India never knew such a power. The Lodi emperor fell in the battle, and thus ended the Lodi Dynasty of India. When Babur

*founded the Mughal Empire in India, young Ananda fled
to the Himalayas where he practised yoga.*

When Sakar finished the first sample, he asked Uttara
and Bhagbati to sit down with him.

They came and sat on the *dari* rug beside him.

"I am not interested in my biography." He said.
"Swanil is implying that such a yogi lived century after
century. Any Indian would be an exception if he or she
lived beyond a hundred years. This biographer is out of
his mind."

"Chacha ji, he might have gotten these ideas from *Autobiography of a Yogi,* which contains concocted stories
such as you see in Hindi films. Swanil might have cooked
up some stories that could make your biography suitable
for a film, thinking the gorgeous Himalayas would en-
chant the film audience. Sure, I will tell him to stop."

"The presence of the Himalayas doesn't prove his
claim. I don't mean Swanil is a liar. It looks to me he
wants my book to be a hot seller like *Autobiography of a
Yogi.* I don't want a book of myths. It should be about my
lived experiences even if they don't resonate with readers." He said this while massaging his forehead. He knew
Pawan was uncomfortable when he heard his biography
news because of his opposition to the exposure of his bastard birth, but he was right about Swanil being an exag-
gerator.

Uttara suggested, "Bhagbati! Before you ask Ramnik
to stop Swanil, be careful. To offend Ramnik would be a
huge mistake. After all, he is our benefactor. We should
never forget that this very comfortable life of ours is due
to him. When Chacha's school was burned down, I
thought he would never overcome his despair." She
wiped her tears with fingers.

"I understand your concern, my beti." Sakar gently put

his hand on her shoulder. "Ramnik did repair my despair, but you don't want your chacha's despair to reappear because of a false depiction. We Paharis are known for our honesty. Imagine a Pahari sadhu lying! Imagine any rational reader believing the projected age of 'Baba ji' in *Autobiography of a Yogi!*"

೮ᴐ೮ᴐ

The next day Bhagbati went alone to meet Ramnik. Ramnik greeted him as usual, and within a few minutes, he brought *masala* tea and snacks. They sat together on the *jhula*, a hanging bench very popular in Gujarat to entertain visitors. They gently began to swing it while talking.

Ramnik brought the wedding topic. "I think that Marci's parents were very much surprised with our arrangements."

"That's true. You did everything. My in-laws have nothing but praise for you." He stopped swinging. "But Chacha ji sounds a little concerned about the sample writing of Swanil."

"A little! He has written awful things. Can you believe in one place how Swami Nirakaranand blessed a childless couple and the following year they had a son! Swami ji doesn't believe in such stupid miracles. I am disgusted with Swanil."

"Really? We didn't read any further after we saw the first sample. You are right. We don't know what other lies he has cooked up. You know we are also a childless couple."

"Then what do you say? I would like to cancel the deal with Swanil."

Bhagbati was moved with Ramnik's Gandhian honesty and for a while he remained speechless.

"You didn't say answer. What do you say? Will Pandit ji be unhappy with my decision?"

"Chacha ji was very unhappy with the sample. He will have no problem with your decision. He respects you so much. You are a true Gandhian, and he tells other friends this."

Ramnik gave a smile of appreciation and proposed, "In that case, you don't have to tell him my decision. I will go with you right now and tell him what a liar Swanil is."

"That's all right. But let me caution. Chacha ji doesn't consider Swanil a liar. He understands all Swanil's good intentions. His motive is only to make a biography that will resonate with common readers."

"You said that he thinks I am a true Gandhian. Bapu never meant his life story, *The Story of My Experiments with Truth,* to be a best seller. In fact, many ridiculed some of his odd experiments. But we know he cared to say openly what he did. It requires much moral courage to always reveal the truth."

"That's right. We have read Kaka Kalelkar's writings on Bapu."

"That reminds me of your request. That is, a meeting with Kaka. I have not yet tried to arrange a meeting with this top Gandhian."

"That's all right. We are very busy now."

Both laughed.

"Bhagvati ji, let us go." Ramnik put his hand on Bhagbati's shoulder.

"On one condition: you will eat dinner with us."

"No need of that formality. Some other evening."

"It will be prepared by Uttara, not me, I assure you!"

They laughed and went out.

When they reached home, Sakar was gone. Uttara explained, "Jhaveri ji himself came in his car to talk to

Chacha. He inquired if everything went smoothly in Lucknow, and then he requested Chacha talk to one of his friends who has some problem. He did not give any indication of what the problem was. But Chacha immediately agreed and went out with him. He will return a little later, but he will be back for dinner. So I have already started to cook."

"Good," Bhagbati said. "Ramnik bhai will eat with us, too. I just invited him."

Ramnik didn't say a word, but Uttara took his silence as acceptance of the invitation. She smiled.

Surprisingly, Sakar was back in time for dinner. Ramnik touched his feet and Sakar hugged him. He said, "Bhai ji and bhabhi ji consider your arrangement in Lucknow a miracle. Harshpat and Marci are so grateful to you, Ramnik."

"All the credit goes to Mota Bhai Jhaveri," Ramnik replied. Unlike before, nobody laughed at the words *mota bhai*, which means "big brother" in Gujarati, not "fat brother" as in Hindi.

Then they all sat on the *dari* rug. Neither Ramnik nor Bhagbati uttered a word about the biography at that time. Nor did Sakar.

Instead, Uttara asked Sakar, "What kind of problem did Jhaveri ji have, Chacha?"

"Nothing serious. But Jhaveri ji thinks the problem was causing his entire family a big headache. His old mother is bent upon a visit to Badrinath. He is worried for her safety on such a trip and he thought that I could dissuade her."

"So did you succeed?" Ramnik asked.

"Very easily."

"I, too, could have convinced Ba if I had told her about my first frightening experience of Badrinath," Ramnik said.

"We thought you liked it very much since you went there twice and have said you wish to go again." Bhagbati smiled as he said this.

"So, about my first awesome visit…"

"What was it like?" Uttara inquired.

"My first visit to Badrinath will remain permanently in my memory. Somehow I reached the temple of Badri Narayan, and then I decided to walk up little higher. I made it almost to the famous ancient city of Alakapuri, which Kalidasa has described in his *Meghadutam*. But I collapsed, lying unconscious due to the lack of oxygen. When I woke up I found two local men helping me. They were from the village of Mana, and they looked like Tibetans. I didn't know that their village was the last Indian village on the border of Tibet. They gave me some pickles. One of them told me, 'Most *desi* travelers feel high altitude sickness here. We Paharis have no such problem.' That's when I learned that the Himalayan people are Paharis and the rest of us Indians are *desi* people. I was totally surprised!"

"That's true, Ramnik bhai. I am a *Pahari* Indian and you are a *desi* Indian. Look at our faces! We are not very different from the villagers of Mana," Bhagbati commented with a laugh. "My father is a specialist in Sanskrit literature. He, too, believes that Kalidasa was a Pahari, not a *desi* from Ujjain. So Kalidasa must have visited Alakapuri and never needed pickles to go further up to Manasarovar in Tibet. Now, go ahead with your story!"

Ramnik laughed and continued, "Right . . . After eating a few pieces, I felt able to walk down but I was still gasping for oxygen. Very slowly I came down to the temple. I told this story to two friends. One was from Ahmedabad and another from Ujjain, both opposite to Badrinath. They were keen to have *darshan* of the Badri Narayan temple. The one from Ujjain returned from

Vishnu Prayag and felt terrible fatigue from walking."

"Ujjain?" Sakar sounded sarcastic."

"And Kalidasa, too, was from Ujjain. Isn't that funny?" Ramnik added.

"It is. Why, I must tell you our Kalidasa story. Since Kalidasa's time, the Badrinath area didn't change much, except the temple, which was not there then. Kalidasa, a court poet, must have lived during the ancient Gupta Empire. Some scholars believe that Kalidasa was a native of Ujjain. These scholars have no idea what the snowfall is like in our high altitude areas, even in the summer. Alakapuri area is one of these areas. No one can imagine a snowfall in Ujjain even in the winter. An Ujjain native wouldn't be so stupid as to dare a trek in that cold, not to mention the frequent landslides. Kalidasa must have trekked the Himalayas for years to give such detailed descriptions in his several works."

"So you mean Kalidasa was a native of your region?"

"Absolutely," Sakar said emphatically. "Ba was convinced that, because I am a native, I know about the inclement environment at high altitude. She was not from Ujjain, but Ahmedabad, which is not too far from Ujjain. I am living in Ahmedabad and can describe its details. But imagine a poet of ancient times, like Kalidasa from Ahmedabad, living in Alakapuri near Badrinath! I told Ba that she can go to Hardwar very safely and take a dip at Har ki Pauri. Now she has decided to visit Hardwar instead and the Jhaveri family is relieved."

Uttara added, "I agree. Maybe she could go even little higher, up in Rishikesh where she would be safe. Beyond Rishikesh there are very poor facilities." Then she moved toward the kitchen.

"Let me help you out, Uttara," Bhagbati said, and he followed her.

In the kitchen Uttara used sign language and Bhagbati understood. Her message was about the decision on the biography. He picked up the rice bowl and nodded his head up and down with a suppressed smile.

"Good job, Bhagbati!" she said quietly.

"All things smell good," he said to verbalize his message. "Ramnik is going to like your dishes."

The couple overheard a big laugh from Sakar as he talked to Ramnik.

When they all started eating there was no sign of depression on Sakar's face. He actually complimented the food. "Beti, you have made such a sweet Gujarati *kari* today. I thought it would be our sour Pahari *kari*."

"Oh, no! I forgot to serve shrikhand. Let me bring it out."

Everyone got a bowl of shrikhand, the last dish of the dinner. Bhagbati took a second serving of shrikhand. "All problems of indigestion are over, Uttara. *Jai Jai shrikhand*," Sakar commented as if shrikhand really needed some sort of "victory."

Chapter 30

Now Nanda and Pawan each knew the other had eaten biryani. Their vow of remaining vegetarian was broken, but Prachi and Sashi wouldn't mind when they found out because they had more non-vegetarian than vegetarian friends. Pawan told Nanda, "If they can accept those friends, then they shouldn't have any problem with us either."

One morning Pawan asked Nanda before leaving for his office, "Would you be interested in mutton *biranji* tonight?"

"Are you?"

Pawan as a lawyer knew very well if you ask someone a question, and that person answers by repeating your question in part or whole, that's not the way you get an answer upon which you can act. You are left alone to decide. He smiled and left for the office.

In the afternoon he walked to Hussain's butcher shop for this time of day was when fresh sheep or goat meat would arrive at the shop almost every day. One could see the skinned corpses hanging from the roof, fresh blood still seeping out of the lifeless animals. The butcher would cut from the carcass any piece the customer requested. Almost all Hussain's customers were Hindus.

The Muslim families were negligible, not more than thirty. They had a little mosque where they congregated for prayers. Some had government jobs, too. They could be easily identified as Muslims as they didn't speak Garhwali, just simple standard Urdu. By their conversational style one could easily guess that they were doing well in their businesses in a small place like Pauri.

When Pawan arrived at the shop he did not find Hussain but his daughter Sameera, who graduated from high school one year ago. Because of her schooling, she knew some systematic accounting that Hussain didn't know.

But social norms clearly discouraged a marriageable girl from living with her parents. Sameera was already seventeen, an ideal age for a Muslim or Hindu girl to wed. Her home would then be her husband's home, her community her husband's community.

Sameera was alone in the shop. She looked very cheerful when she saw Pawan was a customer. She said, "Namaste, Uncle ji."

"Live long, Beti!" Pawan responded with the usual blessing for children. "Where is your father?"

"Abba has gone to Rampur," she said.

"Rampur? What for?"

"That's where all our relatives live. My chacha is visiting us to help us here. Abba has a very important plan for my future to discuss with someone."

"I understand."

"No, you don't understand!"

"What do you mean?"

"Do you have time right now before Chacha returns from shopping? I know your time is very valuable because you are a *wakil* and judge, but you can save me."

"Save you from what?"

She took a deep breath. "Abba wants me to marry a

man from Muradabad." She covered her eyes with her dupatta scarf.

Pawan understood her silence—she was weeping. Pawan, however, wanted to be sure his understanding was correct. He gently put his hand upon her head. "Dear Sameera, I understand your sadness."

She repeated the same refrain, "No, Uncle ji, you don't understand. But let me tell you more and then you can tell me what you can do for me."

"Yes, tell me, and I promise I will help you, my beti."

"That Muradabad man already has a wife who is much older than me—you know a Muslim man is allowed to have up to four women—but they have no children yet. That man is higher-caste Muslim, not like us butchers. Abba thinks our status will go up for the man is rich, unlike us."

"Do you want to get a higher education?"

"Yes, like Uttara didi and Prachi didi. They are lucky their husbands do not have two wives—"

"Don't be so sure. Hindus have no limit on having wives." He laughed, but Sameera didn't show even a faint smile. "So far so good, for my daughters," he said seriously.

Now the judge understood that she was indeed in pain and filled with hopelessness, and she was weeping as if fearing to be eviscerated like a goat.

"I am looking for justice. Why I want justice, you know."

"Yes, I do now. Sameera beti! I am not a specialist in Muslim Law, but I know from my many Muslim friends that Islam requires the consent of the girl. I have very high respect for this requirement. I have a Muslim friend right here in Pauri. Don't ask me to reveal his name. He told me, 'Wakil Sahab, I have three adult daughters with children. All my three sons-in-law are against a man having multiple marriages. They expect that someday India will have the same law for all, just like in European countries.'"

"But I want that law right now, Uncle ji."

"If I understand correctly, you can say no to this marriage, invoking the Islamic requirement. Some of my own relatives have two or three wives. Those wives had nothing to invoke. And worse, some had alcoholic husbands. Drinkers of *daru*, mostly *koda ki daru*—that *daru* is not an ordinary liquor. It's great that Islam forbids drinking this poison."

"But did you know Abba loves to drink, secretly and only with his Hindu friends?"

"I am not one of those friends who would offer him any alcohol."

"Uncle ji, I know how much he respects you. You can tell him that I have said 'no.' I am saying 'no' right now before a judge."

"Beti, I have no power. But you alone have that power given to you by Islam."

It became clear to her the judge would not do anything. He was just like any customer, interested in her meat only. Meanwhile another customer came and she had to maintain her composure. Pawan bought meat, looked into her eyes, and said, "Don't lose hope. Allah will save you, my dear!" And he left.

The following week, Hussain returned home, looking very happy. He had been assured of receiving a good bride price. However, the wedding would be simple and short, and as soon as possible. The groom's people would bring their own mullah, who was willing to perform the ceremony in the local mosque of Pauri. Hussain himself wanted that kind of deal. He assumed that the groom's wife had consented to accept a co-wife. Although Sameera objected repeatedly, Hussain butchered all her cries. Her mother favored her objections, but her voice was as lifeless as a headless animal's.

It was decided that, on the last day of the following month, the mullah would perform the ceremony in the local mosque of Pauri.

಴಴

On the day of ceremony, the mullah and the groom's few relatives waited and waited for the bride to come, but there was no bride to be seen. Hussain and his people had no idea where she might have run away to.

In truth, she hadn't run away. A couple of hours before the ceremony, Sameera's mother Noori told Hussain that she was dealing with a little diarrhea. Hussain was aware of Sameera's nervousness, and so he let Noori escort her out to the latrine. But Noori quietly escorted her about half a block from her house. She saw a man waiting quietly on a street corner, Altaf, who greeted both women. His house was a half block from that point and so was his grocery store. Noori immediately returned, leaving her daughter with him. She was shaking, even though she knew Altaf and his family very well.

Hussain saw Noori returning alone. She told Hussain that she waited outside for Sameera. When there was no response, she opened the latrine's door, but Sameera was not inside. Hussain looked as dumb as his animals waiting to be slaughtered. He waited for Sameera until the ceremony time had passed. Then he left alone for the mosque.

Sameera was totally surprised to see Altaf's wife Banu waiting at the door. She screamed, "Aunty ji!"

Banu put her hand gently on her shoulder. "Come on in, and have no fear, Beti!" she said very affectionately.

"You will meet now your best friend, the man behind your escape."

As soon as she stepped in, she saw Pawan coming toward her with a gun in his hand. She screamed, "Uncle ji!"

Pawan hugged her. "Well done, my beti! Thanks to Altaf. This is the man whose name I had not revealed to you at your shop. You are safe with Banu."

Now Sameera wore a smile. Her shaking disappeared immediately. "Uncle ji, why did you bring this gun?"

"There is a long story behind it. But I will tell you in brief. Let us sit down!"

They all sat on chairs, except Banu who went inside to bring snacks for Sameera.

"So, you want to know why I brought this gun. In fact, I was not supposed to be here. Altaf knows that the gun was meant for him. Suppose your mother, under pressure, discloses your overnight stay here. Then those Muradabad men could come here to beat Altaf. In that case, before they enter this house, Altaf could fire this gun, not at them but in the air. I guarantee they will run away, like jackals, back to Muradabad. I use this strategy to scare monkeys who come to create havoc in our orchards."

Sameera, finally, had a good laugh.

"Can you believe Altaf doesn't know how to fire a gun?" Pawan exclaimed.

Altaf and Sameera laughed. Pawan, smiling, blinked and looked at Altaf. "So I decided to stay with him."

Banu brought out snacks in a *thali* plate. She placed the plate on a table in front of them

"Let us eat the snacks!" Altaf requested.

The visitors from Muradabad didn't do what Pawan had expected. He had assumed that they would return quietly, accepting their loss of face, but Hussain returned home in about two hours, his face bruised and he was limping.

"What happened?" Noori screamed.

"Give me some water first," Hussain requested in a feeble tone.

After drinking a big glass of water, he began to talk about his condition. "Those men beat me up. They would have cut off my hand if their mullah had not intervened. 'He is not a thief. He also is a victim. Stop beating him. Look at his nose, it's bleeding,' Mullah ji pleaded with them as he gave me his *rumal* to clean my nose. Those men then left the mosque along with mullah ji."

Noori brought a wet towel and began to gently clean the blood around his bruises.

"Noori, we are lucky our Sameera didn't go to Muradabad with those hounds. She will go to Rampur to college instead. I will do some other job myself in Rampur. I hope Allah is saving her wherever she is right now."

Noori began to sob.

Chapter 31

Nanda and Murti decided to take a fun trip to Kotdwar, which, like Hardwar, was the last railway station where visitors could enter the Garhwal Himalayas. Most Garhwal natives saw a train here for the first time, but that was not what attracted Murti and Nanda.

Pawan had suggested this trip, and Nanda knew why. To Pawan a small town like Kotdwar was more sacred than any other sacred place of India. He would occasionally tell visitors coming from the plains to see the Badrinath temple, "A visit to Badrinath is good, but have you visited the ancient ashram of sage Kanva near Kotdwar?" If someone said 'no' then he would insist, "You must. Why? King Dushyanta met Shakuntala, the adopted daughter of the sage, and they secretly fell in love and Shakuntala became pregnant with a son, Bharata. Bharata founded his eponymous empire *Bharata*, and thus India's official name: *Bharat* from *Bharata*. The ancient poet and playwright Kalidasa made this story immortal in Indian history. The poet chose Kotdwar for India's founding father because the poet was a native of Garhwal and Kotdwar the gateway to this land for visitors from the plains. The Gupta Emperor, who made Kalidasa his court poet, must have known this fact."

Murti had heard this story many times. She said nothing in response, only nodded her head.

"I am glad that you didn't hesitate to accept my proposal," Nanda said. "I made the same proposal to Saina but she politely declined. Wakil Sahab thinks he knows why Saina has no desire to go to Kotdwar."

"Why?"

"My husband says it is only a possible reason, but Saina is a Brahmin and Mussi is a Rajput. When Dushyanta met Shakuntala he was worried about her caste. He thought, if she is sage Kanva's daughter, then she must be a Brahmin. Dushyanta was a Kshatriya and so didn't consider his attraction to Shakuntala proper. But the next day, he was so happy to know that Shakuntala was sage Vishvamitra's daughter by Menaka. Vishvamitra was a Kshatriya. So there was no caste barrier for Dushyanta and Shakuntala, but the love of Mussi and Saina violated that stupid old tradition. So Saina's visit to Kanva Ashram would be worthless."

Murti surprised Nanda when she said, "Saina told me a different reason, that the love of Dushyanta was not honest. He pretended not to be able to recognize his pregnant wife Shakuntala when she was brought to him at his court from Kotdwar, and for many years, he remained a delinquent father. 'The king was a big thug,' Saina said to me, almost in a fit of anger."

Nanda had a hard time stopping her laughter. Murti joined her.

When she managed to stop laughing, Nanda added one more comment. "By the way, Saina disagrees with my husband's view that a visit to Badrinath is good. Badrinath priests recite the Bhagvat Puran, especially the love of Lord Krishna for his *gopi* girlfriends. Those girls never imagined that he would flirt with them and later have eight wives." That kind of love, she thought, was far more shameful than the love of Dushyanta for Shakuntala. Women are not created to satisfy a man's lustful desires.

Murti looked serious, "Nanda didi! I understand her point of view. But that should not discourage us from taking a trip to Kotdwar. Bharat's founder was created there. A visit there means honoring our country."

🙟🙠🙟

Nevertheless, the next Monday, Murti came to Nanda's house to cancel the Kotdwar trip. Instead she invited Nanda to join her on another exciting trip. For Nanda, it was a total surprise. Murti was going to attend the wedding of her Aunt Sampatti's daughter Purna. Nanda apologized for declining the invitation.

In Murti's absence, an unexpected event took place that Sunday afternoon. Mussi came to visit Nanda and Pawan. He was accompanied by a man who had a full beard and a pair of mustaches. Mussi looked very excited as he stood with this man at the front door of the Kotwal house. Pawan and Nanda came out together. The stranger was smiling as if he was not really a stranger to the Kotwals, who were staring at him without any sign of recognition.

"Have you recognized this man, Wakil Sahab?" Mussi asked Pawan while turning his eyes toward Nanda. Both uttered not a word, their gaze still on the stranger.

"I am Harakh, Wakil Sahab!" the stranger introduced himself and touched the feet of Nanda and Pawan. Nanda had tears in her eyes and Pawan hugged him.

Nanda held his hand in her hand and said, "Let us go inside and celebrate!"

Over snacks Harakh told the Kotwals his story, an odyssey in the real sense.

"Tell us about your experiences!" Pawan requested.

"I have too many to tell you them all, but one I would like to tell you. I survived in the jungles of Burma by hunting."

"You had a gun?"

"No. I was not hunting like you. I would catch frogs and lizards and eat them raw."

"Raw!" Nanda exclaimed with an expression of repulsion on her face.

"I think I shouldn't say any more about my wild diet. Let me enjoy your delicious snacks. All I want to tell you is that we were stupid. We could have avoided this ordeal if we had learned the lesson of the First World War. How many Indian soldiers lost their lives! You know this is true, Wakil Sahab," Harakh said with disgust.

"My uncle narrowly survived when he faced the German guns in the First World War," Pawan said to Harakh while nodding his head.

"In the Second World War, Japanese soldiers captured me in Burma. I was lucky that they released all the captured Indian soldiers to the Indian National Army. Our leader, Subhas Chandra Bose, the new head of the INA, had no military training and was in no way comparable to the founder of the INA, Mohan Singh. Sardar ji was trained in Dehradun's Indian Military Academy. We were destined to lose against the well-trained British Indian Army. More than half unit of the Garhwali soldiers of the INA was wiped out. Some starved to death. One day I ran away and got lost in the jungles of Burma. How I survived is a long story. A Burmese tribe found me and saved me. I am now alive and well due to the kindness of the Burmese people."

"You are indeed lucky, Harakh," Nanda said. "I am

happy that I am here with you. I was supposed to be in Kotdwar."

"To attend a relative's marriage?" Harakh asked.

"No, just to visit the Kanva Ashram. We think the ashram is an important symbol, even more important than your Indian National Army."

"Yes," Pawan said. "The INA was trying to liberate Bharat, and you fought for the honor of Bharat. Bose fought for the honor of Bharata's Bharat. I wish we had more fighters like you and Neta ji Subhas Bose."

"Did you know that Neta ji and Bharata's father, Dushyanta, had similar marriages?" Harakh asked them.

"No," Nanda interjected. "Tell us more!"

"Neta ji met Emilie Schenkl and married her very secretly. Some say she was not really his wife but just a companion. There were many rumors among the soldiers, but I used to tell them that Neta ji and Emilie ji were married in the same way as King Dushyanta and Shakuntala."

"You are right to say that. In the *Gandharva Vivaha* in our religion the couple promises to love each other as husband and wife. After all it is love, not ritual, that makes marriage possible. Neta ji was married to Emilie Schenkl and, like Bharata was the son of such a union, Anita Bose is their daughter. There is no room for rumors and nonsense talk."

"I agree. But some who worked very closely with Bose ji have a different opinion about him."

"What opinion?" Nanda became curious.

"Like he was married but still secretly flirting in Japan. One Indian very close to him was happy that India's freedom was achieved through Gandhi ji and not through Bose. Maybe Gandhi ji had more reasons to oust Bose from the Indian National Congress."

"Many Indians believe that Neta ji is alive and will

come back. What is your opinion?" Nanda looked intently into Harakh's eyes.

"We Indians are religious, and we are very superstitious. He died in a plane crash. It was terrible loss." Harakh sighed. "He sacrificed his life for India's freedom. Let us pay our *sraddhanjali* to him, no matter the conflicting opinions about him. He started a revolution in India and for India, and Gandhi ji couldn't have started that kind of revolution."

"But for Gandhi ji revolution meant making it possible for an untouchable and a woman to head the government of free India," Nanda said with a smile.

"Well, Bose ji appointed a woman to his army, Captain Lakshmi, a move toward fulfilling the Gandhian dream," Harakh responded with a sense of pride in his deep voice.

Pawan's eyes showed some sense of loss. "Bose ji and Gandhi ji died of accidents, but did you know Sardar Mohan Singh returned to India safely?"

"No. Someday I would like to pay him my respects personally. Where is he now?"

"He returned to his native village near Sialkot. There was no Pakistan then, but during partition he was forced to leave his native place and came to India with no money in his pockets. Partition made our fight for freedom worthless. As if the war was not enough to start an economic holocaust, the partition dumped us into undreamt of poverty, which was of course driven by behavioral poverty. If some rogue leaders, like Hitler, had not used race or religion as a pawn for their personal ambitions, we would have saved people and their property."

Pawan wanted to talk more about Sardar Mohan Singh's post-independence life, but Harakh changed the topic. "Have you met Banki?"

"That was my main concern, Harakh," Pawan replied.

"Banki has been waiting for you. She still has her nose ring on. She never believed that you were among the dead Garhwali soldiers of the INA."

"Mussi has told me everything. I fully understand that he was trying to save our family honor by following our Vedic instructions."

Apparently, he was aware of the old Vedic instructions to the bride at the time of her wedding vows, such as *Devṛkāmā bhava:* Be desirous of your brother-in-law. Levirate marriage is allowed if, for example, the husband dies and the *devar* (a cognate of Latin's *levir,* husband's younger brother) is still unmarried.

So Mussi offered his "presumed" widow sister-in-law Banki the levirate marriage choice. She refused this choice because she believed that her husband was alive and would be back someday. That's why she kept her nose ring on, a traditional sign of an unwidowed woman. She left for her parents' home, where she waited for Harakh's return. Since then there had been no contact between her and Mussi.

Some thought that Mussi should have forced her, but Mussi considered such force a case of rape, a despicable act for a Rajput like him.

Banki, too, was a Rajput and was aware of the Rajputana region's infamous practice of *sati,* the burning of widows, in medieval times. Instead she left for her parents' home where she waited for Harakh's return. Her parents abhorred this inhuman tradition of *sati* more than the levirate marriage. They recommended that Banki have no contact with Mussi.

For a while Pawan remained silent. Or was he? Maybe, he was asking questions within. Did his father, a Brahmin, merely followed those Vedic instructions? And when he failed, did he commit rape due to his own uncontrollable desire? Most probably these unanswerable questions were responsible for his sudden pensive silence.

Harakh looked at him. "Wakil Sahab, we have come here for your blessing. I request both of you to accompany me and Mussi to meet Banki. Saina is very much excited to join us. We want to meet Banki as a family and earn the trust of her parents. They might have a sort of hatred for Mussi, and your presence there could be an ameliorating factor."

"Let us proceed tomorrow morning to meet Banki," Nanda proposed.

"Yes. I will not go to my office for a couple of days." Pawan nodded his head.

౸౩౸౩

The following week they all went to see Banki, whose parents could not understand why Banki closed her eyes and began to sob when she recognized Harakh in the unexpected visitors.

"What's the matter with you, Banki?" asked her mother.

Instead of Banki, Saina replied to her mother. "Ma ji, the bearded man is Harakh bhai ji. I am Saina, Mussi's wife," Saina said after touching her feet. Then she touched the feet of Banki's father.

After Saina, Mussi, too, touched their feet and said, "And you know who the other two are?"

"Indeed, we know them, Beta!" Banki's father responded.

They greeted Pawan and Nanda with folded palms.

Mussi looked moved when he heard the word *beta* (son) as a reference for him.

Finally, Harakh touched the feet of Banki's parents. They hugged Harakh and began to cry. Banki, hiding her eyes with her hands, was still speechless.

Pawan took Nanda aside. "Nanda! You have seen the real Shakuntala and Dushyanta meeting after their long separation."

Nanda wiped her own tears. "It has been so hard for both. Stupid wars!"

Chapter 32

In her village of Adhwani, Sampatti and her son, Harit, and daughter, Purna, welcomed Murti. Sampatti was disappointed not to see Nanda with her. Murti told her how they were almost ready to visit the Kanva Ashram of Kotdwar. She was surprised that Aunt Sampatti knew why Nanda's brother Ram Char committed suicide just in a year after his marriage to Raksha.

"Murti!" she said. "Would you believe that our priest, Pandit Shiv Prasad Dobhal, knows all about Nanda's painful loss? His uncle performed Ram Char's marriage to Raksha."

"No. Nanda didi never told me anything about this matter. So what about Ram Char's marriage, Puphu ji?"

"There are so many rumors. But Dobhal ji can tell you more. If you are interested, Harit can request that Dobhal ji tell you what he knows after he completes Purna's wedding ceremony."

"Nanda didi is my best friend. I will never question why she didn't tell me about her painful loss. But I definitely want to know what Pandit ji knows about it."

"Some I can tell you, but let us wait until after the wedding."

After the morning wedding, Pandit Dobhal was relaxed and willing to have a chat with Murti. But their talk took place in the evening, after dinner. Harit and Murti looked very serious as the pandit gave his opinion.

"Those rumors are hard to prove," Pandit Dobhal continued, "But just a few days after Ram Char's suicide, Raksha left for Dehradun. Her relatives there helped her start a primary school. She went to college in Dehradun, where she had a classmate who, like her, was seeking a teaching degree. Two licensed teachers with bachelor degrees are good enough to run an elementary school. She hired him, and that ideal educational partnership opened another window for more gossip."

Dobhal ji skipped earlier gossip about Raksha's premarital love for a local boy of her age, her classmate. His caste was low and her parents objected to her desire to marry this boy instead of Ram Char. After the marriage, however, the boy continued to meet her secretly. Ram Char found out. Some even gossiped that Ram Char was not fit as a husband.

Pandit Dobhal lightened his talk, and he said as he smiled, "There were some differences between Raksha and Ram Char. Ram Char wanted Raksha to follow his family's rules. He would not even allow her to use onions and garlic. The rumor was that he told her these vegetables were *tamasik*, not good for pious living. She even counter-argued with stories of sages who have lived healthy lives by eating raw bulbs, roots, and fruits. None of her arguments changed his opinion."

"What is your opinion, Pandit ji?" Murti interjected. "Nanda didi uses these vegetables in her regular cooking, and certainly with meats."

"Nanda is following the standard cooking procedures. I would say our food is delicious because of garlic and onions, and certainly all meats require garlic and onions!" Dobhal ji laughed. "Our religious beliefs are hard to bend, even if you hammer them with the force of medical facts. Even her Ayurvedic argument failed to change his religious opinion."

"It's amazing how Nanda didi, coming from the same family, changed her food without any problems!"

"Her change might have encouraged Raksha to ignore the religious classification of food as *sattvik*, *rajasik,* and *tamasik*. I heard that her male teacher narrated the *Ramayana* story to students with a different interpretation. He told them that Sita wanted the deer because it was a part of her diet. But he also told them that, according to his family priest, Rama and Sita did eat *mriga* but it was not deer. He said it meant a kind of fleshy fruit, but his priest was not a Pahari Brahmin, though!"

Harit and Murti laughed.

"Now the bad news," Dobhal added. "The school closed after three years and both teachers disappeared. One reason was lack of funds. Another was Raksha's safety."

"Her safety?" Murti asked, looking curious.

"One night a man banged on her door shouting obscenities. She escaped through the back window. A week later, the same man, or so it is assumed, tried to get into her house through the back door but she was not there. That stalker didn't know that she stayed with her partner at night."

"You mean with that male teacher?" Harit asked.

"Yes. Brij Nandan was his name."

Murti put her hand on her forehead as if she was confused. "I wish she had learned from Nanda didi how to scare these men-tigers," she commented. "All she needed was a sickle in that house."

"You mean she should have beat him with a sickle?" the pandit asked.

"Yes, just a sickle."

Dobhal ji looked at her, his expression showing disbelief. But he avoided dwelling on the use of sickle for self-defense and continued his story. "Raksha was going to have a baby. The rumor spread so much that the villagers stopped their children from going to her school, which forced its closure. She and Brij Nandan disappeared and nobody knows where they went. No book of life is complete, some pages from every book of life excluded on purpose."

"What pages could be missing? Any idea, Pandit ji," Harit queried.

"It really is a sad ending to a good school. The school was not exactly in the city of Dehradun. It was quite far from the city. Its location in a rural area made sense, and parents in the area welcomed its presence. They sent not only their boys but girls, too, when they found out the founder of the school was a woman."

"Did the police investigate?" Harit asked.

"That I don't know. There was a rumor that Raksha and Brij Nandan went to an Arya Samaj temple where they got married properly with a Vedic ceremony. I hope they are safe and happy," Pandit Dobhal replied.

"This sounds like the Arya Samaj marriage of Nanda didi's in-laws," Murti commented.

"I know," responded Pandit Dobhal.

Their discourse stopped when they heard people shouting outside. Somebody was calling Harit, too, warning that a female bear with her two cubs was close to Harit's house. Bears frequently came close to their village in search of food, the animals probably attracted by the large quantities of leftovers. Murti, Harit, and the pandit joined others in shouting with raised voices and hands. Some boys threw rocks at the cubs. The cubs ran away, and the mother bear followed her cubs.

Chapter 33

It was raining. "You are late and wet!" Nanda said to Pawan when he came home a little late in the evening. "What happened?"

"Let me change my clothes and I will tell you," Pawan responded and went inside.

Nanda brought a hot cup of tea for him after he came out in the sitting room.

He sat down. "Those two freeloading sons of Bansi are in trouble again. Bansi came to my office just when I was about to close for the day. He begged me to get Digam and Sagar out of the Pauri jail. He told me that their imprisonment had something to do with me personally. When I asked him how so, his response was that he didn't know 'but they want to talk to you.'"

"Have you talked to them?"

"Tomorrow I will find out what they want from me but it looks like a gimmick. You know how these freeloaders behave. So just relax!"

Nanda smiled.

☙❧☙

The next morning, Pawan went to see Digam and

Sagar. It was a windy morning, cold gusts coming directly from the Chaukhamba Himalayan range. The eyes and
noses of Digam and Sagar were streaming, and Pawan,
although he intended to scold them for recidivism, felt
sorry for them in their prison clothes cleaning the front
yard of the prison. But they looked happy when they saw
the judge. Both wiped their eyes and noses and touched
Pawan's feet. Pawan's facial expression softened, and he
asked the police officer to let them stop their yard work
for a short conference with him. The officer took them
inside in to a little room where they sat with Pawan at a
long table.

"So, tell me why you are here?" Pawan said as he
looked at them.

"We are here because of Mattu and Param Singh,"
Digam replied.

"But they had good intentions. They wanted to avenge
Sakar Chacha's insult," Sagar commented.

"What insult?" Pawan asked, looking puzzled.

"We thought you already knew," Sagar said.

"You tell me what you know," Pawan said with a
commanding voice.

"Kundan discriminated against Lachchhu and his son
in his sweetshop. Param Singh told us that Kundan insulted Sakar Chacha ji. Like Chacha ji, he also believed
that untouchability was another form of slavery in India,
agreeing with Gandhi ji. We also believed this. Param
Singh told us that Mattu was willing to give two rams to
anyone who would destroy Kundan's sweetshop. So we
both are responsible for his shop's destruction. We wanted to punish Kundan for practicing this kind of slavery,
enforcing untouchability."

Pawan was furious. "You idiots took the law into your
hands."

The brothers were ready to justify their act anyway.

Digam said, "We were fighting against India's slavery, and our models were Shaheed Bhagat Singh and Neta ji Subhas Bose. They also broke laws to fight the British enslavement of Indians. This untouchability is more shameful because we have made our own people our slaves."

For a minute Pawan couldn't say a word, he was so mad. Finally, he said, "But why is Mattu against you?"

"We went to Mattu and asked for the two rams. He denied that he ever made such an offer. We believed him and left him alone for some time. Later, we needed some money, however, and so we thought to persuade Mattu again. He refused to give us the two rams as our reward. So we took two rams from him at gunpoint."

"What happened to the two rams?" Pawan asked.

"We sold them to Hussain for cheap. Mattu says that Hussain told a few friends how we got the rams, and Mattu has threatened us again and again, threatened to expose us with the help from those friends. One night we entered his house to warn him he needed to not reveal what we had done. But we didn't know his cousin was visiting him, and when he saw us he became Mattu's witness. We had a gun. We didn't want to hurt Mattu, just warn him not to threaten us. Mattu's cousin said that we wanted to kill him. So we are here."

"You are criminals, no matter what you think of yourselves. Bhagat or Bose you are not," Pawan scolded them. "I think Kundan might be responsible for the destruction of Sakar's school, so what do you expect from me?"

Sagar and Digam showed no remorse, which made Pawan madder.

"Sakar was fortunate to leave here and find another way to live," Digam responded. "We want a big favor from you, Chacha ji. Please, get us out and give us a job.

We don't want to be a burden upon our parents, who are poor and old."

That request had some impact upon Pawan. He realized that their parents created these young men's poverty, behavioral poverty, and so these two freeloaders were not entirely responsible for their recklessness. Their parents, like most Indian parents, were reckless, having child after child with no regrets, no remorse.

"Would you both be willing to keep our court area clean and grow some fruits and vegetables in and around the front and back yards of the court? Sakar would be very happy to know that you are producing food," Pawan said as he thought of Sakar's dream of utilitarian gardening. "And don't blame others for your failure; learn to be responsible for your failure. Here is a mantra for you to succeed: Work and do not whine." Pawan knew how freeloaders behaved. Freeloaders were smart enough to blame others for their failure and took no responsibility for it. He paused and looked them in their eyes. "Do you understand what I am trying to say?"

"Yes," both uttered together.

"Good." Pawan softened his stern looks and added, "So I will tell Mattu to withdraw his charges against you."

The brothers burst into tears and fell at Pawan's feet.

"We will do whatever you say, Chacha ji," Digam said. Sagar nodded his agreement.

"Earn money and repay your parents!"

"You stole my words, Judge Sahab!" Sagar reacted.

Pawan laughed and slapped them on their backs. Then he left them alone and talked to the police officer.

Just after Pawan left the jail, the police officer took the brothers to their prison cell. He began to shout at them, "I overheard what the Wakil Sahab told you. You are *kam-chor* sons of your parents. Wakil Sahab is doing you a great favor, but you deserve hard punishment for taking the law into your hands." He kicked Sagar hard in his butt.

Digam didn't expect a *sipahi* to call them freeloader sons. He grabbed the officer by his neck and threw him down. Sagar began to kick him. "You are the one who will get hard punishment. You are not a judge. You are just a petty *sipahi* of this jail, appointed to follow orders. Your order was not to kick us. You are the one who has broken the law."

The officer realized that he underestimated their physical strength and legal argument. He quietly got up and left them into their prison cell.

Within a few minutes, the officer returned with two other police officers. They entered the prison room and beat the hell out of Digam and Sagar. "If you try to go against us, we will lodge a complaint of assault on a policeman. That means no release for you," one policeman warned the brothers.

"You both are *kamchor*. Don't leave a given task unfinished, " another policeman admonished them. "You must keep growing vegetables and fruits as Judge Sahab wants!"

The brothers were unable to respond, and the three officers left them moaning in pain.

ഔഈഔ

A week later, Pawan got their release order. When they came out of their cell, they went straight to Pawan's office to thank him.

When they touched his feet, Pawan was appalled. "I see your faces are bruised. What happened?"

"It's our fault. We provoked the policeman because he provoked us. He asked us a few questions. We answered

all his questions with no offense to him. But then he began to give us his vulgar lecture: 'Your parents are reckless fuckers, India's enemies for having so many children. Tell your parents that, instead of having so many
children, raise more *bhains*, animals that will give a lot of
milk to be food for you and work, too. You can sell that
milk, butter, and ghee and earn some cash. Do you understand, you freeloaders?'" Sagar said, showing no remorse
on his face. "He kicked me and Digam tried to save me
from further beating. He held that *sipahi* down. When he
locked us up, we thought the matter was over. But he
came back with two more *sipahis* and the three beat us
very badly."

"I will get those policemen dismissed." The judge
looked mad, even though he thought that having female
water buffalos instead of several children was a good idea
for any Indian parents!

"No, Chacha ji, we don't want them to be jobless and
become freeloaders like us." Digam touched Pawan's feet
again as he said this.

Pawan felt pity for them. In a way, they were not freeloaders but victims of someone's behavioral poverty, he
thought. "You are not freeloaders; you are victims."
Pawan thought of what that *sipahi* meant. *There are millions and millions who keep having more and more children*, he thought, *and we as a society must pay for their
mistakes. Those who keep justifying their mistakes keep
committing mistakes. They don't want to learn from their
mistakes—*

"We are very excited to tell our parents of the favor
you have done for us," Digam said, interrupting Pawan's
thoughts.

Pawan didn't utter a word, but he looked at them with
his eyes open wide. The two brothers touched Pawan's
feet and left for home immediately.

In the evening, Pawan told Nanda what he had done for Digam and Sagar. But Nanda didn't seem too impressed. "These are freeloaders," she said. "Freeloaders complain that others are not working for them. They don't think the other way around, that they should work with others and for others. I tell you they will soon leave the job you gave them and then whine again that they don't have any opportunities."

"I agree with you, Nanda, but I thought it right to give them a chance to improve their freeloading behavior. Let's see if they can work for themselves and not remain a social burden," Pawan said sincerely.

"I hope they never get married. What if they behave like their parents in raising their own children? That *sipahi* was telling the truth about their parents—the reckless fucking parents of India!"

Chapter 34

After lunch Murti came to the forest alone, going to the slope where she and Nanda would bring the oak branches to slip them down to the creek. She watched the beautiful autumn colors all around the forest while waiting for Nanda to join her.

The Chandrabhaga's raging waters produced far more noise than usual. This year rains created havoc. Even the normally dry creek beds carried considerable water, the flooding making this year's rainy season very inauspicious for areas where pilgrims visited the holiest temples located on the banks of the most sacred rivers of India. The rivers there swelled up and up, and the heavy overflow destroyed the brand new bus road that linked Pauri with other parts of the district. Several houses were swept away by water, and a whole village disappeared along with its people due to a landslide. Fortunately, Pauri and adjacent areas were safe because of its location in the lower Himalayas and because there were no very large rivers nearby.

But Pauri had one disadvantage. It faced the northern Chaukhamba Range, and snowy winds from the mountains started in October and did not end until early March. The Kotwal's forest faced south across Chandrabhaga, and so, except from late December to late February, it was very comfortable to work here most of the year. It was still October and Murti had no complaints about the weather in this forest.

After more than one hour wait, Nanda still had not arrived. Murti began to walk frantically between the nearby big oak trees. She decided to chop a couple of big branches with her axe, and with great effort she was able to bring that branch down.

Nanda was still nowhere to be found. Murti assumed some unexpected job must have kept her very busy. She started to cut another big branch from the center. This branch seemed very difficult to cut. After resting for a bit, she tried to cut it again. Soon she felt exhausted and began to pant, but Nanda finally appeared with her axe and sickle.

"Are you cutting that branch for fuel?" Nanda shouted from the bottom of the oak tree.

"No, it's too green for fuel. But it should be good for chhimi."

"But chhimi season is four months away. This is the month of Kartik, not Chait. Three months from now these branches will be dry."

"You are right. I will use them for fuel."

"All right. Come down and I will help you. You are panting."

Murti came down. Nanda climbed up and started to cut the same branch with her bigger axe. She quickly brought it down.

They both dragged it to the slope. They sat there for rest.

"Didi, you were so late today."

"I didn't want to come, but then I thought you must be waiting. I am ready to go back right now. An emergency has come up.

"What sort of emergency?"

"It is unmentionable."

"No, no. I would like to know." Murti's voice was firm.

Nanda told her that her husband stayed home from work today because he was in excruciating pain due to some serious wounds.

"Did he tell you what kind of wounds?"

"Yes," Nanda answered. "A monkey bit him."

Neither of them spoke for a minute, their heads hung low. Then Murti broke the silence and raised her head. "I am that monkey. Take him to your doctor soon!"

"What?" Nanda raised her head as well and looked into Murti's eyes. "Don't make fun of his pain," Nanda admonished.

Murti lowered her head again. "He knocked the fuel wood I carried from my head after he dropped his gun," she mumbled.

"I don't understand. You mean my husband?" Nanda asked her. "I don't believe you!"

"You will believe if you listen to my full story, Didi," Murti replied as she raised her head again, tilting it toward Nanda. "He began to probe my breasts, and then he dropped his pants and pulled down my sari. My small sickle that was hidden in my waist under my sari fell to the ground. Somehow I got hold of that tiny weapon and cut his *lumru* before he could go any further."

"You did what?" Nanda shouted. She placed her hands over her mouth, her eyes open wide.

Nanda's anger and disbelief got aroused further. Murti realized that she used the obscene Garhwali word *lumru* for penis. She reiterated, "Yes, I hit his *kujaga*, Didi. And I am not sorry for that. I had no choice. He tried to shoot me but he missed. He had only one bullet, perhaps, but I know a smart hunter never keeps just one bullet in his gun and so he might shoot again—and I ran away."

She paused for a moment as she watched Nanda's face, which was all red. But she was unfazed and continued, "The judge violated the rule. I remember once he said: any rule is a balloon which can burst even if slightly punctured. Tell him I am not a *gopi* girl. I am his younger cousin's wife and like a sister to him. He is not supposed to touch me, not even look at my face. He broke this Hindu rule."

Murti didn't expect that Nanda, too, would break the rule in her own way. Nanda hit Murti's fingers with her sickle. "You have ended the only pleasure of my heart," she shouted.

Murti's hand began to bleed. She quickly wiped the blood with the corner of Nanda's sari. She was expecting another strike, maybe an axe chop from Nanda's powerful hands. She got up quickly and ran while shouting in Garhwali, "*Janau ka tana, hola kana* (like father, like son)." She loudly added her meaning of the saying, "Your father-in-law raped his young widow sister-in-law. Sakar is her bastard son." She kept running downward. Nanda could hear her voice echoing: *"Bhainchod* (sister fucker), *bhainchoooood.* Ha, ha, ha, ha, ha!"

After this encounter, the two women never met again. Occasionally they would see each other from a distance while going to the spring or forest, but Murti, scared of Nanda's revenge, would change her path quickly. She worried, "What if we crossed paths and Nanda pushed me down the hill?"

Their neighbors couldn't find out what went wrong between the two partners but they were gossiping about them. The gossip changed, but all stories failed to hit the target—mutilation.

But the judge was trying to find a legal means to revenge. The Pauri district hospital chief received a letter from a lawyer that suggested an investigation of one of its accountants, Murti's husband, Balram Datt. The letter mentioned possible embezzlement of hospital funds by Balram.

When Balram heard this news from the hospital chief, he found out that the lawyer was a very close friend of Pawan. He met Pawan and asked him to warn his lawyer friend to withdraw the complaint. Pawan flatly denied his role in the complaint: "I don't know what you are talking about."

"I know what I am talking about," replied Balram. "I am talking about an attempted rape in our family that must be investigated."

"I had nothing to do with it, bhula, but I will check with that lawyer to find out why he complained."

"Yes, that will help stop the rumor mill, bhai ji." Balram very politely gave a veiled threat to his cousin.

The affectionate exchange of words such as "bhula" (little brother) and "bhai ji" (big brother) loosened the tension of their dialogue. After that dialogue, however, the two fellows were never again seen together and neither was ever investigated.

৵৵৵

The following year, Harshpat and Marci were blessed with a new son. That news somehow reached Murti and Balram, who were not invited for the naming ceremony. Their absence was filled by fresh rumors, not only in the Kotwal community but even in Pawan's Pauri circle.

One rumor was that, on the twelfth day of the baby's birth, an elegant naming ceremony took place. The boy was named Mel, which means "meeting" or "mixture." Many guests, some from the adjacent plains, such as

Marci's relatives and friends, were invited. Nobody was sure if Pawan and Nanda participated in the ceremony.

Another rumor that gossips found highly enjoyable was a question which surgeon treated Pawan. Was he treated initially at the Pauri hospital, which was very primitive and poorly staffed? Nobody from the Kotwal clan was sure. This was the only hospital of the Garhwal region and not easily accessible, not even for the nearby villages let alone for the villages miles away. Sick people were reluctant to walk the uphill trail to the hospital. This government hospital didn't provide transport by horse or litter (*dandi*) even for the patients living within a mile, and as a result, many died walking uphill to the hospital.

The patients had small bamboo beds, all in one hall, and so there was no privacy. The patients beside another patient under examination could see his naked body. The adjacent smaller hall was for women patients.

The hospital had only one surgeon, whose title was Civil Surgeon and he served as the chief of the entire hospital. But the surgeon at the time of Pawan's rumored mutilation was soon transferred to another town on the plains.

Chapter 35

Sakar couldn't figure out who was calling because the voice sounded very different and suppressed. Sakar repeated, "Who is this?"

"Pandit ji, I am Jiva Bhai Jhaveri. I have very bad news. Ba just passed away. Please come as soon as possible to perform the funeral!" Jhaveri hung up, and Sakar wept because he respected Jhaveri's mother so much. She likewise held Sakar, her favorite priest, in high regard.

Sakar quickly went to perform the final rites on the bank of Sabarmati. He wept along with Jhaveri as her body was reduced to ashes on the funeral pyre. After the funeral Jhaveri thanked Sakar and requested that he come for her thirteenth day funerary rite of memorial.

છ૭છ૭

At the memorial, Sakar was in disbelief to see the Jhaveri house full of many distinguished guests and relatives of Jhaveri. After Sakar performed the rite, Jhaveri gave a little speech.

"I am grateful to you all for sharing our pain and paying your respects to my mother. For years Ba suffered from diabetes. She was warned by our family doctor so many times not to eat sweets. But as you all know, every Gujarati food is a sweet, even the pickles."

There was laughter in the audience.

"Ba didn't care for the doctor's advice and resented it whenever food without sugar was served to her. More than any doctor's advice, she believed in prayers. She had made a pilgrimage to many major temples. We all know how difficult it is to travel to the Badrinath temple, and many people die on their way because it is so high and cold! Ba visited not once but twice and nothing happened to her. Well, she had breathing trouble a few times, but she always carried a bottle of *gunda* pickle. That saved her, not Badri Narayan!"

There was laughter in the audience again.

"Ba had no business training, but she gave many people good business advice. One of my accountants, Moti bhai, wanted to leave my business. Someone told him that he wanted to start a caviar business here and he would like to hire Moti bhai. Ba advised him, 'Vasanti, who goes to college, told me something I didn't know. Gujarat is the only region in the world that has a big sea coast full of fishes and full of vegetarians. Moti beta, your caviar business will fail. I believe in the sanctity of life. You don't kill others' babies to feed your babies,' she told him.

"The last thing I wanted to tell you is this. A few days before her death, Ba asked Vasanti, my daughter, not to believe in idols. Idols have no power to save anyone, she said. They are lifeless matter. So our family has decided to honor Ba's wish."

He paused to drink water and then continued, "Like many Vaishnavs and Jains here, she also avoided foods cooked with garlic and onion. She knew that Vasanti didn't avoid such foods whenever available elsewhere, and she often said, 'Oh Dadi, you are missing the best

tasting food if you don't add onions and garlic to it.'
Vasanti would often encourage her to think rationally,
and finally, Ba agreed with her granddaughter, maybe out
of affection. She said, 'Vasanti, it's all right for you to eat
onions and garlic. But be sure you chew some *mukhwas*
at the end.' As you all know, it is very important in Gujarat that your mouth should not expel a foul smell. So
mukhwas spices and herbs are the best antidotes."

There was big laughter all around. Sakar didn't laugh,
however, for he would not be required to do *puja* at the
Jhaveri home any more. Most of Sakar's big clients were
Jhaveri's friends.

Jhaveri continued, "Ba believed in home remedies. In
a *kirtan* one of our relatives was singing the *bhajan* song
of Mira Bai. This relative had terrible weight problem. Ba
told him, '*Bhajan* does not reduce *wazan*. You are singing Mira Bai's line *Rama ratan dhan payo* and what you
have is *Rama ratan wazan payo*. You don't want to get
weight as your gem. Right? Mira Bai was slim because
she danced while singing *I have earned wealth, the gem
Lord Rama*. Son, to lose weight, you should dance and
eat a small red apple before going to bed at night. More
important than that, leave eating *puris* filled, don't fill
them with *basundi*.' He really followed her advice and
lost weight, and became a slim and trim man. But Ba,
who was a patient of diabetes, continued eating those little fried puffed breads filled with that sweet fatty milk
cream pudding *basundi*. 'You are not an honest Gujarati
if you hide *puris* and *basundi* from your diet,' Ba used to
say."

But he ended with an unexpected criticism. "Ba's advice was not always liked. Before giving advice she
would criticize the person. She would say, 'You are stupid and lack common sense. Pay attention to what the
doctor has recommended for you.' Advice like this would

be more likable if the irrelevant criticism is left out. She would have been better served to just say, 'Pay attention what the doctor has recommended.' She would ask, 'Who spilled oil on the floor?' She would not rest until she knew who the spiller was. To know who messed up the floor is less important than cleaning up the mess on the floor."

The audience didn't react one way or the other, and Jiva bhai ended with praise. "But Ba would boost the morale of any person who felt failure. Her motto was: 'There is no such thing as unhindered success.' I will miss her." He wiped his tears.

When Sakar returned home, he looked depressed to Bhagbati and Uttara.

"Are you feeling well, Chacha?" Uttara sounded concerned.

"Well, Ba's memorial was painful."

"She was a big admirer of you and loved your pujas," Bhagbati said, trying to cheer up Sakar.

"Not exactly so, Bhagbati! Ba said something disturbing to her granddaughter before she breathed her last."

Sakar told them what Jhaveri's mother thought of pujas.

"Certainly, it's disturbing," Uttara replied.

"So disturbing that I have decided now to go back to my village," Sakar said. "On my way, I brooded over her wish. I want to get out of this puja business. Prayers produce nothing. I didn't want to be a *purohit* in the first place, but I always believed this: For a happy life, don't be rigid and don't be lax either; just remain flexible but remain productive. In my case, let me be literal: grow plants that produce edible fruits and vegetables. Prayers produce nothing edible. I plan to start utilitarian gardening, not only in my Kotwal land but also in other neighboring villages, and certainly in the town of Pauri. In

Pauri every home has some vacant land around it, and that little piece of Mother Earth can provide some fruit and vegetables. Some use that little piece for the *linga* worship of Lord Shiva. It's a myth that this *linga* will produce anything you wish. Its worship is old like stale food, unhealthy to consume."

Bhagbati was baffled a bit but he expressed his frustration, "Chacha ji, you don't have to take Ba's wish so seriously. Just like other women, she didn't know what the scriptures are about. She had no knowledge of Sanskrit. Her prayers were in Gujarati and Hindi. Just forget what she said!"

"To be fair to Ba, she didn't have the same opportunities men are offered in our male-dominated society. She was born in Khambhat. She told me that her main job was to collect rainwater and save it in big clay pots underground. That was their drinking water, not the salty sea water of Khambhat coast. We should use that method in our town of Pauri, too. You know how long the lines of men and women are early in the morning to get water from a single water tap at the Pauri bus station! It's a shame."

"That drinking water from the sky is available everywhere. What's wrong with India when the Gujarat model has been known for such a long time?" Sakar wondered aloud.

"And Ba gave Vasanti the right advice," Uttara added. "Didn't your priests instruct that you never utter the *gayatri* mantra near any woman or untouchable!"

"Yes. Even my father took Manu's instruction literally. At my sacred thread investiture, the priest whispered the *gayatri* in my ear and warned me as you have said. I understood. Women are not allowed to use the Vedic mantras."

"Religious idiots hurt the progress of humanity," Uttara said. "The authors of scriptures don't accept that their religion promotes hate. India's partition is proof of hate, religious hate. Most haters cannot read their scriptures but claim that their holy books promote love. Love unites humans; it does not divide them."

Bhagbati also commented in support of Uttara, "Religions hate *Shudras, infidels, heathens, and kafirs* and harbored so much hate that they loved to kill them. God's representatives prove that there is no God, otherwise, He would have killed anyone He disliked. If God does not love His created beings, then don't claim your religion has love for humanity."

"I agree with you both. Every religion despises the other religions," Sakar said with a nod.

"Chacha, you may like to know what Vasanti told me one day after you performed a puja for Ba."

"What is it?" Sakar inquired.

"Hers were very much like your thoughts," Uttara responded. "Religious people tend to be removed from reality. For example, a deity becomes a reality and removes the believers from reality. Like when games are taken as natural by the players they are removed from nature's reality."

Uttara added further, "Clearly, her education and classmates are impacting her. She studies physics. She told me that she has a bunch of classmates who were much older than she was, some as old as thirty-five, yet they were unmarried. Their parents couldn't afford the large dowry so common here. Those girls felt lucky to remain alive. Their vegetarian mothers are as beastly as the man-eating tigresses in our Himalayas. Those tigresses don't kill their cubs. Here vegetarian mothers kill their infant daughters by feeding them poisoned milk until the infant breathes her last. And parents feel relief at her death and justify it. 'They tried so hard to save her, gave her so much milk!' What kind of cruel justification is that?"

"That's it. Vasanti is the lone anti-religion rebel that I know in Gujarat," Bhagbati said.

"She said to me, 'My protests against religion have earned me no supporters. Even women are not for women. Women are under the spell of scriptures. None of those girls in my circle were able to read any scripture. And these are college girls, not like my grandmother.' Vasanti's conclusion is: Women must leave religion or live by male prescriptions delivered in sermons. I hope someday women everywhere will wake up and use their brains," Uttara said, showing her disgust by her rolling eyes.

"Her wake-up call will have no impact. The spell will continue for long time to come," Sakar responded. "Most men also need to wake up and use their brains. I am trying to wake myself up. In my observations, most priests couldn't literally translate the Vedas in Hindi for their audience."

"Most priests I know repeat the mantras like parrots with no understanding of their meaning," Bhagbati said. "If a priest cannot translate the Vedic mantras, then he is cheating his audience. But that tendency goes for any religion. Do you think your Christian principal understood the original Bible? The head mullah of our town couldn't pronounce the Arabic word *Ramadhan*. It's not *ramzan* in Arabic!"

"And in our region, we always pronounced the word *jñāneśvarī* as *gyāneswarī* and the priest never corrected us because he himself pronounced it that way. And you are right on the mark, Bhagbati! Our Christian principal didn't know a word of Hebrew or Aramaic. Jesus would not have understood the King James' Bible," Sakar added with a slight smile.

After a few moments' pause Sakar continued, "But Bhagbati, don't worry too much about the correct pronunciation of the prayers. You and Uttara don't have to leave the priestly business because of that. Try your best to translate the mantras word for word for your audience. Your audience will have more confidence in you, and you will earn more respect, and *dakshina*, too."

Bhagbati said with a funny smile, "Chacha ji, my father tried that method, but his audience didn't pay much attention to his oral translations and explanations. Most of them would merely gossip in lowered voices during my father's performance of the ceremony. Women would talk about the forthcoming marriages of their relatives and friends. And if not others' marriages, then they would talk about their own marriage or jewelry. Men would talk about politics and economic problems. I heard two of my male relatives giving advice to each other for how to solve the problem of poverty. One had five children and the other had seven!"

Sakar laughed. "Very good observation, Bhagbati. That should not discourage you, though. You had better continue the puja business here. You need a continuous source of cash flow. You will not find more religious people elsewhere."

After nodding their agreement husband and wife remained quiet. They looked satisfied with Uncle Sakar's practical advice!

But Sakar's silence was for a different reason. This whole discussion they just had, he thought, would not impress anyone if they knew about his birth. Is a person fit to be priest whose married father was forced to marry his widow mother? What if Ba had known about his background?

Their silence was broken by a knock at the front door. It was Ramnik.

They greeted each other. Ramnik seemed to be in hurry as he said, "Do you remember, Pandit ji, that young man Swanil Trivedi?"

"Don't tell me he wants to write my biography again!"

"He would feel obliged if you allow him, but right now, he wants a big favor from you," Ramnik said with folded hands. "This morning his wife gave birth to their first child, a boy. He respectfully requests that you perform his son's naming ceremony. Do you think you can forgive him and bless his son? He thinks you are an incomparable priest."

"That's wonderful news. Give his son my heartfelt blessings. I would have come but I will be out of town then. Is Bhagbati all right in my place?"

"Sure, if Bhagvati is willing."

"I will come if he is willing," Bhagbati said with a smile. "And I will not accept any *dakshina*."

"That matter I cannot handle. It's between him and you, Bhagbati!" Ramnik responded, smiling. "Swanil wants a unique name for his son. And he joked, 'Not like my name *Swanil*. Too uncommon. The name must be meaningful. Do I smell as a *good wind,* Ramnik? Not when I burp raw garlic or onion,' Swanil joked with me," Ramnik said while blinking.

They all laughed.

After Ramnik left, Sakar went out in the yard for a walk. He felt relief that he was still Swanil's preferred priest. He realized that he should not worry about Swanil's lies in his biography, but what if he himself had been truthful with Swanil?

He never told Swanil about his own birth. Who would use a bastard Brahmin as his priest? He was fed-up with his religion-related proselytizing. Living by lies might pay, but no amount of money was worth saying those lies.

He felt his redemption must be in his return to his native garden.

Chapter 36

When Sakar arrived at the Pauri bus stand, no one was there to greet him there. He looked around for any acquaintances. He found some—the snow-covered majestic Chaukhamba Range between Tibet and India. He was very happy to breathe the cool late afternoon Himalayan air. He was eager to see his Kotwal home as soon as possible. So from the bus stand's teashop he took a cup of tea and a few *pakoras*, quickly finished the tea and saved the *pakoras* for the road. Before he started to race down the path, however, he placed one big *pakora* in his mouth.

He didn't even notice that he passed the famous Christian Messmore High School, his alma mater, situated in the middle of a plush green wooded area. By Indian standards, the school building was huge, the biggest in the entire district of Garhwal. Nevertheless, during the cold months of late February and early March, the teachers held classes out under the sun near huge pine trees. The students sat on rocks in a circle and the teacher had a chair near the trunk of the pine tree. The rustle of the pines and the sun's rays would compel some students to doze, forcing the teacher to be mad at them. Memories after memories.

By chance he looked up and saw a white horse with a rider. He knew that there were only two men who had horses, a prestigious symbol in those days. He concluded that the rider couldn't be other than the principal, the petite Chinese-Indian headmaster going up to his bungalow on the wooded trail. He saluted him with his folded hands with no fear.

The head master sat high upon his horse and had no idea that one of his disciples was paying him respect. Every student feared this Christian head master, a strict disciplinarian, the kind needed to make Pahari kids smart enough to go to the top colleges in India.

His bungalow and big guest house were surrounded by wild and cultivated flowers and fruit trees. Pear and apple trees were the most common. These fruit trees all around the school had inspired Sakar, convincing him of how easily they could be grown at this altitude and climate. There was no school lunch for hungry students. They could climb those trees and eat even unripe fruit, costing them nothing, except dysentery once in a while.

Feeling strong because of these memories, Sakar didn't realize that he was already home, and in less than one hour. It would have been dark if he had traveled at his normal speed, which would have taken him more than one hour.

His ranchette was not the same home, though it was the same physically. Slowly he moved toward the front door and knocked on it, shouting as well. He repeated this at the back door. No response. He started to peep through every window while shouting many times, "Bhaiya, bhabhi." He heard only his own voice. There was no Pawan, no Nanda.

He made his way toward the other house. He shouted again, "Balram bhaiya." Murti came out to welcome him.

"Sakar!" she responded loudly. "Come on in! Bhaiya will be back any time. Sakar touched her feet. By 'bhaiya' she meant her husband Balram, not Pawan as she informed him that Harshpat and Prachi took Pawan and Nanda to Lucknow.

"Why?" Sakar asked with amazement.

"Bhai ji needed medical attention. That was the reason. But then something terrible happened."

"No. What is it, Bhabhi?"

Murti remained quiet as tears began to roll from her eyes.

"Bhabhi, you shouldn't hesitate to tell me even if you think I will not like the news. You are crying, and so I understand it must be terrible news."

"Harshpat and Prachi requested that we not tell anyone what happened with their parents. Bhai ji is being taken care of by them, but Nanda didi is gone."

"Gone where?"

"She cut her wrists," she said.

"Did you say she cut her wrists?" he asked, his disbelief apparent in his widening eyes.

"Yes, she committed suicide."

Sakar sat down on the ground and wept like an orphan.

Just at that time Balram returned from his office and saw Sakar weeping. He embraced Sakar. Sakar kept crying on Balram's shoulder. Balram also had tears while consoling his cousin. "Mussi went to Lucknow to see bhai ji. But Harshpat told him that visitors were not allowed. It looks like bhai ji has TB."

"TB?"

"Some sort of contagious disease." Obviously, Balram knew better than anyone of Pawan's affliction. But he was not ready yet to disclose Pawan's real problem.

"I should inform Uttara and Bhagbati by telegram."

"Sakar, you should ask them to come here soon. That would be enough in a telegram. They shouldn't go directly to Lucknow. We can give them all the bad news when they come here. Maybe you should check with Mussi before you send the telegram."

వ౩౩

The following morning Sakar went to meet Mussi. He walked all the way and arrived at the front door of Mussi's house. Mussi was not home.

He was greeted by Saina, who was accompanied by Ghosa and her three-year old son. She introduced Ghosa and her son, Bimal. Ghosa touched Sakar's feet. He blessed her. "I know all about you. You have a beautiful boy. I would like to know more about him."

She was surprised that he was interested in her story, but she looked embarrassed as she looked down at her own bare feet.

"Let's go inside and have some tea," Saina intervened. They all went inside. Sakar sat in the sitting room with Saina. Ghosa went into the kitchen to prepare the tea. Bimal followed her.

Saina sighed deeply as she faced Sakar. "One day an old man and woman accompanied by a young man appeared at Ghosa's door," Saina said. "The young man said to her, 'The father of your son belongs to us. The father of your son is my older brother. These are our parents. We request that you give us your son.' Surprisingly, Bihari consented to give them the boy. The parents of Bihari were relieved to get rid of the bastard boy and his whore mother disguised as a nun.'"

Sakar reacted by uttering *humm* while resting his chin on his hands with his fingers interlocked. He was pondering his own birth.

If Bimal was a *bastard* for them then what was he? His face was down, looking at the zigzag pattern of rough stones of different sizes set into the floor.

Saina continued, "But gradually Ghosa began to feel guilty until guilt began to eat her up. She wanted to get Bimal back. After all, she is his mother. Those folks were so kind to Ghosa. They understood that a child needed his mother. So they handed Bimal over to Ghosa. Now we think that a child needs a father, too. Let me be quick before your tea comes here. Mussi has gone to meet Mattu."

"You mean they intend to ask Mattu to adopt Bimal as his son?"

"And take his mother as his wife!"

"That's very good thought. Did Mattu show any interest in your ideas?"

"He didn't, but Mussi is visiting him again to give him some food in the hospital."

"In the hospital?"

"You didn't know that he is disabled. He can't walk because of a fracture and a couple of wounds. Mussi saw him yesterday. He seemed to enjoy our food. Mussi thought to persuade him that it would be good for him to get married and get that good food regularly. Ghosa prepared *bhari rotis* and *alu gutkas* for him."

Sakar smiled. "Of course, he would be so happy again and again. But tell me how he got into this trouble!"

"Let me go to the kitchen to see if Ghosa needs any help."

She went into the kitchen, and in a couple of minutes, Saina brought a cup of tea.

Ghosa and Bimal remained in the kitchen.

"Ghosa is planning *parathas* for lunch. You must stay for lunch and I will tell you the story of Mattu's fractures. He will listen to you if you support Mussi."

"Yes, I will visit him tomorrow. Is he still raising cattle?"

"The murder of his goats and rams hurt him. As you know, occasionally people would buy a *bakri* or *bakra* from him for sacrifice at the local temples."

"That was part of his business."

"But he never sold any lambs, not ever. A couple of gundas wanted to buy lambs for curry. He refused. So they barged into his barn and got two lambs. Before Mattu could get hold of his gun they grabbed him by the neck and threw him down. He was beaten badly, very badly. While he was lying there the thugs grabbed a goat, too, and ran away with three animals. And Mattu had to be rushed to the Pauri hospital. Sakar bhaiya! You can do something to protect Mattu's property. I know that your first occupation was law."

Sakar smiled. "I have been in several occupations. Before I became a lawyer I was a gardener. Now I am that gardener again."

Saina laughed. "Whatever you choose to be, you can persuade Mattu to think of Ghosa so her boy can grow up with a father."

Sakar smiled and said, "Let me be clear. Mattu's decision must come from him. The thought of marriage under social pressure goes against my legal mind. If Mattu is not enthused about this prospect, then it will be hard for me to persuade him. But I will tell him what you and Ghosa think."

After lunch Sakar passed by Mattu's home. He saw a young man in the barn. Sakar met him. The young man identified himself as Mattu's cousin, his mother's nephew. "I am in charge of Mattu's house and animals," the man said.

Sakar said, "That's very kind of you. Do you have any

message for Mattu? I am going to see him tomorrow afternoon."

He responded, "Just tell him that everything is good here."

ⓔ✑ⓔ✑

Sakar visited Mattu the next morning. The first thing Sakar did was served him samosa and chutney on a leaf plate. "Wah! I never ate such tasty samosas and chutney! Who prepared them?"

"Ghosa. I overheard her telling Saina in the kitchen: *samosa aur chutney jaise pati aur patni.*"

Mattu spilled out a morsel from his mouth with an uncontrollable burst of laughter. Knowing that samosa was masculine and chutney feminine grammatically, he cleaned his lips and added his comment. "I never heard before that samosa and chutney are like husband and wife. How does she know? She never had a husband."

"Could you believe that Saina asked her the same question! She confessed that it was not her saying. She heard it from a snack-shop owner in Srinagar."

Sakar continued, "She has packed lunch too for you. And guess what else? She and Saina had gone to our local temple and brought some *prasad*. They wanted to share it with you for your healthy life."

"I will eat the samosas and the lunch, but not that sacred *prasad* of lifeless statues. Statues of the dead don't do a damn good. Why don't they spend that money on hospitals and help patients live longer? Only dumb people believe in the worship of deads and their temples and tombs. My father believed in the power of dead Lord Rama and dead Lord Krishna, even in his dead father's spirit. None could save my young mother." Mattu sighed.

Sakar took the *prasad* packet with him and left the hospital. He entered the trail that went through the wooded area of the hospital. It was evening but not quite dark yet. Suddenly two men came out of a wild raspberry bush and ambushed him. They had no idea that Sakar had learned karate from his lama guru. Sakar slammed them against a huge oak tree so hard that their heads were bruised. He kicked them in the groins so hard that they fell to the ground. He left them crying in pain and went back to the hospital. Soon two staff members of the hospital came down and escorted them to the hospital for treatment.

Then Sakar immediately ran back to Mattu and asked him to identify the two men and the man in charge of his house. Mattu was surprised to know that someone claiming to be his relative was looking after his home. He was sure that Mussi and Saina were doing that job. Mattu had no knowledge about these crooks.

The two thugs were given treatment, and an hour later the hospital released them. As they came out of the hospital, they were met by two police officers with their guns pointed at them. They were handcuffed and taken away to the Pauri jailhouse.

Chapter 37

Behind every individual's back is a room where people make gossip about that individual," the lama guru had said to Sakar at the time of his initiation. "That room may exist even when you don't exist. Your initiation could keep many visitors entertained in that room for long time."

Sakar was never concerned about who entered his room of gossip, but when he returned to his Kotwal colony, he entered Murti's gossip room a couple of times. "What is this gossip about Murti bhabhi?"

"It's a fact, not a gossip," Mussi said in a conspiratorial voice. When he told him the whole story, however, Sakar developed tremendous respect for her. "It's a fact, not a gossip," Mussi said to him again.

This is the story he told: Murti and Maheep used to treat each other with love, a love that should ideally be between sisters and brothers. Every year that love would be refreshed by the ritual of *Raksha Bandhan*. Murti would send the sacred thread of *rakhi* to Maheep. He would be very sentimental as he tied that colorful string around his wrist. But after Maheep got married to Janki, the bond created by the sacred string began to be some-what loose. The cost of that string was almost zero com-

pared to the jewelry that the widow mother had left. It
was with Maheep. That means it was with Janki. Only a
woman would use jewelry. It was family jewelry and a
daughter-in-law is expected to maintain the continuity of
that family by having children.

Murti thought otherwise. A mother's jewelry must
pass to her daughter. She was fair in her own way, and
when Janki became pregnant, Murti sent a *rakhi* to Maheep with a note. She wanted half the jewelry. Maheep
was angry. Janki had sowed the seeds of his anger. She
thought that Murti already got a lot of jewelry at the time
of her marriage and now she had no right to claim a single piece of that jewelry that was left with Maheep. Murti
thought that her brother received much land and a house
and she got no part of that inheritance.

The feud became very ugly. Murti began to observe a
sacred fast to achieve divine intervention in her favor. A
swami had recommended this fast, which required its
practitioner to sacrifice his or her favorite food to achieve
their wish. Murti's favorite food was meat.

Murti lost much weight, which made Balram very
much concerned. He told her, "Murti, leave your fasts.
Sacred fasting is for fools." But Murti continued fasting
and did not eat or cook meat. Balram yearned for meat.
He was so angry that he wrote a letter to Maheep.

His letter made Maheep so mad that one afternoon he
visited Balram in his office. He pretended that he was out
hunting in the Adhwani forest and that on his way he
wanted to drop by Balram's office. Balram told him that
Murti was upset, and that she was justified. Maheep became argumentative. Balram advised him not to shout in
his office. So both men came out and sat on a bench in
the open. They had harsh exchange of words. Balram
took it as a fake threat when Maheep pointed his gun at
his head. He said, "Don't show me your gun!"

"Guns are not made for show. They are made to shoot." As Maheep said that he began to comb Balram's head with his gun. Balram quickly got up and ran back to his office. Maheep, too, ran away. He was afraid that Balram's colleagues might come out to beat him up. He then went to the Adhwani forest where he shot a deer.

That year, on the day of *Raksha Bandhan* Murti didn't send *rakhi* to Maheep.

Everything changed when a few months later she heard that Janki delivered a premature girl. A week after the delivery Janki died. Murti rushed to her parental home to take care of Maheep's infant daughter. Her help changed Maheep dramatically.

Janki had an unmarried cousin, Sumitra, who was four years older than Janki and considered too old to get married. She was born as a *mangli*. A girl born in an astrologically determined position of Mars, called *mangli*, can marry a boy only if he is born in the same astrological position of Mars. The boy is called *mangalik*. Around that area there was no *mangalik* boy.

Murti was determined to defy the astrological practice for the welfare of her brother and his daughter—and for the welfare of Sumitra, too. Murti was successful. Sumitra's parents had no objection to Murti's proposal. Maheep didn't care for the stupid belief of *mangli*. A few months after the proposal, Sumitra and Maheep happily became husband and wife in a small ceremony. Sumitra agreed to raise Maheep's daughter as her own daughter. After all, Janki's daughter was a blood-relative to her for Janki was her cousin.

Balram also attended their marriage. He even brought Bharat Ram, the pandit, along with him to perform the marriage. An hour before the marriage, the pandit asked Balram, "Do you have the horoscope of Maheep and Sumitra?"

"Why you need their horoscopes at this time?"

"I have to know what *gotra* they belong to."

Balram was happy that he inquired only about the *gotra*, the name of their traditional lineage. But his happiness didn't last too long. When they arrived at Maheep's home he did ask him for the horoscopes. Maheep had no horoscopes. The priest was not willing to perform the ceremony without horoscopes, and so, Balram took Bharat Ram in a corner where nobody could see them. Instead of horoscopes Balram gave him two notes, each a one-hundred rupee note. The pandit didn't inquire anymore about the horoscopes. But Balram did tell him that Sumitra was a *mangli*.

Balram had brought those rupee notes for the bride as a cash gift, but those notes were far less valuable than what was in the tin box he brought with him for Sumitra. It contained Murti's jewelry that she had received from her mother at the time of her marriage to Balram.

Mussi surprised Sakar when he said, "Maheep deposited his gun at the Pauri police office. Could you believe that he and Sumitra have become vegetarians! They have heard about you. They showed their desire to meet you some day. Maybe you can convince them to join you in utilitarian gardening!"

Sakar smiled. "I remember how Maheep learned to shoot correctly from Pawan bhai ji. And both men abandoned hunting!" He paused for a few seconds as he thought of Pawan's dubious interest in hunting. He continued, "Anyway, much more important is that Murti bhabhi's relations with her brother are restored."

"That's true. I know this year she sent him a *rakhi* and a box of clothes for her infant niece. I was the one who delivered the box to Maheep. He cried."

Chapter 38

On Sunday morning, Sakar rushed to the Pauri hospital where Lachchhu's mother was in a diabetic coma. The doctor had already told Lachchhu that she had no chance of coming out of her coma.

When Lachchhu saw Sakar, he began to cry. Sakar also cried. They sat on a bench near the front door of the hospital and talked about her funeral arrangements.

"You should burry her beside your father," Sakar suggested.

"My father was buried because he belonged to the *dom* community, but I would prefer to cremate her like you and the Rajputs do. Moreover, my father used to beat my mother. I was fifteen when I hit him on the head with a rock because my mother collapsed on the floor after he beat her with a log. The log was rough, which caused bleeding scratches as well as bruises on her body. That was his last day of beating her."

"I understand your point," Sakar said.

"In my Gandhi ashram days, we had to treat the untouchable residents just like any other high caste residents. If Gandhi ji could be cremated, so can your mother be. We will cremate her in Srinagar on the bank of the Alakananda."

"With Vedic rites? You know the *doms* are not allowed to use the mantras of any of the *Vedas*."

"We will do just like our pandit did for our parents."

"But how will you get a pandit for a *dom* woman's rites?" Lachchhu exclaimed with a puzzled look.

"Don't worry about that. Bhagbati and I have done funerals in Gujarat, but frankly speaking, neither burial nor cremation is useful. A utilitarian funeral is a lot better."

"I don't understand." Lachchhu looked even more puzzled. "What is a utilitarian funeral?"

"A dead body should be used for the good of others. Burial and cremation do not provide anyone a benefit. If my lama guru had his way, he would have recommended cutting up every dead body and feeding the pieces to other animals."

"You mean I should cut up my own mother's body?" Lachchhu had a look of disgust on his face. "It's not like cutting nails or hair. I cannot do it."

"Not you, but doctors can. Let me explain. I have told my doctor-nephew Harshpat to use my dead body for medical purposes. You must have heard that medical students use cadavers to learn…"

"Now I understand your view. But that does not make *doms* equal to you Brahmins!" Lachchhu looked sharply into the eyes of Sakar.

"You are right. I will do the Vedic cremation. We will use your Sanskrit name Lakshmana at the funeral. Lakshmana, Rama's brother, was a Kshatriya. Is that agreeable to you?"

"No, Lakshman was a coward. Lakshman cut up a beautiful woman's nose and ears, mutilated her. He was not different from my father. My mother was beautiful, but my father disfigured her face so many times. A man's manhood is not tested by how he hurts a defenseless woman. Please don't call me Lakshman!"

"Then how about calling you *Lakshya* instead of *Lakshmana*?"

"That sounds good to me if it is a Sanskrit name and higher castes use it. You can call me just *Laksh*. The shorter the better. Easier for everybody."

"How about Balasubrahmanyam?"

"What? I never heard that name. Who has that kind of long name?"

"It is just a guess, but at least a million men in south India! If they remove *m* in the end, then that change will make it a correct name for men. And short, too."

"Short, too!"

They both laughed.

"The south Indians must be highly educated. My people here are not educated enough to pronounce such a big name," Lachchhu said. "You better leave my name Lachchhu alone!"

Sakar smiled, nodding his head. They both were silent.

Sakar was expecting that Lachchhu might discuss the way untouchables did their funerals. Their religion was different but resembled the folk paganism most Hindus practiced. Yet the untouchables claimed that their god was *Nirankar*, which literally meant *nirakara* or no-form.

Sakar reminisced about what Swami Tirthanand had discussed of death and funerals. When Tirthanand died, he was given a yoga burial. In this burial, the dead body remained in the *samadhi* meditation pose, which was meant to indicate that the dead person had not just died because he had already achieved "nothingness" while still alive. Once he had talked about nothingness. He quoted the most ancient Vedic hymn, *Nasadiya Sukta,* to the effect that the cosmos originated from no-form, nothingness, existence coming out of non-existence. He told Sakar that his initiation name, Nirakaranand, fit well with the belief in nothingness.

But the yoga guru had also given Sakar a hidden pronunciation of his name: Nirahamkaranand. It meant "a
person with the joy of no *ahamkara* or ego." Egolessness
meant nothingness. Swami Tirthanand had received his
yoga training from another lama, a lama from Tibet, quite
close to Uttar Kashi.

Sakar recollected how his lama guru had taught him
that *aham-kara* literally meant "I-ness" or the sense of
personhood. But there was no such thing as personhood
or self. When there is no "I" then there is no sense of
"mine." The lama guru strongly believed that the elimina-
tion of I-ness is the way to eliminate *dukha,* suffering.
Sakar found his advice so true in his life: one should not
believe in I-ness. Or despair will continue. Instead, keep
trying to repair despair because every moment is different
from the preceding one. No existence of I-ness, no per-
sonality, just impermanence of *atman.*

Sakar was aware that his *sannyas* primarily implied
the renunciation of mine-ness, possessive-ness. Indeed,
mama-tva, the Sanskrit word for "mine-ness," has always
been considered a hidden poison for "Good" or *Shiva.*
Shiva alone is capable of drinking this poison to destroy
it. The meditation mantra given to Sakar, therefore, was
om namaḥ shivāya: Absolute salutation to good. But any
word meaning "good" in any language, or just the Sanskrit *Om*, were as good for meditation. No ritual, no religion. The objective of yoga meditation is to feel "good."

Sakar now had no *sannyas* name now. That name,
Swami Nirakaranand, could have impressed the untouchables: a Brahmin swami was named after their god, a
formless creator of all. He wanted to explain these philosophical speculations of his gurus to Lachchhu, but he did
not think he would be able to comprehend them. As they
say here, don't play lute in front of water-buffalos.

But he began to brood again, "But does it really matter how the body is disposed of when there is no life or *I* in it? His dead mother would be 'nothing' anyway when she is dead. But wouldn't it be 'good' to utilize her 'nothing' body the Tibetan way?!"

Lachchhu noticed Sakar murmuring and so felt encouraged to unmute him. "I will go along with your plan for my mother's funeral, Pandit ji!"

ೞೞೞ

Five days later, Lachchhu's mother died. The next morning, because of such short notice, only Param Singh was available to join Sakar, Bhagbati, and Lachchhu to carry the dead body to the *ghat* reserved for cremation on the banks of the Alaknanda.

Sakar, assisted by Bhagbati, started performing the standard Hindu cremation, the rite reserved only for the higher castes. A few yards away another cremation was taking place. After that cremation was over, four men came to attend the cremation of Lachchhu's mother. They asked Param Singh, who was quietly standing nearby, who was being cremated. As soon as they learned that the two pandits were performing the Vedic rites for Lachchhu's untouchable mother they retreated.

After the rites were completed, the four men left for Khanda where they had planned to eat late lunch. There were only two small street shops, *dhabas*, where fresh hot food was available. The smaller *dhaba* had no guests, unlike the other big one, which had over a dozen customers at that time. Lachchhu's party chose the smaller *dhaba* and sat on a bench facing a long serving table.

As soon as Lachchhu paid the bill, he turned around to find the four men from the other *dhaba* behind him. One of them came forward and picked up ashes from the clay oven of the *dhaba* and threw them into his eyes as he said, "These are the ashes for your funeral." Then he slammed him on the ground. Lachchhu fell on the floor crying. He could not see because some ash had fallen into his eyes.

Param Singh grabbed the neck of that perpetrator and thrashed him on the ground. The man's three friends jumped over Param Singh. Sakar saw that Param Singh could not handle them alone, and he signaled to Bhagbati. The two of them proceeded to beat the hell out of all four men. They held the four flat on the ground and waited until Param Singh could wash Lachchhu's eyes. As soon as Lachchhu was able to see partially, Sakar told Param Singh and Lachchhu to run away with him and Bhagbati.

Before leaving, Param Singh looked at the man who had thrown ashes over the face of Lachchhu. That perpetrator was still flat on the ground. Param Singh had brought a fistful of ashes, which he wanted to throw into that man's eyes. He kicked him hard and ordered him to get up. Sakar understood Param Singh's intention for revenge, but he stopped Param Singh by staying his hand. "Let's leave this place! Let's run away!" Sakar announced to his party. They obeyed him and started to run on a trail.

After a few minutes they came to a creek, drank its fresh water, and then crossed it. They rested under a pipal tree nearby. Lachchhu thanked his saviors. He asked Sakar, "How did you two pandits beat those four men so badly and manage to hold them on the floor until I could see?"

Sakar smiled and responded, "Actually we didn't beat them so badly as you might think. We stunned them as we grounded them. We didn't even slam them."

"But how did you do that feat?"

"When I was young, my lama guru had taught me non-violent self-defense. Some call it *karate*. Bhagbati learned this art from me. My guru told me to never be violent while defending myself against the attacker, and when the attacker is momentarily down, to just run away. That's what we did. Otherwise they might have brought more attackers from the other *dhaba*. We could not have tackled over a dozen men so easily."

Param Singh interjected, "They would have made *chutney* out of me." He paused. Then he turned toward Lachchhu and asked him, "Lachchhu, did you like the food?"

"Not really. I could have cooked better than that *dhaba* cook!" Lachchhu laughed. "But you would not have eaten the food cooked by a *dom*."

"Lachchhu, we would be fools to miss a chance to eat your food!" Sakar said.

Param Singh and Bhagbati nodded their agreement.

Chapter 39

Bhagbati invited his cousin, Giri Raj Pokhriyal, to meet Sakar. Giri Raj had just finished his Ph.D. in agricultural botany from Allahabad University. Bhagbati thought that, with his expertise, Giri could advise Sakar on utilitarian gardening.

Bhagbati remembered how his father once had a big argument with Giri about using foreign foods, especially those which the British used to eat in India. Bhagbati knew his father was a nationalist and nationalists feed on historical distortions.

That day, when Giri Raj arrived at the Pokhriyal residence, it was raining. He had brought a basket of freshly roasted, shelled *mungphali*. Bhagbati greeted him. His parents thanked Giri Raj for the *mungphali* basket.

"Giri," Bhagbati's father Shailesh Pokhriyal said, "Let us have warm tea and eat *mungphali* while they are still warm. This food is good for a rainy day!"

Over tea, Bhagbati's father, began to praise the *mungphali*.

"My parents were addicted to these nuts. So we, too, became addicted. I am sure our ancestors were addicted to *mungphali*."

"Tau ji, our ancestors did not know about *mungphali*

until Portuguese traders brought them to India from South America. And *mungphali* is not a nut. It's like *dal* legumes, even if its English name is groundnuts or peanuts."

"Did you mean that the Portuguese introduced them here?"

"Yes, Tau ji."

"Then why do we call them *mungphali*? Aren't they called *mudgaphala* in Sanskrit? I think they were ancient Indian food."

"Many non-Indian foods are given Indian names. India welcomed foreign foods whenever possible. *Taste buds* gradually tend to resent discrimination against foods of foreign lands. And hunger adopts any foreign foods. One way to integrate them is give them some native names in Hindi such as *alu* for potato and *mirch* for chilies."

Giri knew that Sailesh, like a typical Pahari, loved to eat potatoes, but Pahari potatoes were considered the best. Poor people would simply bake them and mash them with ground chilies and salt. So he first asked Sailesh, "Can you avoid potatoes in your daily diet?"

"Then how would we survive?"

"How about crushed chilies with some salt over a baked potato?"

"Unbeatable combination!"

"I assure you, your great-grandfather never ever tasted that combination. Potatoes and chilies were brought to India by the Portuguese from the Americas."

"Chilies, too? Giri, tell me then how Indians made their curries hot?"

"With other spices, such as peppers. Actually pepper is from India, but now it is served in the restaurants of other countries. Most probably only a few diners in those restaurants would know that the peppers they are sprinkling over their food originated from India."

"Many in India wouldn't either."

"You know Sanskrit. Pepper is from Sanskrit *pippara* or *pippala*, from which we get the Hindi pi*pal*. The Portuguese introduced many other popular fruits and vegetables from the Americas. How about maize?"

"Maize! Don't tell me my favorite *makki ki roti* is not of Indian origin?"

"The natives of Mexico have been eating corn since before God created Adam and Eve!"

Giri named dozens of other food items brought to India from the Americas: cashews, guavas, papayas, tomatoes, to name a few.

"Then what was left for our ancestors to eat before the Portuguese arrived? Just grass?" Saliesh asked Giri as he placed his palm on his forehead.

"A lot. I will give you an interesting example. The majority of the population of India eats rice. We call it *chawal*. That is our word. But did you know that 'rice' is also our word?"

"I always thought it was English in origin."

"No, *rice* is an Indian word, actually an anglicized Tamil word *arisi*. It is believed that India is one of the first regions of the world where rice was grown. Didn't you see how many varieties of rice dishes are eaten in southern India?"

"How about wheat? The Sanskrit word for wheat is *godhuma*. It must have originated in India."

"Words sometimes imply and sometimes don't imply the origin of what they refer to. The Levant Valley in the Middle East is where wheat originated, and it eventually spread to Punjab. Punjab's major crop is wheat, and the best *roti* varieties are eaten there."

Mr. Pokhriyal became quiet, and he looked humbled by Giri's Ph.D. in agricultural botany.

Giri, however, had no intention of making him feel humble. So he gave a big list of Indian foods that became international. Then he added another list of spices. At the same time, he warned Mr. Pokhyriyal that these lists should not be associated with nationalism. "Foods grow where they do because of a favorable climate."

Giri then pleased Sailesh Pokhriyal as he commented, "India's greatest ideal has been *vasudhaiva kutumbakam*."

"Your list shows that ideal: the world alone is the family. Another older ideal is the Vedic mantra *Mātā bhumiḥ:* Mother is Bhumi."

"Yes, my father, too, told us about this ideal: Mother is Earth. I am the son of *Prithivi*. Thanks to Ma Bhumi. Thanks to Ma Prithivi. Thanks to Ma Vasudha. Don't we contradict our own ideal? How many times do our scriptural mantras repeat this ideal using various names for our Mother Earth? All people of the world are her children and are united by sharing her foods."

"Then we should salute Mother Earth when we say *vande mataram*. This salutation is fit for Mother Earth, not for Bharat. As you know, *Bharat* is masculine and *Prithivi* feminine. To call Bharat a 'mother' indicates poor grammar on the part of the national fanatics," Shailesh said with a sigh.

"Even if you make those fanatics aware of their irreverence for grammar, they will not stop calling a father a mother. Imagine if Bhagbati called you 'Ma' unless you change your gender!" Giri said with a laugh. "There is always a lot of conflict between research opinion and public opinion."

"Yes, we call them *gyaan mat* and *jan mat*. They have been in conflict for ages. Recently India suffered from the 1947 partition because of the traditional conflict between *jñaana-matam* and *jana-matam*."

"I agree. It happens not only in India, but even in the West. Galileo's shameful treatment by the ignorant

church is an example. Public opinion becomes a farty behavior when it politicizes research opinion," Giri said.

Sailesh laughed. He was impressed. "Let's finish our
tasty *mungphali*!"

Giri smiled.

Sakar had heard the conversation. "A very impressive
story," he assured Bhagbati

Bhagbati said, as if confessing," I tried my best to re-
construct it, but I am happy you liked it."

"Every story is reconstructed when narrated the second time. I got the gist and it serves my purpose. Well, I
am interested in growing apples, which were not native
fruits to India, either. Maybe Giri could suggest some
other fast growing fruits not necessarily of local origin."

୧୭୧୬

Two weeks later, Giri, who had accepted Bhagbati's
invitation, came to visit the Kotwal colony. Sakar gave
him a general idea of his plan at breakfast. Then Bhagbati
took him to the Kotwal forest and around the banks of the
Chandrabhaga. Giri collected a big bundle of *lingura*
ferns from the swamps of the Chandrabhaga.

In the evening Murti included the *lingura* curry in the
dinner. "Giri," Sakar asked while eating, "what do you
think of the *lingura* curry?"

"Very uncommon and so tasty!" Giri replied.

"Can you commercialize it?"

"Chacha ji, it grows all over the world, wherever there
is wet land, especially in hilly swamps. People can be
made aware of its edibility, or someday a Pahari could
accept the challenge to grow it and market it all over.
Anything can be marketed, after all. Unknown foods have
spread around the world because of marketing.

"So what other fruits do you think can grow fast like
apples?" Bhagbati asked Giri.

"I suggest peaches. Apricots are even more useful because they yield not only pulp but also sweet and bitter nuts. Their sweet nuts are just like almonds. You know how costly almonds are in India! The apricot nuts can compete with almonds."

"Will you join us in our plans for utilitarian gardens?" Sakar looked him in his eyes.

"Chacha ji, currently I am doing some research on the chromosomes of other local crops."

"What crops?"

"*Jhangoru, kodu, china,* and *kauni,*" Giri replied. "Most of my time will be spent in experimentation. But I can always give you advice."

"Anything else you think we can add to the fruits you have suggested?"

"Let me recommend some beans that are easy to grow."

Before Giri could name those beans, however, there was big noise from the neighboring village of Malli. Men were shouting, "*Hwa hwa.*" Gongs and drums accompanied those shouts. It was clear some tiger was seen in the village. Sakar, Bhagbati, and Giri came outside where they heard someone crying, "My cow is gone! My cow is gone!"

"I wish Pawan tau ji was here. He would have gone after that tiger." Bhagbati let out a deep sigh. Sakar also sighed deeply. Tears began to drop from his eyes. When Balram and Murti came out he tried to wipe his tears.

"What's the matter, Sakar?" Murti asked very affectionately.

"Just feeling sorry for that cow," Sakar replied.

"You know that tigers maul cattle here often, and I never saw you shedding tears before for such attacks," Murti said, hoping to find out the true reason for his sadness.

Sakar knew the true reason, but he remained quiet.

For Giri, it was an awful experience. He didn't expect the kind of ruckus he was witnessing. "Chacha ji, I have more ideas for utilitarian gardening, but can we discuss them inside?" he requested of Sakar.

"Not tonight. I will forget whatever we discuss because I am not able to concentrate at this moment."

Chapter 40

Bhagbati had gone out to Dehradun to visit his old friends at Dharm Samaj School. He also met the headmaster, now called the principal, who surprised him with an offer. The principal wanted Bhagbati and Uttara to return to the school. But when Bhagbati told him about his association with Sakar, the principal surprised him with one more offer.

Bhagbati returned to the Kotwal colony. He told Uttara and Sakar about the offers.

"Bhagbati!" Sakar sounded somewhat puzzled. "Why does the principal want me to be his vice principal? He doesn't even know me."

"Chacha ji, I have told him all about you. He was very much impressed by your attempt to have a borderless school. He was sorry that it burned down."

"But I have no real administrative experience. Moreover, I don't believe in what that school believes. I mean, their religious beliefs. Their concept of Sanatana Dharma creates walls between other religions. They don't even recognize the Arya Samaj as a part of the Sanatana Dharma. The Arya Samaj tradition of *shuddhi* is not acceptable to them, as it is not for me too. No humans are impure. Nobody needs *shuddhi* unless they are a trader in our high Himalayas. You know some traders don't take bath for months, courtesy of the severe cold weather. They smell awful!"

Bhagbati and Uttara laughed.

"Chacha!" Uttara interjected. "Prachi also had differences with her Arya Samaji in-laws. But I admire them. They believe in educating girls just like boys. I consider that borderless education—no borders between genders. Under the ancient *stridhan* laws, Prachi and I cannot own our parents' land and house. Harshpat bhaiya will inherit them.'"

"Chacha ji, when I told the principal about your borderless education, he agreed. 'Knowledge has no borders,' he said. If you accept the offer he is willing to give you, in writing, complete freedom."

"What happened to his vice principal?"

"The vice principal was expected to succeed him, but he did something that forced him to resign. The principal is going to retire next year, and you will succeed him. He assured me that you will have complete freedom. You can even rename the school."

"That's an unusual offer. But I am curious. What if I am also forced to resign like their vice principal?"

"There is no possibility! Their vice principal left his wife and son for a Christian woman who was his son's music tutor. Her singing and beauty blinded him. The school was shocked when it was discovered that he was living with that woman. Lots of gossip began to float among the teachers and students, and most of them began to sympathize with his wife and son. His son ceased having any contact with him and his mistress and his dada and dadi took over his custody. The grandparents consider their son a criminal because he abandoned his son. So his resignation became inevitable."

"My goodness!" Sakar looked stunned.

After lunch he went to see Mattu. He was surprised to see Mattu smoking *bhang*.

"I never expected to find you smoking *bhang*, Mattu!"

"It's a necessity. After my release from the hospital, I began to lose sleep because I was in too much pain. Then a sadhu came here, and he recommended *bhang*. First I flatly rejected his recommendation, but he explained to me why Lord Shiva is called Bhole Nath, the sinless lord. Bhole Nath ji loves *bhang*. Just say his mantra, *bam bam Bholenath,* and take a few puffs. So I smoked it, but without the mantra, and my pain was gone."

"I know how the sadhus promote *bhang*. Anyways, forget *bhang*. I have a purpose for meeting with you. Would you be interested in taking care of our gardens?"

"What do you mean? I thought you were expanding your gardening beyond your gardens."

"That I will explain to you later. I am happy that you are feeling better, but you can grow anything you know how to grow in our gardens."

"I would very much like to grow *bhang* and provide it to anyone who needs it to get rid of their pain."

"You are talking like the Buddha. His goal was to end the suffering of all. But you can grow it just like they grow it in Eastern Garhwal. They grow it for fiber out of which they make rugs, clothes, and sacks, and they use the dry stems for fuel. The *bhang* seeds are popular as spice. The roasted seeds beat any roasted nuts in taste. I am talking about its potential for commercial use."

"Any objections from any Kotwal?"

"I am now in charge. Bhai ji is represented by Uttara, and she would like you to lease our gardens from us."

"Two questions. Uttara is a married daughter and she cannot permit me. Did you check with her brother?"

"Dr. Harshpat will never say 'no' if I say 'yes.' More-over, you will pay us nothing for the lease. I am just using the legal word for *tihar*. You keep our one 'third share' as long as you and your partner sell the produce of our gardens."

"My partner?

"Yes, your partner."

"Who is my partner? You don't mean Mussi?"

"Not him. I will tell you who your partner could be."

"So half of my earnings go to my partner. Is that right?"

"No. All the earnings will be yours. I will explain to you later. But a partner is necessary for your success. You will have more sales and you may not need to smoke *bhang*."

Mattu laughed and Sakar smiled.

When Sakar returned home, Murti handed him a letter that the postman had delivered in the afternoon. He was delighted to receive a letter from Jiva bhai Jhaveri.

Then, during dinner, he discussed his plan for Mattu with Murti, Balram, Bhagbati, and Uttara. They all supported him.

The next morning Mattu paid an unexpected visit to Sakar. He was not sure if Sakar was serious when he heard his plan, and Sakar understood his doubts. So he went inside to check with Murti, who was alone working in the kitchen.

"Bhabhi! Mattu is waiting for us in the sitting room. Tell him what we discussed last evening."

Murti covered the cooking pot, which was on the stove, and came out. She greeted Mattu. Then she added, "I am cooking whole *tor dal* and basmati rice. Mattu, I want you to join us for lunch."

"Any reason for this sort of auspicious lunch?" Mattu asked her with a suspicious look in his eyes.

"Yes, I am happy to know that you are managing your pain. But I will be happier if those culprits are caught."

"There is no need to arrest them," Mattu replied with a smile. "Harakh bhai has already taken care of them."

"You mean he used his World War II tricks?"

"I think Banki bhabhi encouraged him. What she recommended is not mentionable."

Murti smiled. "Then let us discuss the plan we have for you."

Mattu quietly listened to her. He was flabbergasted over how much these Kotwals cared for his welfare and he agreed to their plan.

After Mattu left, Sakar wrote a reply to Jhaveri.

Chapter 41

The new morning was also a new dawn for the colony of the Kotwals. As the sun rose above the horizon, all the Kotwals and their guests assembled under a canopy at the front yard of Sakar's house. Sakar introduced Jiva Bhai Jhaveri to as many guests as possible. The guests seemed to be impressed by Jhaveri's simplicity, a rich jeweler but dressed in Gandhian *khadi* clothing: *dhoti* and *kurta* with a Gandhian *topi* (cap). Like Jhaveri, Sakar also wore a white *khadi* outfit: *kurta*, pajamas, and the same kind of *topi*. Jhaveri was surprised to see many adult males wearing Western pants and shirts in khaki, an influence of their military jobs—none of them in *khadi*. In contrast, all the women wore saris and blouses. Not a single woman was in *khadi*.

Sakar had told him that Paharis liked Mahatma Gandhi, but they also liked the British, whose rule created an unprecedented number of military jobs and developed famous modern Westernized towns such as Nainital, Mussoorie, and Dehradun. However, Paharis were also aware of the signs posted in many modern hill stations like these: *Dogs and Indians are not allowed*. Nevertheless, Jhaveri was impressed that the Paharis were following Gandhi's request to remain truly friendly with the British people after Independence.

Noticeably, one of the guests was missing, but he was kind enough to send a message that he was sick. Pandit Bharat Ram was not, in fact, sick. He just was not willing to perform the wedding ceremony of Mattu with Ghosa. Sakar knew that the pandit had performed a couple of marriages of married men with children, however Hindu men were allowed to marry again and again, but not Hindu women, even when no miscegenation (*varṇsaṃkara*) was involved. Bharat Ram, like other priests, had very poor critical thinking with which to challenge bigotry. Fortunately, he was able to bark but not bite. No overt challenge was heard from him.

Bhagbati did challenge this inegalitarian tradition and volunteered to replace Pandit Bharat Ram. He was dressed up like Jhaveri except that he put on a traditional white turban of Pahari priests. Following his advice, Sakar acted as the father of Ghosa to offer her hand to Mattu. Mussi and Saina stood by the bride as her brother and sister to do the *homa* ceremony with her and Mattu.

The last part of the wedding ritual was completed by Murti and Uttara. They placed a gold nose ring on the bride's nose, which meant that Ghosa was a married woman now. At that point all of the guests stood up to bless the bride and threw rice grains and flower petals toward the altar (*Vedika*). Some guests went to the altar and showered the bride with gifts.

Saina went with Bhagbati to meet Jhaveri ji. She touched his feet and then began to tie a red-yellow *rakhi* on his wrist while Bhagbati pronounced the sacred *Raksha* mantra.

Bhagbati didn't translate the mantra but added his own blessing. "Jiva bhai ji, May Badrinath save you with her *rakhi*."

"I am so happy I have a Himalayan sister!" And he took his gold ring with a big ruby set in it from his finger. He placed it in Saina's palm with his hand over it. She said 'no' several times and tried to give it back to him, but Jhaveri kept on saying 'yes' and pressed it firmly into her palm. He won the match. The ring didn't fit her fingers, but she was persuaded by Jhaveri to keep it and have it adjusted later.

Then he met Ghosa and Mattu to bless them. Jhaveri gave Ghosa a jewelry box, which contained two earrings with a nose ring, a necklace, and a bracelet. The jewels contained gems set in twenty-two carat gold. A short congratulatory letter was also inside the box. The letter ended with one instruction in Hindi: Use these jewels for your son's college education.

Sakar was totally surprised. He took Jhaveri aside. They sat on a bench. "Such a generous gift!" he said to Jhaveri. "Your magnanimity is as wide as the seacoast you come from and as deep as the ocean."

"She deserves these gifts. You told me that her marriage was like the love marriage between Shakuntala and King Dushyanta. Any educated Indian would tell you that the ancient sacred *Gandharva Vivaha* is our modern love marriage. One silver lining to this love marriage is that there was no dowry involved. Imagine if Kanva, a poor sage, had to give a fat dowry. Most probably that's why he quickly accepted the notion of love marriage because he had to pay nothing in dowry."

Sakar couldn't resist laughing.

"Look, I am not trying to be funny. You and I know very well that in India women have been committing suicide either because they don't bring enough dowry or don't produce a male child. Shakuntala was fortunate that she didn't go through the tortures of the greedy in-laws. However, I am not trying to justify Dushyanta's cheating

on Shakuntala. Dushyanta cheated not only Shakuntala
but also the head queen he left behind in his capital. A
married man forcing a woman to have sex with him could
be considered a rape and her son a bastard!"

Jhaveri suddenly saw Sakar's face exhibiting sadness.
He misunderstood Sakar's sadness.

But Jhaveri continued, "Somehow Dushyanta came to
his senses. He finally recognized Shakuntala, and he recognized Bharata, not as her son, but their son. What if he
had recognized Shakuntala but considered Bharata as
some other man's son? An average person could have
raised that kind of question without realizing that no baby
is a bastard. Can you say that India's founder, Bharata,
was born as a bastard baby of Shakuntala?"

Sakar's eyes were wet and his head down. Jhaveri's
sunny analysis had enabled him to melt his own frozen
sense of inferiority for being of "bastard birth."

A few minutes later Bhagbati announced to the audience that it was time for sweets. All the guests sat in the
big yard on the *mandra* mats. Sakar and Jhaveri sat together.

When *samosas* and *chutneys* with big *laddus*, the traditional sweet balls for a celebration like this, were being
served, Sakar got up and thanked the audience. "I want to
say a few more things," he said loudly, facing the audience while clapping for attention. "This marriage was
made possible by Ghosa's *samosa* and *chutney*, which go
together like *pati* and *patni*. Mattu tasted them while he
was in the hospital. Now they are husband and wife like
samosa and chutney."

There was big laughter, which made it clear the audience understood his grammatical joke—*samosa* is masculine and *chutney* feminine and *patni* and *chutney* (*chatni*)
rhyme.

"In the hospital, while he was enjoying this hot spicy

snack, I was thinking of my guru's advice. Not to know a remedy is bad enough, but worse is to ignore a known remedy. Today he could not afford to ignore it. I appreciate his courage."

Sakar did not tell of his own remedy, getting Mattu's attackers jailed. Instead he said, "Let me explain what I mean by courage. Today Mussi and Saina were followed by Mattu and Ghosa, who broke the barriers of age-old tradition. Intercaste marriage is welcome. So is the right of a woman to marry and remarry, just like men—"

He was interrupted by applause from the audience.

Then he continued, "Now let me express my gratitude to our chief guest: Shri Jhaveri ji, Jiva bhai ji from Gujarat."

The audience applauded loudly. Sakar continued, "I learned a lot from Jiva bhai ji. Even from his daughter Vasanti I have learned so much that I am changed now. Do I look like a swami or a pandit?"

There was laughter all around. The attendees could see Sakar's white *khadi* outfit, not a single thread of ochre. One senior man said loudly, "For us you are always Pawan Kotwal's younger brother, Sakar Kotwal."

Sakar folded his palms to salute that older relative who had identified him as Pawan's younger brother. He felt clean and energized as if that man's authentication washed away his muddy past. "Let me tell you a little more about Vasanti," he said with a smile as he looked toward Jhaveri, who responded with a smile and nodded his consent. "Vasanti is likely to grow up to be an influential woman. She was influenced by the destruction of Gujarat's Somnath statue by Mahmud Ghaznavi. Once, after a Ganesha Puja by Bhagbati, she told him that Lord Shiva couldn't save himself because his son Ganesha failed to remove his father's obstacles. So, some of you might have noticed that Bhagbati didn't include Ganesha

Puja in today's marriage ceremony. It is this unknown Gujarati girl's influence on him, not the influence of the two well-known disbelievers of idolatry from Gujarat, namely Swami Dayananda and Mahatma Gandhi—"

He saw a hand raised in the audience. Sakar paused and said, "Yes, Altaf bhai sahab!"

Altaf said, "Ghaznavi was an insensitive looter. Fortunately, he didn't break Lord Buddha's statues in his own country, Afghanistan."

Nobody reacted to Altaf's statement as if they agreed with him. Then Altaf added, "I, too, feel that Saina and Ghosa broke religious barriers. They are lucky they were not in Pakistan. They could have been stoned to death."

At the mention of Pakistan, Sakar remembered what Vasanti had said in a school debate on partition when someone asked her if India and Pakistan would ever be able to walk together: "It's possible when the two countries realize that religion is a poisonous tree and its roots can be cut by secular axes."

Sakar looked around to see if anybody else had a question. He thought that someone could say that the Swami and the Mahatma of Gujarat destroyed their sacred Hindu tradition, namely idolatry. His audience, like other Pahari people, believed very strongly in idol worship. But nobody seemed to mind what Sakar just said about the worship of Ganesha.

He continued. "Like Jiva bhai's Vasanti, our Saina and Ghosa, too, are unrecognized revolutionaries. They cut some rotten roots of our religion and put a dent in the tradition strongly opposed to intercaste marriage. Two Rajput men walked with them. These ladies hit a nerve for our pandit, who refused to perform their intercaste marriage."

Sakar didn't mention that some had threatened to beat Lachchhu and even start a social boycott of the Kotwals when they found out that Lachchhu was going to be the cook instead of a *Sarola* Brahmin. Param Singh had already counter-threatened.

Sakar was following the Gandhian path. He was not in favor of Param's counter-threats of beating any trouble-maker. Nevertheless, Param was a formidable guest at the wedding and his presence was enough to keep the boycotters at bay.

After Sakar finished his speech, Param Singh announced that the lunch would be ready on time, at one p.m.

Sakar joined Jhaveri and requested that he accompany him to see his orchards. Jhaveri agreed. As the two began to step down, however, a man came from behind and faced Jhaveri while touching his feet. Jhaveri greeted him simply, "Namaste."

"Jhaveri ji, don't take Param seriously. I just checked with Lachchhu. Param's 1:00 P.M. means one-thirty," the man said with a smile.

Jhaveri also smiled. The man quickly went away.

"I feel embarrassed. That man touched my feet and I didn't even ask his name. I wonder why he contradicted Param Singh's announcement. Very funny!"

"Kartar Singh is here because he is Param Singh's friend. He is a rebel for good reason. I like him for what he did." Sakar could not resist telling Jhaveri Kartar Singh's story. They sat on a rock.

This is the story he told: Kartar Singh was from the Jaunsar area in the western corner of the Chaukhamba Range. Kartar Singh was the third brother. His wife, by their polyandry tradition, should have been the common wife of his two elder brothers. But he independently married another woman. That was allowed in their tradition. Nevertheless, his parents and brothers, and even the common wife of his two brothers, were very unhappy with him. The common wife and Kartar's wife began to quarrel over this matter. The common wife very much wanted Kartar to be her husband, even though he was seven years younger than she. Kartar always thought that she was his bhabhi, but she never thought that she was his sister-in-law for she thought Kartar was the most handsome among the three brothers.

One day the common wife beat Kartar's wife, and he decided to leave the joint family. He, with his wife, left their home in disgust and settled in Pauri.

Jhaveri was shocked by this story. "Did the common wife have children by her two husbands?"

"Yes. It's like the story of Draupadi. As the *Mahabharata* epic says, Draupadi was forced to accept the five Pandava brothers as her husbands. Then she had sons from each of them. And imagine the stupidity of the Pandava brothers! Each of them had their own independent wives after marrying Draupadi. Unfortunately, Kartar Singh's community authenticates their *parampara* by citing the Pandavas' marriage with Draupadi."

"They shouldn't cite Draupadi's polyandry case to justify their tradition. Her case is a story of rape. Draupadi's consent was for only one Pandava brother, Arjuna. I don't know how Vasanti would react to Kartar's story, a woman with two husbands in this day and age!" Jhaveri covered his eyes for a few seconds.

The words "two husbands" and "rape" struck a nerve for Sakar and he, too, covered his eyes but for different reasons. His mother had two husbands. Was she raped by his father?

He said to Jhaveri, "Let's go back to Shakuntala's case. What do you think would have happened if Shakuntala had married another man before Dushyanta recognized her as his wife?"

"Dushyanta was already married before he married her

at the Kanva Ashram. I think Shakuntala would have been justified if she had married another man later. Dushyanta was dead to her the moment he refused to recognize her."

Sakar thought of Saina. For her, too, the first husband was like a dead man, a divorced husband. She was justified in taking another man.

The word "dead" gave Sakar a sort of relief. He thought of his mother, a widow. He thought that the second husbands of Saina and his mother were not like the two husbands of Kartar's sister-in-law.

Then Jhaveri got up and remarked, "Forget about the stories of Kartar and Shakuntala. They are a matter of the past and not productive in our time. Your orchards look so beautiful! Let me see what else you are growing here."

Sakar's eyes lit up, and he led Jhaveri to the next orchard.

Chapter 42

After their tour of the orchards, Sakar and Jhaveri came to a stone bench under a cedar tree that was standing tall on the hump of a saddle. For irrigation, a little garden canal flowed from the saddle and passed through all the orchards on the slope. Its soothing noise attracted Jhaveri. He picked up its water in his cupped hands and washed his face.

"It's not glacial water. You can drink it," Sakar said.

Jhaveri collected the water in his cupped hands and sipped a couple of times.

"So refreshing!" Jhaveri remarked.

Then both sat on the bench.

In front of the bench Jhaveri saw a little section that had *jhangoru* plants. "Is this a variety of *bajra*?" He pointed toward the plants.

"It does look like a variety of sorghum. We call it *jhangoru*. We eat it as a substitute for rice. You will taste it today."

"How did you get *jhangoru* here?" Jhaveri asked with a smile.

Sakar couldn't think of a proper answer, except this one: "According to my lama guru's folk etymology, the word *jhangoru* comes from the name for China:

Zhongguo. Thus *jhangoru* means 'of China.' Many crops here are of Chinese origin: lychees, loquats, soya beans."

"I have eaten lots of lychees in Dehradun."

"You can see our lychee trees from here." He pointed toward a row of lychee trees below in his huge orchard. "My lama guru's guess is that these lychees came to us via Tibet. But the Tibetan climate is not suitable for lychee trees. They came here from a different route."

Jhaveri moved his eyes from the lychee trees toward the Chaukhamba. "Your guru must have thought of Tibet because it is just over the Chaukhamba Range. What a panoramic view! Put all the shiny jewels of the world together and they will not match the brilliance of this Himalayan roof of the world." He turned his face toward Sakar and said, "You are lucky to be born here!"

Sakar replied, "The credit goes to Mother Nature. I think all parts of Prithivi Mata are beautiful. You, too, are lucky to be born on the sea coast. So beautiful, and so useful!"

"At some point perhaps someone will attempt *lychee diplomacy* to unite China and India, dig a tunnel from here and travel underground all the way to China via Tibet."

They stood up and made their way across the orchard. Jhaveri took a couple of deep breaths. "It smells so good here. It must be from these orange trees," Jhaveri remarked.

"Yes, this is the season of orange blossoms."

"Let's sit down here."

They sat on a wooden bench and Jhaveri looked around. Then suddenly he noticed a bee on Sakar's head.

"I see a bee sitting on your head, Sakar bhai," Jiva bhai exclaimed, raising his hand to make it fly away.

"Don't be panicked by its presence. It will fly away. It must be from our beehive. We are used to them."

"You have a beehive?"

"Balram bhai and Murti bhabhi have one. It's very common here to have a built-in hive in your house. Balram bhai wants me to include beekeeping in my utilitarian gardening plan. He thinks every house in Pauri should have a built-in hive. Lachchhu is in the beekeeping business. He sells a lot of honey."

"Beekeeping is good business for landless people. The bees can own any land. A beekeeper needs to own no land and still gets honey, and he pays bees nothing for their hard work."

"Bees teach us borderlessness and a good work ethic."

"That's why that bee landed on your head. Your head is no land!" Jiva bhai joked as he stared at the bee still sitting on Sakar's head.

Sakar laughed.

The two Gandhians didn't even think of smashing the little bug with a slap.

Sakar said, "Balram bhai compares bees with women. They work harder than their male counterparts. Yet they are abused. 'No bee in the hive must be hurt' is his advice to us."

"It's strange. Honey is considered sacred, but not the honey-makers. I haven't heard yet from any priest that the bees are holy mothers, like holy cows," Jhaveri said as he looked at the bee sitting still on Sakar's head.

"So, you were right when you said in one of your lectures in a college, 'It's time to consider panditology an illogical scholarship.' How did you name the pandit business as panditology?"

"I got this idea from the bogus science of astrology. Pandits would say, if you worship this god your obstacles will disappear now, or if you worship this goddess you will be rich very soon. The knowledge created by the pandits lacks reasoning."

"That's true. Some relatives refused our invitation as soon as they found out that Lachchhu, not a Sarola Brahmin, was going to cook the food."

"Wait a minute!" Jhaveri interrupted. "I hear drums and see a line of people on a trail moving toward that hilltop across the way. See? Over there!"

"Yes, I do see. Those are dhol-damau drummers," Sakar responded in an unconcerned tone and looking the other way.

However, Jhaveri continued his inquiry. "But why is a man behind them dragging a goat by a rope? I am sure you know why!"

Sakar felt compelled to explain. "They are going to worship Devi and her son Lord Ganesha. Do you see a little temple at the high end of the trail?"

"Yes."

"So, they are going there to sacrifice that animal in front of the statue of the angry goddess?"

"Angry goddess! I am angry at those Paharis who can't understand that a statue is a statue. They are dumber than that dumb statue. Can't you stop them?"

"I wish I could stop this cruel act. The hilltop looks very close, but the loopy trail takes more time because it disappears partly in the currents of the creek water gushing down from that mountain. From here the distance is about one mile, and those people are coming from Godhar village, which is on the other side of the mountain. The creek is not on their way."

"You mean there is no way to stop them?"

"Suppose we reach the temple and the ceremony is already over. Or suppose you and I or someone else reach there before the sacrifice and try to stop it. There would be serious opposition. The temple priest will argue that animal sacrifice is our *parampara* since Vedic times, and—"

"What is this stupid *parampara*?" Jhaveri interrupted.

"Tradition, or *parampara,* is the cultural hard wiring of human behavior. It's very hard to cut these wires. So, they will sacrifice the animal. This tradition is long and will continue. If you physically try to stop the slaughter, you will be shoved away."

"I have an idea. What if Vasanti comes here with her classmates and surrounds the temple to block the entry of the sacrificial animal. This could be a sort of grassroots movement to cut the cultural hard wiring of Paharis."

"In theory, this kind of *satyagraha* of Vasanti would be a powerful tool to cut that cultural wiring. But I am afraid of the safety of the girls. What if someone throws rocks at them? Did you know that some temples don't allow women if they are in their menstrual cycle?" The goddess temple was no exception.

Jhaveri placed his hands around his ears and lowered his head with closed eyes.

After a short pause, Sakar began to speak. "Some of our folks were expecting Bhagbati to start our ceremony with Ganesha worship in the morning. One of our relatives had already brought some fresh cow dung to make the Ganesha image, but Bhagbati refused to do the ceremony."

"What do you mean? A Ganesha image of fresh cow dung?"

"The fresh dung is molded into a mini-pyramid, about three inches tall. Then a few *durva* grass leaves are pinned on its top. This Ganesha symbol is considered very sacred and it removes all obstacles sooner than other kinds of idols."

"The traditional myth says that Ganesha ji was created by his mother Parvati out of her body's dirt. The dirt was not cow dung, though," said Jhaveri.

"Parvati means Pahari woman. She can do anything." Sakar smiled.

"I understand your humor. No offense, but no Pahari woman can produce a being out of fresh cow dung. I don't understand why these two Paharis, Parvati and Ganesha, couldn't remove the plight of their own Pahari people!" Jhaveri said seriously.

"And then you see their temples throughout India where the pandits are fooling even many college-educated Indians."

"That proves my point. Panditology lacks reasoning. Believing in temple magic is disbelieving in human endeavors. My mother believed in such temples and their pandits, but Vasanti doesn't visit these temples. For her, every bow one makes in a holy place is a lie."

"If you meet Pandit Bharat Ram, ask him why is it that devotees bow to Ganesha and not to his mouse who brought the lord to their temple? Why don't they feed some *laddus* to that mouse?"

Jhaveri laughed at Sakar's joke.

"I am laughing, but I should feel sorry for those people. This myth teaches us that big people ride on the backs of small people and have fun at their expense. Rich people's pleasures are produced by poor people."

Jhaveri now looked quite serious. Sakar couldn't guess the reason of his momentary silence. He wondered why Jhaveri closed his eyes, pressing them with his thumb and forefinger as if in pain. To keep his mood light Sakar engaged him again in the Ganesha mythology.

"So, I would rather advise Bharat Ram not to believe that a mouse could be the vehicle of fat-bellied Ganesha with an elephant head," he said with a smile. "Now suppose Lord Ganesha is sitting without his mouse in a *puja*. The mouse is now without the obstacle of carrying the heavy weight of the lord. But then that poor animal must face other obstacles alone, like snakes, foxes, and hawks. Can't he request that his boss stop the plight of his fellow mice? They are even a staple in the diet of some human societies!'"

Jhaveri was still serious.

However, Sakar continued, "Vasanti would have liked this joke. And another one, too. I told Bharat Ram once, not about mice but about a man with two wives. I asked Bharat Ram, 'You performed that man's two weddings. Each wedding started with the worship of Lord Ganesha. How is it that the lord created more obstacles for the first wife by giving her husband the second wife?' His answer was the lord himself has two wives! I didn't want to argue with him as my lama guru had cautioned: Don't argue with people who are not important to you, unless you think that could make international news!"

Jhaveri said, "Vasanti should have listened to the advice of your Guru ji. She frequently argues with her girlfriends that holy men exploited women by creating divine myths. She said, 'How could a man with more wives become holier! God is a joker who faked the monkey law of polygamy.' Ba always thought that Vasanti was talking nonsense with her classmates!"

"Vasanti is right, Jiva bhai. It's true, men priests have authored scriptures to their advantage. All scriptures are full of male mythology. Male mythology is like a canal whose water irrigates panditology's gardens."

"Vasanti hopes that eventually college girls discard junk male mythology. Our modern English-style colleges don't proselytize panditology. Vasanti wants to meet Pandit Nehru for whom panditology is not the right source of knowledge for India's modernization."

"India's complete modernization will be confirmed when no Hindu puts one single drop of holy cow urine in his mouth!"

As Sakar opened his mouth, Jhaveri had a good laugh and looked at the bee on Sakar's head, which still had not moved away.

Suddenly he got up, fear in his eyes. "A crocodile, Sakar! Over there!" he shouted, pointing with his index finger.

Sakar calmed him down quickly with a smile. "It's not a crocodile but a giant lizard. It is of crocodile size but harmless to humans. In Garhwali, we call it *gaulu*. This lizard shies away from humans. That's why it disappeared quickly down in the bushes. The dangerous animals here are bears and tigers. We are used to them, but I still hope they are not around."

"You really live in the wilderness, which is highly enjoyable but also terrifying."

"Look at the northeast corner the highest peak of the Garhwal Himalayas. Do you see it there?" Sakar tried to divert his attention, pointing.

"Yes, it is distinct from the other peaks," he responded.

"It's the Nanda Devi peak. Close to twenty-six thousand feet in height from sea level. It's named after Goddess Nanda, whom folks believe is also Ganesha's mother Parvati and lives on that peak. In her honor, there is a sacred festival, *Nanda Devi Raj Jat*. It occurs once in twelve years."

"I never heard of this festival!"

"This festival requires a four-horned ram, which is worshipped but not sacrificed. The Nanda worship starts at Nauti, a village near Karna Prayag. After the worship the devotees force that ram to travel almost to the base of that mountain. This travel is called the Royal Travel, or *Raj Jat*. This is the local pronunciation of *Raj Yatra*. After additional rituals, the ram is given freedom to roam around as long as he lives."

Jhaveri slapped his forehead with his palm and said, "Do you understand that poor ram would not survive at that altitude because of the bone-breaking cold! It's stupid to believe that up there a goddess will keep him safe. You Paharis are insensitive to consider such a cruel act worship of a goddess that never existed. That reminds me of the ancient Greeks who worshipped their goddess, Athena, at Mount Olympus. They sacrificed animals to please her. When they adopted Christianity, they abandoned this sacrifice. It is so strange that you Paharis are still torturing animals in this day and age to please your Athena, your Goddess Nanda!"

"Mattu had a ram that looked like it was four-horned. In addition to two regular horns, the animal had two small growths that looked like two more little horns. At first Mattu was somewhat tepid about requests for his ram, but then he became bold. He refused to donate that ram for this festival. Fortunately, this festival comes only every twelve years. The local pandits do this ritual during warm weather."

Jhaveri continued, "Panditology creates gods to serve its diverse self-serving needs and interests in different places. The same god who loves sacrifices in your area hates them in our area. Sorry if I am being too judgmental, but I think that the people of the Garhwal Himalayas must adopt the Gujarat model of non-violence. I am pleased that the Garhwali food to be served today will be non-violent food."

"I believe a time will come when the future generations of the world come closer to the Gujarat model. This model will also help animal welfare. Gandhi's name is the best name for this model of animal welfare!" Sakar predicted.

"But don't think that our Gujarat model is flawless. Look, how do we get our staple food? By violence. Gujarati farmers plow their fields with oxen. Not only in Gujarat but everywhere in India, farmers whip oxen. I have seen whip marks and bleeding bruises on the backs of oxen. Panditology wants protection of Gau Mata but allows her male children to be castrated and later tortured in the fields. Just imagine somebody castrating and beating your nephew or leaving him alone at the base of Nanda Devi!"

Sakar commented, "What bothers me is that Nehru ji never said anything against slaughtering defenseless animals at the temples."

After clearing his throat again, Jhaveri said in gruff voice, "Well, Pandit Nehru is also a Himalayan Brahmin like you. Even though his parents moved to Allahabad from Kashmir, they weren't vegetarians."

"You are from Gujarat. If you see animal sacrifices in Pahari temples, you will call them butcher houses, places of *sacred slaughter*."

Jhaveri coughed with a disdain. "Yes, that's not acceptable to us in Gujarat."

"I know. Gujarat is under the heavy influence of Jainism and Vaishnavism. So, they have no concept of sacred slaughter. And here we have the best-known temple of Lord Vishnu but no influence of your kind of Vaishnavism." Sakar shrugged.

"Do you mean the temple of Lord Badrinath? I never heard of sacrifice at that temple."

"But there are others where Paharis offer sacrifice. But some Paharis do change. Mattu is an example. His goats were frequently stolen for temple sacrifice. Now, due to Ghosa's influence, he is out of the goat business. You have to sacrifice at least one goat at the temple or shrine of the local god or goddess to celebrate a marriage, but this is a goat-less marriage."

"You mean godless marriage."

They both laughed.

It was close to one p.m., when Jhaveri reminded Sakar, "Well, should we slowly move toward the gathering now?"

"I trust that man, Kartar Singh. So let's stay here a little more."

Chapter 43

A little after one, Jhaveri heard music. "Do you hear the *dholak*?"

"It's time to join the wedding entertainment," Sakar responded.

Hurriedly they got up and began to walk up the trail. Suddenly, Jiva bhai stopped. "I left my bag down there," he said.

"Do you remember where?"

"No!"

"Never mind. I will get it and you can proceed ahead. I will be back."

Sakar ran down toward the orchards.

Jhaveri saw Param Singh coming toward him. "I was looking for you to dance with us before the food is served. Lachchhu is sorry for his slow cooking," Param said with folded hands."

"To be honest with you, I have lost my appetite."

"I am sure you would like our special Pahari dishes."

"It's not your dishes but your animal sacrifice. See that Devi temple over there! We failed to take any action to stop that sacrifice."

"Jhaveri ji, I will not fail you."

"But that cannot be undone now."

"I mean for any future slaughter. We will save a little over one hundred sacrifices per year—"

"A *little*, eh?"

"I assure you, I will break the statue of the goddess."

"Please don't do that. I am a Gujarati. Mahmud Ghaznavi gave us a costly lesson when he destroyed the golden statue of Lord Somnath. Most Gujarati Hindu leaders didn't learn the lesson, but Swami Dayanand and Mahatma Gandhi were exceptions."

"The Pahari people, too, are like Gujaratis. They love temples and their statues. If you don't want me to destroy that goddess, then I promise not to be another Mahmud Ghaznavi." Param held Jiva bhai's hand to escort him up the trail.

Sakar came up running and handed Jhaveri his handbag. Then they joined the crowd in the front yard. The guests were being entertained by a *baddi* and a *badini*. The *baddi* (the male player of the *dholak* drum), clad in his loose red kurta and gray pajamas, was quite muscular and tall. He looked taller because of his long hair assembled and raised spherically in the form of a pyramid-shaped topknot on the center of his head. A saffron band tied between his ears and his topknot kept his *baddi* status distinct. With *ghunghrus* (anklets) on her bare feet, his young beautiful wife (*badini*) was dancing, acting out their Garhwali song. Her multi-colored bandana, matching her colorful *ghagri* (long Pahari skirt) and frequently flowing upwards in whirls, made the audience clap. Unlike higher-caste women, she didn't observe the custom of *ghunghat* (veil) to cover her face in front of men. Like other married women assembled here, however, she had a red bindi on her forehead and a nose ring. Her wrists were full of multi-colored *churis* (bangles).

Sakar explained to Jhaveri, "Though uninvited, these musicians know well ahead of time where a celebration is to take place. People welcome them. They are untouchables, but they are treated slightly better than other untouchables because it is believed that Lord Shiva favored them. The lord wanted the males to grow beards, mustaches, and topknots to distinguish them from other untouchables who earn their living by manual labor rather than by music."

"What is the song about?"

"It's a love song about how a young woman and a young man fell in love secretly. They were not compatible because their castes didn't match. So one day they eloped and got married in an Arya Samaj temple of Punjab and never returned."

"A very simple love story with a good end." Jhaveri didn't expect some *Kamasutra*-style touches in a Pahari folk story, not even a single instance of kissing and so no possibility of acting it out. Nevertheless, he was impressed not only by the musical composition but also by the Arya Samaj that was established by a Gujarati, namely Swami Dayananda, who cut some of the hard wiring in the Hindu caste system. He tipped the musicians with a number of rupees. The *baddi* fell on the feet of Jhaveri ji.

The entertainment halted when the lunch was announced at two-thirty. Nobody seemed bothered by the delay. They understood that Lachchhu, despite the assistance of Murti and Uttara, had never before cooked so many dishes for so many people. Moreover, everyone had eaten enough *laddus* and potato *pakoras* along with waterless milk tea earlier.

All the guests sat in the big yard on the *mandra* mats made of dry wheat stems. Sakar and Jhaveri sat together. When Murti came out of the kitchen, she noticed that the *baddi* and *badini*, as expected by the tradition, sat quietly in a corner, maintaining sufficient distance from the guests. She moved toward the musicians and requested that they sit with other guests. Apprehensive of possible disruption due to their untouchable status, they flatly refused. Instead, they moved further back into the corner, thus refusing nonverbally as well.

Murti realized that her coaxing them would not work. She quickly left the couple there and walked to Sakar. She explained the situation to him. Sakar agreed with her and together they made their way to the musician couple to speak with them, but they refused again. Then Sakar dragged the *baddi,* who was laughing as he was being dragged, very gently. The *badini* agreed to eat later with Murti.

With much hesitation, the *baddi* agreed to sit with Sakar. Tears came in his eyes when Jiva bhai patted him on the back while praising him. "You remind me of our Gujarati folk musicians." Sakar's eyes were also teary as he was overwhelmed by the unprecedented courage of Murti. The *baddi* couldn't utter a word, but he folded his palms and bowed to Jhaveri. He was unable to absorb the shock of the honor of sitting and eating with a higher-caste guest from Gujarat and a local Brahmin.

Sakar also complimented him. "Gujarat's folk music is so rich, so fascinating. There is nothing like their *dandiya* and *ras* folk dances," he said to the *baddi*. The *baddi* had never heard of these foreign-sounding Indian dances! The trio became quiet as volunteers placed leaf plates in front of them. Just then Murti came out and whispered into the ears of the *baddi*. He nodded his head and got up. Murti led him to the kitchen.

The *baddi* was surprised to see the *badini* working there without the ankle bells on her feet. Before starting his work of cleaning pots, he whispered into her ears, "Should I compose a song that a Sarola Brahmin was replaced by an untouchable?"

His wife whispered in reply, "No. Just be quiet. Nobody will welcome us if you sing your stupid song! And Murti ji would be in trouble."

So, the *baddi*'s revolutionary song about three untouchables, one of them a woman, working in the kitchen of Brahmins would go unheard.

After all other guests received leaf plates, Kartar and Param began to serve the *urad dal* pakoras topped with sesame seeds, the sacred food to begin the lunch for marriage. Harakh Singh and Banki followed them with other food items.

Kartar told Jhaveri that Lachchhu had cooked the whole lunch. Jhaveri began to taste each unfamiliar dish like *jhangoru*, *chainsu*, *kaphli*, etc. He was expecting the classy Pahari dishes like *basmati* rice with whole *tor dal*, not the dishes that were part of poor people's diet like Lachchhu.

As soon as Jhaveri chewed a morsel of the dry *jhangoru* mixed with the soupy *chainsu*, he asked Sakar, "Do you eat basmati with *chainsu*?"

"*Chainsu* would be an insult to basmati. This distinguished rice is eaten with distinguished beans, whole *tor* or whole *urad*. *Chainsu* is made out of ground *urad* beans and that lowers its status to be a basmati partner."

He smiled. "It happens. A sociologist told me that he was thinking of introducing a new scholarly field called *Food Dialectology* and applying it to India's food diversity. For example, an *urad dal* derivative is your Pahari *chainsu*, not sugared. But the same ground *urad* derivative is soupy and sugared *dal* in Gujarat. The same foods but their serving styles vary. And there are so many shades of the same food, like those two different food languages, or dialects, derived from a common parent, *urad dal*."

Pausing momentarily, he continued with a smile, "Sakar ji, are you missing Gujarati food."

"You are asking a lion if he is missing meat."

Jhaveri laughed. He said, "You know, meat is rare in Gujarat. I never tasted any meat, but Muslims are famous for meat dishes in Ahmedabad. I have been told that their meat dishes are slightly different, though."

"Yes, your sociologist friend might consider varieties of meat dishes for his idea of food dialectology. He might divide Indian food not only by geographical dialects but social dialects as well. I don't know what the difference is between the Muslim-style spicy chicken called *Murgh-Mussalam* and the Hindu-style chicken, but I should know. Like any Pahari Brahmin, I was raised a non-vegetarian and ate chicken. No vegetarian dish can match the taste of any meat dish," Sakar said with a smile. After swallowing another morsel of dry *jhangoru* mixed with *chainsu,* he continued, "Our Paharis don't cook as good as the Muslims of Lucknow. The Muslim vegetarian dishes are as good as their meat dishes. So, my nephew Dr. Harshpat has hired a Lucknow Muslim cook."

"Brahmins can eat the best food by breaking the religious barriers," he said while sucking his peppery saliva. He was missing sugar, which was not only a good for suppressing the taste of hot chilies but an essential additive to Gujarati food.

"Gandhi ji would have liked to eat Lachchhu's food— less frying, fewer spices, less salt, and more roughage."

Jhaveri coughed and then put a small morsel of *jhangoru* with *chainsu* into his reluctant mouth.

Harakh Singh brought some yellow fried vegetable rice. "This is *biranji*, meaty but meatless," he said. He poured several scoops on their plates. "Murti didi prepared it."

Sakar tasted it. "True. Meaty without meat. Murti bhabhi's special dish, vegetable *biranji*."

"I wouldn't know what meaty *biranji* is, but it's very

spicy, chunky and hot," Jhaveri remarked as he ate some by mixing it with the soupy spinach *kaphli*.

Param Singh brought another round of *jhangoru*. Balram followed him with *kaphli*.

"No, thanks! I am full." Jhaveri spread his palms over his leaf plate. But Param Singh insisted he take more.

Sakar intervened in Garhwali, "*Param, we ka gaula lag gi syu jhangoru. Bas!* (Param, that *jhangoru* is stuck in his throat. Stop!)"

Param didn't serve him any more of that dish. Jhaveri understood only the last word *bas* and its instant effect. He smiled to hide his disgust.

Just as the guests were being served the sweet dish of *halwa*, the last celebratory item, a three-member team of dhol-damau and bagpipe players appeared in the yard and started the music with an auspicious song in Garhwali: "*Siri Badarinatha ji, jhamako! Jai Jai bola Jiba Jhaberi ji, jhaaamako!* (Lord Badrinath, a joyful dance! Pronounce victory and victory to Jiva Jhaveri ji, and dance!)" The damau player sang partially, "*He Jhaberi ji, jhaaamako.*" The dhol player sang the next line: "*Gujrat ko maha dani jauhari* (the big benevolent jeweler of Gujarat)." The damau player repeated, "*He Jhaberi ji, jhaaamako.*"

Mussi, Saina, Bhagbati, Uttara, Altaf, and Banu began to dance, holding each other's hand and moving circularly around Jhaveri, singing the rhythmic dance word '*jhamako*' with the damau player.

Sakar was moved. He got up and grabbed Murti's hand, "Come on, bhabhi! Let us dance!"

Sakar remembered how Murti refused to wear a veil even when her mother-in-law insisted. But so strict was her mother-in-law that dancing with males was out of the question for Murti, an example of how women have placed roadblocks in the forward march of women.

But Murti didn't show any hesitation to dance with her brother-in-law. They joined the dancers, singing with them '*jhamako.*' Other Kotwals and guests began to clap, singing with the damau player just that one word: "*Jhaaamako.*"

That dance-song, which was only offered for community celebrities, was a surprise tribute. Jhaveri had no idea of this secret plan to honor him as a celebrity of their community. He was highly impressed by the bagpiper, who was not from Scotland but a local Himalayan man and so overcoming the barrier of combining two diverse folk traditions.

He expressed this sentiment to Sakar. "I like this fusion model of the highlanders." The bagpiper wore pants and a shirt with a round cap. The drummers wore small *achkans*, jackets like long Jodhpurs, and tight slate-gray pajamas. They also wore white khadi caps. All of them had red tilaks on their foreheads.

After the dance and music ended, Jhaveri thanked the musicians. He gave each of them ten rupees out of his handbag. The dhol player, older than his partners, cried as he touched Jhaveri's feet. Then with his folded palms he said in Hindi, "*Thakur ji, hamko itna paisa kabhi kisi se na mila* (Lord! We never received this much from anyone)."

Jhaveri understood the plight of the lowest castes. He hugged the three musicians one by one. While Jhaveri was talking to them, Bhagbati took Sakar aside. "Chacha ji, Uttara and I have a gift for you," he said in a very low voice.

"What gift?" Sakar asked with a smile.

Bhagbati whispered in his ear.

Sakar heard the news and instantly hugged Bhagbati. He speedily went to the musicians and said to the dhol player, "I just learned that I am going to be a nana. Uttara is expecting her first child. I am going to name him or her 'Jiva' to honor Jhaveri."

The dhol drummer instantly and very quietly passed the news to the other two musicians and they began to play. The bagpiper began to bloat his mouth and pump air into his bagpipe. The dhol player sang, '*Siri Badarinatha ji! Jhaaamako! Jai Jai bola parbati Jiba, jhaamako!*' (Lord Badarinath! Dance! Speak victory and victory to the hilly Jiva, *jhaaamako!*)

'*He parbati Jiba, jhaaamako!*' the damau drummer sang, and Bhagbati and Sakar sang, too, while dancing with tears in their eyes.

Jhaveri saw them with stunned looks. He wanted to make sense of why they were dancing and crying while speaking his name. The music continued as other men began to join the dance, but Jhaveri remained speechless and remained standing just where he was. "I am an outsider, anyway," he thought.

ॐ

Two days later as the sun was rising and he was ready to leave for the bus at the Pauri bus station, Bhagbati showed up to accompany him and carry his luggage. Slowly they topped the rise where the trail met with the bus road.

Below where they stood they saw the Devi temple. It was completely charred and still some smoke billowed from the ruin.

"Who burned the temple? Param Singh promised me he would not harm it!" Jhaveri said with a look of disgust on his face.

"Param Singh has nothing to do with this temple's destruction," Bhagbati said with a smile. "Saina and Ghosa did it. They heard from Sakar Chacha ji that you were upset when you saw a goat being dragged to that temple and you felt helpless."

"So, did he ask them to burn the temple down?"

"No. Those two women feel indebted to you."

Jhaveri took a deep breath and sat down on a rock.

Bhagbati also sat beside him, placing the luggage on the ground. "Are you sad?" he asked Jhaveri.

"Give my thanks to those two Pahari women. They are my little sisters. Let me know if they are in legal trouble for arson. Is Sakar bhai able to help them?"

"When he saw the temple in flames, he decided to start his law practice!"

"What? Literally his re-incarnation! He didn't tell me about his decision."

"He didn't tell Uttara and me either."

"Then how did you know?"

"He was out in the yard shouting mantras while watching the temple's raging flames at midnight. We came out and saw him chanting the first Vedic mantra: 'I praise Lord Fire, the first priest.' He repeated the mantra again and again: *Agnimīḷe purohitam*. In his delirium, he also said, 'I will start my law practice again. No Dehradun job, no utilitarian gardening.'"

"Did he say anything about me?"

"Not a word. Not about us either. Just those sentences."

"Strange!"

"Then he quickly left. Maybe he had to run to toilet."

"I thought *jhangoru* caused his dysentery."

"No. He should not have eaten those green apples."

"By the way, how are those two women reacting?"

"They are happy because this is revenge of a sort, I guess."

"Revenge? Against whom?" Jhaveri looked curious.

"For the untouchables and women in their menstrual cycle."

"You mean, they were not allowed to enter the temple?"

"Right. Saina and Ghosa had failed to persuade the priest."

"And then my desire to stop the sacrifice ignited their anger!"

"Undoubtedly. You are their big brother from Gujarat."

"My Vasanti must meet these two new revolutionary relatives."

"The sooner, the better. Chacha ji would be very happy."

"Now let's move on so you can catch the bus."

Bhagbati picked up the luggage and placed it on his shoulders again, and they left the narrow winding trail to join the bus road a few yards above.

After a half-mile walk, they finally reached the bus stand. The bus was on time. Jhaveri entered the bus and took a window seat. Bhagbati handed the luggage to the bus driver, who placed it up on the bus roof.

As soon as the driver started the bus engine, Jhaveri peeped out from his window and yelled, "Bhagvati, will you ask the temple priest if he ever saw the temple goddess menstruating?"

Bhagbati remained quiet as he placed his palms behind his ears and pushed them forward, but still he had no success in hearing over roar of the old engine.

The End

Author's Note

This novel is based on interviews with the individuals mentioned below (all interviews were done in Hindi and then reconstructed in English).

Bimal, Ghosa's son, was married to Jiva, the daughter of Bhagbati and Uttara. During his formative years, Bimal learned Sanskrit from Sakar. His knowledge of Sanskrit enabled him to become a college professor of ancient Indian history and religion. Jiva became a gynecologist with the help of her aunts, Dr. Prachi Kotwal Bharadvaj and Dr. Marci Jacob Kotwal. She participated in India's family planning. Information provided by Bimal and Jiva made up the bulk of this novel.

Kusla, Lachchhu's son, became a school teacher known as Upali Kausalyayan, a name he adopted when he converted to the neo-Buddhism of Dr. Bhimrao Ambedkar, an untouchable and chief framer of India's new constitution. Along with his wife, Kusla became active in the Dalit movement of India's untouchables.

Binti, Param Singh's daughter, became a zoologist working with India's wildlife preservation program.

Vasanti, Jhaveri's daughter, ran her father's jewelry business.

Sameera, Hussain's daughter, and her husband Gautam retired as veterinarians. They both acted as reviewers.

Glossary

Achha: Okay, good

Achha tamasha: Good show

Ahimsa: Non-violence

Alu gutka: Fried spicy potato balls

Arti, arati: Worship with lighted candles

Arya Samaj: A branch of Hinduism (literally: Aryan Society)

Ashram: Retreat

Atman: Self

Aurangzeb: A Moghul Emperor of India (1618 AD to 1707 AD)

Ba: Mother (Gujarati)

Baba: Father, a holy man

Baddi: The male folk musician in the Garhwal Himalayas

Badini: The female folk musician in the Garhwal Himalayas

Bakra: He-goat

Bakri: She-goat

Bal: A sweet

Bali: Animal sacrifice

Barat: Bridegroom's party

Bas: Enough!

Basundi: A creamy milk pudding

Bater: A kind of quail

Ben: Sister (in Gujarati)

Beta: Son

Beti: Daughter

Bhabhi: Senior brother's wife

Bhagavad Gita, Gita: The eighteen chapters of the Sanskrit epic *Mahabharata* containing the philosophical dialogue between Krishna and Arjuna (literally: *Divine Song*)

Bhai: Brother

Bhainchod: Sister fucker

Bhains: female water-buffalo

Bhaiya: Same as *Bhai*, used as an affectionate term

Bhajan: Devotional song

Bhang: Cannabis

Bharat: India's name

Bhari roti: Fried stuffed flat bread

Bhat: Cooked rice

Bhiksha: Alms

Bhula: Younger brother

Bhuli: Younger sister

Bhusa: Garbage

Bhusu: Snacks of Gujarat

Biranji: Pilaf, biryani

Biryani: Pilaf

Chai: Tea

Chainsu: A dish made with crushed or ground black beans

Chat: A spicy snack

Chaukidar: Guard, office boy, peon

Chutney: Chutney, a sour or sweet spicy dip

Chhaunka: Spicy seasoning in hot oil

Dada: Father's father

Dadi: Father's mother

Dal: Beans

Dakshina: Cash gift for priestly service

Damau: An Indian timpani drum

Dandi: A litter to carry humans

Dari: Hand-made mat or rug

Darshan: View

Daru: Liquor

Desi: Indian, any Indian not from the Himalayan region

Dev Bhumi: Land of gods

Dhaba: A small street restaurant

Dhol: An Indian bass drum

Dholak: A small barrel-like drum with two heads

Dhoti: An unsewn cloth used by men as a lower garment tied around the waist

Didi: Older sister

Digchi: A round cooking pot

Dipavali: Festival of Light, same as *Diwali* (literally: line of lamps)

Dom: A person from the lower castes (a derogatory word used for the untouchables)

Dupatta: Scarf

Dukkha, dukha: Sorrow, pain

Gahath: Horse gram beans

Gaja: Elephant

Gandharva Vivaha: "Love marriage" with no formal wedding ceremony

Ganga jal: Ganges water

Gayatri: A Vedic mantra used mostly for daily prayers

Ghagri: Long loose skirt

Ghat: The part of a river bank reserved for rituals or sacred bathing

Ghunghru: Anklet (tied on a dancer's ankles)

Gita: Same as *Bhagavad Gita*

Godan, go dan: Ceremonial gift of a cow

Gopi: Lord Krishna's cow-girl friends

Gori: White woman, a woman with light complexion

Gotra: Lineage, clan

Graha shanti: Planetary peace (via worship)

Graha puja: Planet worship

Gulab: Rose

Gyaan mat: research opinion

Hawaldar: Sergeant

Harijan: God's person, the name used by Mohandas Gandhi for the untouchables (Dalits)

Holi: A festival of colors

Homa: Fire ritual

Jan mat: public opinion

Jai, *Jay, Jaya*: Victory

Jamadar: Janitor

Jhanda Mela: Flag Fair (organized by the Sikhs of Dehradun)

Jhangoru: A Himalayan millet

Jeth: Husband's older brother

Jogis, jogi: a male mendicant, an ordinary monk (derived from *Yogi*)

Jogini: a female mendicant, an ordinary nun (derived from *Yogini*)

Kamchor: Delinquent, freeloader

Kari, kadi: Yogurt curry

Khadi: Homespun coarse cloth

Kamasutra: A treatise on love in Sanskrit

Kanya dan: Giving away the daughter at her wedding

Khadi: Homespun coarse cloth

Khunkhri: A Himalayan dagger

Kshatriya: The second *Varna* or group of the class system, a person belonging to this class

Kujaga: Genitalia (literally: bad place)

Kurta: Tunic, a long loose shirt

Laddu: A ball-shaped sweet

Lakshmana: The third brother of King Rama in the *Ramayana*

Lassi: Sweet yogurt drink

Ling, linga: Lord Shiva's creative symbol (literally: phallus)

Linga puja: Phallic worship

Lingura: Edible ferns grown in swamps

Lumru: Penis

Lwekhuru: A dish made with heated coagulated blood

Machan: A sitting place in a tree made with its branches and ropes and used for hunting

Mahabharata: The ancient Sanskrit epic containing the story of the Kuru dynasty and Krishna

Mahant: Head of a temple or monastery

Mahmud Ghaznavi: An Afghan king (971 AD to 1030 AD)

Mandra, mandru: Mat made with dry stems of wheat

Mangli: A girl born in an astrologically determined position of Mars (*Mangala*)

Masala chai: Spicy tea

Mata: Mother

Mashak baja: Bagpipe

Meghadutam: An ancient poetic work by Kalidasa

Mirch: Chilies

Mitha bhat: Sweet fried rice cooked with nuts, raisins, etc.

Mota seth: Senior wealthy man (in Gujarati)

Mukhwas: A spicy mix chewed at the end of a meal (Gujarati)

Muhurt: Auspicious time to perform any happy ceremony

Mungphali: Peanuts

Murabba: Jam

Murgh-Mussalam: A spicy chicken dish

Namaste: Greeting for welcome and farewell (literally: a bow to you)

Nana: Mother's father

Nani: Mother's mother

Nastika: Atheist

Nautanki: Hindi folk theater

Nagara: A drum

Nirakara, nirankar, nirakar: No-form God

Niyoga: Surrogate parenthood in which the father is other than the husband by consent

Pahari: A native of the hills, Himalayan people

Pakora: Spicy fritters deep fried in a batter

Pan: A popular spicy chew wrapped in a *pan* leaf

Panchgava: A sacred drink made of five ingredients—cow urine, cow milk, cow ghee, cow yogurt, honey

Paṇi-grahaṇa: "Hand-holding" of the bride and the bride groom, wedding

Pāpa Yoni: Sinful life

Parmatma: Supreme Self, God

Parampara: Tradition

Paratha: Fried flat bread with or without stuffing and spices

Pati: Husband

Patni: Wife

Patraul: Forrest ranger (English: patrol)

Prithivi: Earth

Pranam: Special bow or greeting

Prasad: Sacred food

Puja: Worship

Puphu: Father's sister

Puran-panthi: Believer on the path revealed in the later Hindu scriptures, the *Puranas*

Puri: Fried bread

Purohit: Priest

Purush dan: Giving away of the boy

Rajput, Rajaputra: A higher Hindu caste (literally: royal progeny)

Rakhail: Mistress

Rakhi: A string tied to the brother's wrist by the sister for his protection

Raksha Bandhan: A ritual in which the sister ties a string, called *rakhi,* around the wrist of her brother to protect him (literally: protection tying)

Ramadhan: The holy month of Islam (pronounced *ramzan* in India)

Ramayana: The ancient epic story of King Rama

Roti: Indian flat and round bread

Rumal: Handkerchief, cloth napkin

Sadhu: Saint, holy man

Sadhukkari: a dialect of medieval Hindi used by saints

Sati: A widow burned alive (Suttee)

Sahab: Sir, an honorable term of address, an important man

Samadhi: Thought-less meditation, the eighth and last stage of Yoga

Samosa: A fried stuffed spicy fritter, most commonly in triangular shape

Sannyas: Renunciation (Sanskrit *Saṃnyāsa*)

Sasur: Father-in-law

Sati: A widow burned alive (Suttee)

Satsang: Religious gathering

Sattvik, rajasik, tamasik: The three traditional qualities—pure, mixed, impure

Satyagraha: Civil disobedience, the movement of Gandhi (literally: *true resolve*)

Sehra: Wedding crown

Sevak: Servant

Shabash: Bravo, a term used for appreciation and encouragement

Shahnai: Indian clarinet

Shasthi purti: Sixtieth anniversary

Shikha: A topknot as a mark of a high caste Hindu

Shiva: God Shiva

Shiva Ratri: A sacred night to worship Lord Shiva

Shrikhand: A sweet yogurt dissert

Shuddhi: Conversion to Hinduism by the Arya Samaj. (literally: purification)

Singori: A sweet

Sipahi: Police officer, soldier

Swadishth: Tasty, delicious

Tamasik: Impure, stale

Tarka: Spicy seasoning with hot oil

Tau: Father's older brother

Thug vidya: Thug knowledge (art of cheating)

Tilak: A colorful sacred mark on the forehead

Topi: A kind of men's cap popularized by Gandhi

Tor: Pigeon peas

Upaya: Solution

Urad: Black beans, black gram

Varna Saṃkara: Miscegenation

Veda: The first four Hindu scriptures in ancient Sanskrit

Vedika: Altar

Wakil: Lawyer

Wazan: Weight

Yogasutra: An ancient treatise of Yoga in Sanskrit aphorisms authored by Pantañjali

Yamuna jal: Yamuna's water

Yoni: Female genitals

About the Author

Anoop Chandola is an Indian American linguist-anthropologist educated at the universities of Allahabad and Lucknow. His last two degrees in linguistics include an MA from the University of California, Berkeley, and a PhD from the University of Chicago. He has taught Indian literature, culture, and religion at several universities in India and the USA, including Sardar Patel University, the MS University of Baroda, the University of California at Berkeley, the University of Washington at Seattle, the University of Texas at Austin, and the University of Wisconsin at Madison.

Currently he is Professor Emeritus of East Asian Studies at the University of Arizona. He is a member of numerous professional associations, including the American Anthropological Association, the Association for Asian Studies, the Linguistic Society of America, and the Linguistic Society of India. Chandola has published sixteen books and numerous papers.

His scholarly books and articles are in the areas of linguistics, music, religion, and literature, including extensive interdisciplinary and theoretical analysis. Among his five novels, *The Dharma Videos of Lust* published by UKA Press, London received two finalist awards: Best Books Awards of USA Book News and the National Indie Excellence Awards. His novel *In the Himalayan*

Nights, released in 2012 by Savant Books & Publications (USA), received a Great Northwest Book Festival award and is a finalist listed in ForeWord Reviews. His latest novel *Myth and Punishment* was released by Black Opal Books in July, 2017. It received an award from the New England Book Festival of 2018. He lives in Tucson, AZ and Seattle, WA with his wife Sudha. More details about him are available in Wikipedia.

www.ingramcontent.com/pod-product-compliance
Lightning Source LLC
Chambersburg PA
CBHW070535260626
47161CB00002B/390